About the Author

M. H. Lowe grew up in Sydney, Australia. After leaving school she trained as a nurse before concentrating on music and singing studies, and for twenty years juggled family and singing commitments.
In later years she worked in various nursing and administrative roles including assistant to the Dean of St. Andrew's Anglican Cathedral, Sydney.
M. H. Lowe is married with two children.

For my family

M.H. Lowe

IN GRIEVOUS TIMES

AUSTIN MACAULEY
PUBLISHERS LTD.

A CIP catalogue record for this title is available from the British Library.

ISBN 9781785549175 (Paperback)
ISBN 9781785549182 (Hardback)
ISBN 9781785549199 (eBook)

www.austinmacauley.com

First Published (2016)
Austin Macauley Publishers Ltd.
25 Canada Square
Canary Wharf
London
E14 5LQ

Printed and bound in Great Britain

Acknowledgments

My sincere thanks go to my family who have supported me throughout my literary endeavours. My special thanks go to Peter for his unfailing support, to Sarah and Elizabeth for their enthusiasm and encouragement, and to Daniel for his advice on all things military. To this I must add my gratitude to the Venerable Terry Dein and Reverend Robert Jones for their theological guidance, and to Shirley whose willing assistance with administration made my life easier. I would also like to thank Gillian for her guidance, Stewart Angell for sharing with me his amazing knowledge of the Auxiliary Units and to the many people I interviewed about life in Britain during the Second World War.

Chapter One

ENGLAND
Tuesday 3rd September 1940

'Clement!'

He heard her calling but he did not lift his head.

'Clement! There's a telephone call for you!'

He took in a deep breath and looked up. Of course he would go. That was his job. He laid the shovel down and reaching for his handkerchief, mopped his brow. 'One day I will finish this garden,' he muttered as he shuffled down the path between the potatoes and the climbing roses towards the back door. Perhaps it was the warmer-than-usual September weather, but he felt every one of his fifty-five years.

His wife had already left the doorway and returned to her task. She was standing beside the table peeling beans as he entered the house. He glanced at her hands. It always amazed him how her fingers peeled the vegetable, the swift, deft action of the sharp kitchen knife cutting and slicing with the precision of years. He walked along the corridor to the small table by the stairs and lifted the Bakelite receiver.

'Hello?'

'Reverend Wisdom?'

'Speaking.'

'Clement, this is John Winthorpe.'

He thought for a second. The name was familiar but he just couldn't remember why.

'Johnny Winthorpe. Say you remember seminary school, Clement?'

'Of course, forgive me. It must be twenty years, Johnny.' He paused. All the fun and fellowship of his younger years at Oakhill Theological College flooded back and he found himself smiling at the memories. Johnny Winthorpe, voted the man most likely to advance. Intelligent and good-looking, the man could always attract the attention of people. And his charm was equally effective on men as it was on women. But Johnny was fifteen years his junior and so had not served in the Great War. At times that distinction, much more than the difference in their ages, had created a gulf between them. War did that.

'Is everything all right?' he asked.

'Absolutely! Archdeacon Winthorpe, actually, Clement.'

'Congratulations,' he said. Nothing has changed then, he thought. 'What can I do for you, Johnny?'

'I've put your name forward for inclusion in a new initiative. Can't say much about it at this stage. I wonder if you would come up to London on Thursday?'

'Thursday?'

'It may be best if you stay overnight, what with the blackouts. You can stay with the rector of Christ Church, in Mayfair. He's a friend of mine. Can you be at Victoria Station around eleven on Thursday? I'll have a driver pick you up. Just stand at the cab rank. He'll find you.'

'I suppose so,' he stammered.

The Archdeacon hung up.

He replaced the telephone receiver. A council, one that wanted him! He had finally admitted to himself that *All Saints*, Anglican Church, Fearnley Maughton, East Sussex and tending the potatoes were his present and his future. But the war was changing everything. And the unexpected call from Johnny Winthorpe had made his heart race. He felt the smile fall from his face. Perhaps it had more to do with shortage of manpower than any special ability he may possess.

'Clement?' Mary called. 'Are you going out?'

'That was Johnny Winthorpe,' he said, walking into the kitchen. 'He's an Archdeacon now.'

She had stopped peeling the beans, the knife held in suspended readiness. 'What did he want?'

He stared at the peeled beans floating in a bowl of water on the table in front of him. Whilst admitting, even if only to himself, that he felt excited at the prospect of finally being involved in something bigger than the Church Wardens' Committee, he remained perplexed at receiving such a call at all. 'He has put my name forward for some committee. I have to go to London on Thursday.'

'What sort of committee?'

'He didn't say.'

He glanced at his wife as the peeled bean dropped into the water, her left hand unconsciously reaching for the next bean to be peeled. He saw her lips tighten at the corners. It was the smallest of reactions but he knew from experience what it meant. Thursday was their day together.

'Well, I'd better get the rest of those potatoes dug,' he said.

'Lunch will be ready in half an hour,' Mary said.

He nodded. Placing his hand on the doorknob he paused. 'Perhaps we could go to Lewes on Saturday?'

'You have a wedding and a baptism on Saturday, Clement,' she said without looking up.

Leaving the house, he walked back along the path. He would make it up to her. And her disappointment would not last. That was one of the things he loved about Mary. A vicar's life was never routine and she knew that. Especially so in wartime. He picked up the hoe, pondering the new initiative. He could not imagine why Johnny would ever think of him. Swinging the implement, he chipped out another cluster of potatoes. He had been the vicar of *All*

Saints for twenty years and he had long given up on career advancement. He raised his head and looked over the rooftops of the village houses and shops. Fearnley Maughton was a pretty village. Every season brought its own special delight; in winter the snow made the village like a Christmas card scene, while in spring and summer the potted flowers and long hours of daylight brightened the most tedious day. But spring was past, and the autumnal leaves were already changing colour in nearby Maughton Forest. Up to his left, the church and surrounding graveyard stood on top of the low hill. It was only a short stroll from the lych gate to the front door of the vicarage. Down Church Lane was the High Street and turning left, past the police station, was the common. But Fearnley Maughton was more than just bricks and mortar. The villagers were his family. He knew them all. Well, almost all. During his twenty years at *All Saints*, he had shared their sorrows and joys, held their hands and their confidences, baptised, married and laid to rest more than he cared to remember from almost every family in the district. But lately there were too many memorial services for mere boys for whom there would never be a funeral. He reached forward, grabbed a fistful of potatoes and tossed them into the nearby wheelbarrow.

At twenty-nine he had been considered old when the first insanity swept the world. But the current madness worried him. Clive Wade, the village baker, had lost two sons already. Just boys. He shook his head thinking about them. One had been a soldier, lost in Norway; the other was a merchant seaman, his ship blown to pieces in the Channel. As children those boys had both been choristers at *All Saints*. He visualised their eager young faces, as innocent as fresh snow in their white choir robes. What had their deaths accomplished? Sometimes, especially when he was alone walking on the Downs, he silently wrangled with God about the loss of innocent life. Yet despite the unanswerable questions, he truly believed that God had a plan for His world and that it would, in God's time, not theirs, be achieved. He smiled, remembering his own conversion and the man who had changed his life. Chaplain Edwin Ross had been the priest at the hospital in Paris where Clement had been sent after being wounded at Marne in '14. He recalled the man's words as though he had heard them only yesterday. 'Generals', Edwin Ross had said, 'do not concern themselves with the fate of the individual soldier or they will lose sight of the battle. But God works in reverse. God uses the individual to reach the many.' Those words were etched on his mind like the sound of his own name. Initially, they had spurred him on, convincing him that the Almighty's purpose for him was as a chaplain in the trenches. But by the time he had finished his theological training the war was over. Age blunts enthusiasm, he told himself as he swung the hoe again. Or did it just make one aware of one's own shortcomings? Either way, his time for adventure was past. He was not unhappy, but he often wondered if he had done enough to reach the many. 'A time for all things,' he muttered, quoting Ecclesiastes. And that included war. He bent down again, his fist grasping three more potatoes. He stared at the soil beneath his feet, his boots sinking into the earth. In his mind he could see the trenches. Death and dysentery. He would never forget the smell or the sight of hands and boots protruding through the brown slime, the man submerged beneath the endless mud. In his mind's eye he could see the injured and maimed returned soldiers whose bedsides he had attended at St Thomas' Hospital in London. It seemed a lifetime ago. And it was. Ross had helped him to secure the chaplaincy at St Thomas' when his attempts to re-enlist had failed. Although his tenure at the hospital was not much more than eighteen months, it was during that time that he had met Mary. She was feeding the ducks in St James' Park. The memory always gladdened his heart; the way she leaned on the railings, her hair spilling over her shoulders and shining in the sun, the curve of her back, her slender ankles. Those were his happy memories of those months. He tugged at a potato half-concealed in the dirt, and brushing the clods of soil from the vegetable's pink skin tossed it into the wheelbarrow. War. There is no honour in war. There never was. Yet despite the suffering of the first war, it had been a soldiers' war. This war was different. Every day the newspapers told of the latest Nazi outrage against the conquered peoples of Europe. There was something sinister about this war that he had not felt in the first. He swung the hoe with extra force, the potatoes uprooted from their earth-bound bed. Even the way men died was different in this war. Raw and instant. Machines, never imagined in the first war, raged and killed in the skies above them every day since the middle of August, one man against another, one on one. Nothing could be more different to trench warfare. He checked his watch. He had already seen three squadrons in the air this day, and it was not yet one o'clock. War went on above his head while he dug vegetables. 'You're too old anyway,' he muttered to himself.

Thirty minutes later he arched his back and leaning on the handle of the shovel, looked up at the sky. The lovely thing about summer is the long hours of daylight. But with the arrival of autumn, although only just September, the evenings were shortening. He glanced at the growing mound of potatoes in the wheelbarrow. There were enough for several days. Delivering the produce to the scullery door, he collected the tools and wheeled the barrow back towards the garden shed. Beside it was the Anderson Shelter. Not everyone had been provided with one. Only those in certain professions and those living near railway lines or airfields qualified. He had been embarrassed about the distinction and he hoped the villagers would not think him elitist for erecting it. Although, in his opinion, erect

6

was not quite the correct verb. The shelter was half erected and half buried and he wondered whether, if bombed, the thing could in fact prevent death. Or was it more likely to contribute to it?

He scrubbed the soil from his hands in the washhouse sink and went into the kitchen.

Mary placed the plate on the table before him.

He stared at the sausages. It was the third time this week. He had hoped that they would have some real meat. But then the newspaper pictures of the destitute children of Europe flashed into his mind, and he felt guilty for ever thinking such a thought.

'I'm sorry, dear,' Mary said. 'But young Stanley says that we are lucky to have sausages.'

He didn't know how she did it. The woman had a sixth sense that the British Army could only hope to emulate.

'No doubt his father has better fare for his dinner,' he said.

The kitchen was silent.

'I'm sorry, Mary. That was uncharitable of me.'

'Well, I wouldn't want to say anything about that,' Mary added.

'For what we are about to receive, may the Lord make us truly thankful,' Clement prayed. He picked up his knife and fork.

'I'm not happy about you going up to London, Clement. And it has nothing to do with Thursdays being our day out. You know the Germans are targeting the airfields, especially those in the south, and the train line is too close to Kenley Airfield. If only one Nazi bomber was even slightly off-course, the railway line would be destroyed.'

'I think it would be good for me to see what others are suffering while we live in our quiet and safe corner of England eating home-grown vegetables. Even Stanley

Russell's sausages would probably be considered a treat in London.'

'I would hardly call East Sussex a quiet and safe corner of England.'

'What our boys are doing in the skies is nothing short of extraordinary. Mr Churchill said we owe them much. But it seems to me that the raids are decreasing every day. Who knows, it may all be over by Christmas.'

'Just don't volunteer for anything that is dangerous. You did your bit for King and country last time,' Mary said.

He reached across and patted her hand. 'They must be hard up for clergymen if they have called on me.'

Chapter Two

Thursday 5th September 1940

His friend Peter Kempton had offered him a lift into Lewes. Crossing the Ouse River they motored through the narrow streets and down the hill towards the railway station. The place was congested with people. From his timetable he knew a train from London had recently arrived, but the numbers of people astounded him. For a moment the noise of the excited crowd sounded like the squawking seagulls he remembered from his childhood home in Rye. 'Poor souls,' he said remembering that people were being encouraged to leave the major cities. It was just a precaution, so the authorities were saying. He made a mental note to raise the issue of billeting evacuees at the next warden's meeting.

But there was something about the group, and it was not excitement at being resettled in the country. Anxiety had orchestrated a degree of chaos. It was palpable. He stared at the disenfranchised group, his heart sinking. Photographs in the newspapers, of European refugees with defeated eyes, flooded his mind. It was unthinkable that the Germans should invade. Yet here, before him, was the portent of things to come. It was the civilian deaths in this war that he could not reconcile; the indiscriminate bombing that killed soldiers and children alike. For a year now the war had gone on elsewhere. Young men fought and lost their lives in the skies above them, but life in Fearnley Maughton had hardly changed. Only the ration books and the memorial services told them that they were at war. Yet at this moment, suddenly, the war was on their doorstep and the realisation shook him. He held no personal dislike for the Germans. In fact, his memory of the only German couple he had ever known was a happy one. In his youth he had taken a job on a large farm near his home. The farm manager and his wife were German. But that had been before the first war. He hadn't thought of them in years. Frowning, he felt mildly guilty that he did not know what had happened to them. They had been interned in '14 the same day he had joined up, but they had shown more kindness to him than his own father. Perhaps they had been the exception. The Germans had been the enemy before, and now they were again. He shuddered, visualising the people of Fearnley Maughton being subjugated under the Nazi boot. He had never really believed the Germans would reach England, but now he began to feel that it may be unavoidable.

The car pulled up in the only available space, a little distance from the station entrance.

'I'm sorry, Clement, this is the closest I can safely park without running over someone,' Peter said.

'So good of you to drop me off,' he said, opening the door of Peter Kempton's car.

'My pleasure, Clement. I had to come through Lewes anyway. I'm in court in Brighton for the next three days.' Peter closed the boot, the thick, wide fingers grasping the handle of Clement's worn leather suitcase. 'Take care, Clement. Don't forget your gas mask,' he said, reaching for the small box. The two men shook hands.

Clement watched his friend drive away. For the country vicar, friendships are easily formed in a close-knit community. But only real friendships survived the bane of village life; gossip. And Peter Kempton, the village solicitor, had been a good friend. They had always been on good terms, but the bond between them had not been forged until after Peter's wife's death. Muriel Kempton had died before the war in a car accident in Switzerland, while

10

visiting her mother. The broken-hearted man had made an annual pilgrimage to his wife's grave in the Swiss rural township of Thun. But that was before the war. Twice now, on the anniversary of Muriel's death, they had held a memorial service at *All Saints*. It had been the beginning of their true friendship, for not long afterwards Peter had become Clement's chess companion. Little is said during a chess game, but understanding one's opponent is paramount. 'If only the world played chess,' he muttered.

He saw the billowing smoke of the approaching train. Despite the dirt and soot of the large, noisy machine, it smelt to him of excitement.

For the first hour he read *The Evening Argus*. Censorship kept local papers uninteresting, particularly those around the coastal towns. He put the paper onto the seat beside him and stared through the window at the passing countryside, contemplating what lay ahead in London. Although he imagined that if the Germans invaded, the council would be short-lived. He did not believe Hitler to be a religious man. In fact, he had heard that Herr Hitler was removing the Cross from churches and replacing them with swastikas. He pursed his lips at such heresy. Leaning his head back he closed his eyes, the rhythmic sway of the train lulling him into a half sleep.

A loud noise and the sudden jolting of the train woke him. Clement checked his watch and saw that nearly two hours had passed. Above him the sky was a pale, washed-out blue. As a boy he had loved to watch the seabirds loop and dive over the Camber Sands near his boyhood home. Now, his eyes searched for aeroplanes. The train inched forward, the carriages clunking and jerking as it rolled towards the station, where the tall metal roof of London Victoria arched above him. A booming voice was announcing to the terminal that the train from Eastbourne via Lewes and Haywards Heath had arrived. He alighted and joined the flow of people heading for the ticket collector.

Outside, a queue was forming for the cabs. His eye panned the surrounding crowd. He had not expected to see so many people in military attire. Even women wore uniforms he did not recognise. His eye passed from one to another. Glancing at the buildings on the opposite side of the street, he saw that all the windows were tapped and walls of sandbags surrounded doorways. He thought London an alien world.

He saw the face in the crowd. The energetic gait, the broad smile, the extended hand... Even at several paces' distance, he could see that Johnny had not changed. But the Naval Officer's uniform surprised him.

'Clement! How good to see you! You haven't changed a bit!'

'I never took you for a perjurer, Johnny. Or should I say Archdeacon?' he replied, eyeing the naval uniform.

John Winthorpe laughed aloud. 'From you, Clement, I would consider it an insult if you did not call me Johnny.' Johnny waved his arm in the air and a car parked at the top of the street, outside a public house on the corner, swung out into the traffic. Turning, it pulled up beside them and Johnny held the door open.

'How is Mrs Wisdom?' Johnny asked.

'She is well, thank you. But not too happy about me coming up to London.'

'And you have family?'

'No. We were not blessed that way,' he added. He turned to stare out the window, the subject of children one he did not wish to continue. In the early years of his marriage it had been the source of much sorrow, especially for Mary. But as the years had passed, anguished tears had been replaced with stoic acceptance until finally age denied parenthood.

'She worked at the Admiralty before you took her away, didn't she?'

He nodded. 'A secretary. So what is this council about, Johnny?'

There was a slight pause.

'We are on our way now to meet a man who has had an idea which we all believe is feasible,' Johnny said.

His eye followed the line of sandbags surrounding the great Abbey and the Houses of Parliament. The threat of forthcoming invasion had transformed London into a creature he hardly recognised. If the crowds at Lewes station had not convinced him that the war was coming to England, London's streets left him in little doubt. But Johnny's prevaricating words resounded in his ears as the car crossed the street and entered Whitehall.

'I wasn't aware that to be an Archdeacon one also had to be a politician.'

Johnny laughed. 'I have arranged for you to stay overnight with James Moore, the rector of Christ Church in Mayfair. You shouldn't experience any problems there for your wife to worry about.'

He didn't believe that encountering street villains was what Mary had in mind. But while he did not reply, he began to wonder what lay in store.

Just short of Trafalgar Square the car turned into Whitehall Place and pulled over. Clutching his small overnight suitcase, Clement followed Johnny to a featureless stone building with an elaborate doorway. Inside was a narrow entry foyer. Clement sensed that whoever held the offices above rarely saw the general public. Johnny strode ahead up the stairs and led him through some hallways to a room on the second floor. Without knocking, Johnny thrust open the door and they went in.

Sitting behind a desk was a neatly dressed woman. She glanced up and smiled as they entered.

'Commander Winthorpe, he is expecting you. Please go in,' she said.

Clement nodded in greeting but although the woman's smile remained, there was no attempt at introduction. Johnny opened the second door and he followed.

He wasn't sure if his mouth fell open but he found himself staring at a man sitting behind an enormous desk. He wore the largest collection of service ribbon bars Clement had ever seen on one chest.

'Sir, may I introduce the Reverend Clement Wisdom. Clement, this is Colonel Colin Gubbins DSO MC.'

Chapter Three

'I am supposing that you are not replacing His Grace Cosmo Lang, Colonel?' Clement said.

Gubbins laughed. 'No, I think the Archbishop of Canterbury can rest easy. His is the one job for which I would never be considered. John, from that remark I am supposing you have not informed Reverend Wisdom of our operation?'

'I thought I would leave that to you, Sir.'

Clement watched the friendly banter between the two men. From the disparity in their ranks alone, not to mention that they were from different services, he would not have believed there could be such camaraderie. He felt a sigh rising, but he suppressed it. Times were changing and formality was almost a thing of the past. He looked at the battle-hardened Colonel. The man had a serious visage with a high forehead, prominent brows, deep-set eyes and a full moustache, the epitome of the decent and courageous man. Clement had seen such men before, in the last war. They were a breed apart; they were not only brave but there was something else about them. They loved their job. It was as if God had made such men for the hour.

Gubbins gestured towards the chairs opposite his desk.

Clement sat down. He should have realised the meeting was not ecumenical when Johnny arrived at the station in uniform. And then when they did not cross Westminster Bridge for Lambeth Palace, he should have been more than suspicious. *Why would you be summoned to Lambeth?* He swallowed. He was a mature man and still his self-doubt, in the form of his father's disapproving voice, could reduce him to a twelve-year-old boy.

'Reverend Wisdom,' Gubbins began. 'As you will be aware, the Royal Air Force has been keeping the Hun at bay for some weeks now. I'm sure the skies in your part of the country have been teeming with more than just rain.' The Colonel paused, shuffling some papers on his desk.

Clement thought of his little community. Ned Cooper had lost his fourteen-year-old son to shrapnel wounds when a Stuka crashed into the man's south paddock. Ned had blamed himself for sending the boy out to plough the field that day. But despite the growing numbers of grieving families in the parish with whom he had consoled and prayed, Ned Cooper's boy was for him, thus far, the only war casualty on English soil.

Gubbins was speaking again. 'A little while ago, I was asked by the Prime Minister to set up a new group. But due to recent escalating enemy activity, we have decided to increase recruitment, and John here has put your name forward. Of course, what we are about to discuss is strictly top secret and not to be shared with anyone not associated with the enterprise. I have prepared some papers for you to sign.' Gubbins slid a document across the desk for Clement to see. 'While I must ask you to sign these, I would also like to have your word on it, Reverend?'

Clement looked at the papers. Before him was The Official Secrets Act. He glanced at Johnny. He wasn't sure if he should be flattered or concerned, and for some inexplicable reason he visualised Mary's beans. 'Of course,' he said reaching for the proffered pen.

'The Battle of Britain, as the Prime Minister is now calling it, would appear to be entering a new phase. Intelligence informs us that we can expect the Germans to step up their attack on us. This could be in the form of aerial bombardment, and will probably be the precursor to an attempt at invasion. We don't know when it will be exactly, but it will be soon.'

'Invasion?' he muttered. It was unfathomable. But the words were coming from someone in the know, not just *The Evening Argus*. He felt a hollowness developing in his chest.

'Yes. We must expect it. But we must not be like the ostrich. Preparation is the key, Reverend. So,' Gubbins said, voicing the word like a punctuation mark. Placing the signed documents in a file on his desk, Gubbins stood and wandered over to the window, his back to them. 'We must be ready for them when they do come. To this end we are establishing auxiliary groups within the Home Guard. These special groups will be completely autonomous, answerable to me but set up independently of each other. We are envisaging groups, or cells, of approximately six to eight men per cell with a fifteen-mile radius of ground to patrol. Each cell will have a leader, and an intelligence officer liaising between the group and us here at GHQ. You will have an underground Operational Base, which the Royal Engineers will build for you in some local woodland close to your village. It will be constructed so that you can live and plan underground, and patrol at night.'

Gubbins turned to face him. 'Reverend, these groups, which the Prime Minister somewhat euphemistically calls *Scallywags*, will only become operational on the broadcast of a word. That word is "Cromwell". If you receive a telegram or hear that broadcast, invasion is imminent and you must leave everything and go to your designated Operational Base. As you would already know, in the event of an invasion the church bells are to be rung to alert the people. This would still happen. But what we are envisioning for certain selected men is more than Home Guard defence and raising the alarm. Kent and Sussex are our top priority as the likely places for an amphibious German invasion. We expect there to be some kind of air support for their invasion, so lookouts and Observer Corps members will be on high alert. The closest to you will be at

Firle Beacon. This will give you some warning but not much. Yours and those further to the east may be the only groups not to get much advance notice.'

Clement wondered if his face showed his bewilderment. He heard the Colonel and he understood what the man was saying, but as Gubbins continued to speak his brain was no longer taking it in. His mouth was dry and he could feel his heart beginning to pound in his chest. He licked his lips, trying to feel normal and look intelligent.

'Reverend, you may be wondering why you have been chosen. Your involvement with and leadership of your local Home Guard makes you an obvious choice. However, Commander Winthorpe has told me of your record of service in the first war. I have, of course, checked the information, but to turn down a Military Cross because you consider that what you did was what any man would do is either the heroics of an extraordinary man, or the actions of a naive fool who has no place in the real world.'

'I did not expect to live, Colonel. I did what I thought I should.'

Gubbins nodded. 'It leads me to another issue. One of life. And death. These groups, as I have said, will be activated upon imminent invasion. Your job would be to act behind enemy lines, targeting and killing high-ranking German officers as well as blowing up bridges, railways, petrol depots, in fact anything the Germans could use to expedite their advancement to the capital.'

He stared at Gubbins. What the man was saying astounded him. He knew well enough what it meant. 'It is a suicide mission,' he heard himself say.

'We would prefer to think of it as guerrilla warfare, Reverend, but be that as it may, we do not believe you would survive long before being captured. They would, of course, shoot you. But you would be expected to take your own life, if captured. There is one other issue of importance, but we can discuss that tomorrow.'

Gubbins stood and came around his desk, his hand outstretched. 'Given the nature of the assignment I cannot force you to be involved, Clement, but I would ask it of you as one patriotic man to another. We are in the midst of what the Prime Minster is calling grievous times. We must anticipate the worst. It can only then get better. Think about it tonight. I would need your answer tomorrow, first thing.'

Johnny stood and waited by the door.

Clement stood and reached for his gas mask and suitcase. He stared at Gubbins, his heart sinking. 'You think they are that close?'

'Yes.'

There was no conversation in the car as they headed for Mayfair. He hoped Johnny didn't think him rude, but his mind was reeling. What he was being asked to do was something he had not thought about in years.

'Get some rest, Clement. I will collect you at six o'clock this evening. I have arranged for us to dine at St James' Palace. Guests of the Grenadier Guards.'

He knew it was an honour. He felt himself smile. But he could not process it all. Perhaps dining with one of the oldest and most prestigious regiments in the land would be his Last Supper. Everything he had heard this day was spinning like a whirlpool in his brain, and he felt himself being sucked into its vortex. He needed time to rest and think, and above all, pray.

'See you tonight,' Johnny called as the car drew up outside Christ Church.

The door to the vicarage opened and a man stood before him.

'You must be Reverend Wisdom,' he said.

Several young children ran towards the opened doorway, squealing and laughing. Two clung to the vicar's legs as he struggled to remain upright.

'Sorry. James Moore,' said the man, extending his hand in greeting. 'We were expecting you. You knew John from Oakhill, I understand?'

'Yes.'

'Helen, come and get the urchins,' Reverend Moore called.

A fair-haired young woman appeared in the hallway and the children ran off.

'We can talk privately in here,' James said, motioning Clement into his study. 'Helen will bring us some tea shortly. John has told me not to ask why you are in London. It must be marvellous to be so involved with all that is happening. Nothing so exciting about my work. I am just a London vicar.'

Clement heard the disappointment.

'I am just a country vicar myself, actually,' he said. At least, I was yesterday, he thought.

James Moore was a pleasant young man. Clement wanted to be gracious but all he could think about was Gubbins and the Auxiliary Units. Small talk was something he, as a vicar, had had to learn but given the age difference between himself and James Moore, and that James had a young family, they had little in common. Pleading tiredness from the journey, he finished his tea and retired to his room to unpack and have a nap. He lay on the bed and closed his eyes.

Did he doubt he would accept the post? He tried to imagine England ruled by the Nazis. No one had succeeded in invading the island in almost a thousand years. Napoleon had tried but failed, and Clement prayed that Hitler would suffer the same fate. Suffer. It would be they who would suffer if the Germans succeeded. Despite his tiredness, he rose and knelt by the bed, his hands together, his fingers intertwined. He whispered the Lord's Prayer, his eyes closed and his head bowed. But his mind was reeling and his prayers and thoughts jumbled, flitting between the theological, the practical and the unimaginable. He would need help at the church. He was already stretched with just routine church duties and the captaincy of the Home Guard. If the church bells rang... he stopped. *When* the church bells ring, he corrected himself, the village will be in uproar. His villagers would look to him, and if they couldn't find him they would believe themselves abandoned. He decided to arrange an exercise with the villagers on his return. At least that way it would not leave too much to Mary. Mary. It was all top secret. He had signed The Official Secrets Act so he couldn't even discuss it with her. Yet he knew she could be relied upon to carry out his instructions. He would organise the drill whichever decision he made. And he would place Mary in charge and he could be the observer. It was possible. But how would it be when the church bells really did peal? He paused, his eye staring at the floral pattern on the bedspread. Gubbins had avoided the term 'suicide mission', but that was what it was. Mary would be a widow. He rested his head on the quilt. She was a capable woman and resourceful. She visited her sister in Windsor regularly and was not afraid of travelling alone to carry out what she saw as her duty. She had also spent some months the year before with an aged aunt, in a remote house near Combe Martin in the West Country, before the old lady died. Perhaps this was his life's purpose. God raised up men like Gubbins in an hour of need, why not him? Killing. Gubbins had said it would involve killing. Killing the enemy, of course. But they were still men, made of flesh and blood. He had taken up the sword as a young man, but since his epiphany he had devoted himself to his calling. Killing was something he had not envisaged since the mud-soaked days of France.

He reached for his Bible. He knew the words of Ecclesiastes chapter three about a time to kill and a time of war, but he wanted more guidance. He held the Book and closed his eyes. The Germans were the aggressors. They had marched on Poland. And Czechoslovakia. His mind rattled off all the countries that Hitler had invaded and conquered. All of Western Europe from Norway to the Spanish border was under the jack boot. And now it was their turn. Yet the sixth commandment resounded in his head. Opening his eyes he turned to the pages of the New Testament. It fell open at St Paul's letter to The Ephesians. At the top of the page his eye read, "Put on the whole armour of God that ye may be able to stand against the wiles of the devil". He closed his Bible. Even though he knew St Paul was referring to The Spiritual Enemy in the passage, was taking up the sword really what God wanted him to do? He sighed, feeling the tension between his faith and his duty. And what of taking his own life? He had given his life to God, and it was for God to determine the time of his death. Yet it was part of the entrenched Christian ethic to give one's life for others. If the deaths of his team and even his own death by his own hand saved others, did that violate God's commandments? There was no tidy answer. He prayed for a sign from God.

There was a knock on the door. Brushing his suit trousers, he reached for his hat and coat. He glanced at the clock on the dressing table. Johnny had probably arrived.

Weaving his way through the boisterous children in the front hall of the rectory he stepped outside and joined Johnny on the footpath.

'You have met the brood, I see, Clement?'

'Nice family,' he said. But he was pleased to be away from the house. He was not accustomed to the total confusion of family life. How was it possible that something as small as little children could make so much noise?

In Cleveland Row, Johnny flashed a card to the guard on duty and Clement followed Johnny through the internal streets of St James Palace, to the entrance to the Officers' Mess of the Grenadier Guards.

He had not expected it to be palatial. After all, they were in the Mess, not the Palace itself. But the Officers' dining room had an understated elegance, which to his mind symbolised everything British. He drank vintage French wine. Actually, it flowed like the river of life in The Book of Revelations. 'Why leave it for the Germans?' a young lieutenant had told him. And there wasn't a sausage in sight. Tradition, ritual and order were observed at all times. He listened to their stories and laughed at their humour. He admired their youth and bravado. And as the war was specifically a taboo subject in the Mess, he had no idea where these men had served or when they would return to active service. If Johnny had arranged his inclusion as a Last Supper for a condemned man, then Clement enjoyed it, for he imagined that Johnny would surmise he would not refuse the position.

Around midnight, he climbed into the car and closed his eyes. They were on the steps of the vicarage in Mayfair within minutes. Or so it felt.

'I'll collect you at half past nine tomorrow morning, Clement,' Johnny said.

He watched the car drive away, then let himself into the vicarage. All was so quiet that he wondered if the family had disappeared in the evening for parts unknown. He climbed the stairs and, making as little noise as possible, he prepared himself for bed.

A loud and violent noise woke Clement. The children were screaming and he could hear Helen's frantic voice in the hallway. He jumped out of bed and opened the door to the corridor.

'Do you know what is happening, Clement?' James was shouting, trying hard to remain composed.

He knew it was not a thunderstorm but something much more serious. 'James, do you have a crypt in the church? Get everyone into it, as fast as possible.'

With each passing second the low droning increased until it roared in the darkness above them; the unstoppable barrage, so loud that it passed through one's very core. Then came the detonation. He closed his eyes, the sound of bombardment impossible to forget.

Clement grabbed his dressing gown and wrapping it around himself, reached for his gas mask then ran to help Helen usher the children downstairs.

Opening the door to the street, he watched as James shepherded his family through the darkness. The sight of the local vicar opening the church was enough to convince many to leave their homes and follow. He looked up. The sky was dark, with less than a quarter moon. A single beam from a nearby searchlight swept across the night sky and crossed another, some miles distant. Caught in its ferocious glare were the dark and ominous shapes of aeroplanes, hundreds of them passing through the piercing shaft of light. The incessant noise thundered on, punctuated only by the long screeching sound of falling bombs as they wailed towards the earth. People stopped where they stood, rooted in fear, staring into the darkness. Explosions and flashing light in rapid succession lit up the sky. It was raw and powerful; death was raining down. James opened the door to the church and people ran for its shelter.

'This way!' James was shouting as frightened people – women, children and the elderly – descended the dark stairs in complete silence.

'Clement, do you have any matches?' James asked.

He shook his head as a man beside him produced a match and James lit the lamp hanging on the wall beside the staircase.

'Is that the only lamp?' he asked.

James nodded. 'I have several on the bookcase in my study. Useless now.'

'I'll go back,' he said.

'Are you sure, Clement?' James asked.

James handed him the keys to the rectory. Clement held no illusions about his own mortality. People had said he had been lucky in the trenches. At least some said it was luck. He did not believe in luck. A line from his favourite Shakespearean play, *Henry V* popped into his head. *We are in God's hands, brother, not in theirs.* It was just as truthful for them in London now as it had been for the English at Agincourt.

He hurried up the stairs and out into the night.

The noise was intense. Overhead the search lights still scanned the night sky. Sirens were wailing but it was impossible to decide from which direction. The long piercing sound of falling bombs increased, going silent only for a heart-stopping second before detonation. Then the earth shuddered. He had no idea how far away the hit was. He ran into the house and opened the door to James' study. Walking straight to the bookcase he felt for the lamps. He grabbed them, swinging each of them to hear if they held enough paraffin. Food. Food would be a good idea. Hanging the lamps on his left arm, he felt his way into the kitchen and hurried towards the tiled wall of the scullery. A blast roared in the night, and even with his back turned to the blacked-out scullery window his eye caught the flash. He jumped with the fright of it. Close. Too close. On the dresser shelf above him two large containers hurtled to the floor with a crash of metal on tile. Two bread bins had disgorged their contents onto the floor. He stared at the five loaves. 'Alright, Lord,' he said. 'I hear you.' Gathering them, he piled the bread into the crook of his arm.

He turned, stumbling down the pitch-black corridor and out of the house. Sirens were shrieking. Standing on the top step he glanced up. A faint orange glow was starting to rise in the east. He heard the clanging bells of the fire brigades. He remembered the docks. They would be the target. That made sense.

He heard the sound of a car, although he could not see it. He stood on the footpath and, straining his eyes, stared into the darkness. From the sound of the motor it was only crawling along the road. He waited as it pulled up in the street. A policeman ran towards him.

'Have you seen the vicar?' the Constable asked.

'I am a vicar. Clement Wisdom. Reverend Moore and his family and about fifty others are in the crypt under the church. Do you need a priest?' he asked, still clutching the bread and paraffin lamps.

The man nodded. 'Some houses in Trebeck Street have been hit. Is there room under the church for more?'

'Of course. Let me give these to the people underground and I will be with you directly,' he said.

He looked up at the large dark form that was Christ Church. Flashes of reflected light from the incendiaries were bouncing off the stained glass windows. He ran across Down Street and into the church. Inside, the great edifice was dark and cold. He hurried towards the narrow steps to the crypt and descended them like a five-year-old.

Within two minutes he was back at street level, and climbed into the waiting car. It had barely turned the corner before they were confronted by another world. Whole buildings had been obliterated. He felt his jaw drop. The damage shocked him. While Down Street looked exactly as it did yesterday, Trebeck Street was nothing but rubble. The car stopped, and he and the policeman got out. Shells of houses were all that remained in Shepherd Street but fire was taking hold in some of the ruined houses. He stared at the gutted dwellings that only half an hour ago had held sleeping families. In the flickering light of the flames he could see that complete walls were missing and upper floors had disappeared. A picture still hung on a wall thirty feet above him. A man of his own age stood shaking on the footpath; a woman was sitting on what was left of some front steps, the remains of their home behind them.

'Anyone else in the house?' he asked.

The man looked up at him. The face was devoid of reaction.

He had seen that expression before. Its cause was shock.

'Anyone in the house?' he shouted.

The man stared back.

He ran up the steps to the non-existent front door. He saw the bottom stair tread and the first three balustrades of the staircase. Lifting his gaze, he saw the night sky, the search beams still sweeping above them.

'Reverend!' the policeman shouted.

He turned, more from instinct than any sense of self-preservation. He felt the shudder. It was more a groan than anything resembling impending doom. He ran back into the street just as the side wall of the house collapsed. Falling bricks, cracking timber and shattering glass crashed around them. The clanging bells of an approaching fire brigade filled the dust-laden air. Clement held his hand to his mouth and nose.

'We were going into our neighbour's house for tea,' the woman said.

He stared at the empty space where once there had been a house. 'Come with me,' he said to the man and woman.

Behind him, the policeman was telling the ARP warden about the crypt in Christ Church.

'As soon as you hear the All Clear, vicar, we could use you up here,' the warden called to him.

'Not before?' he asked.

'We have enough to worry about, without a missing vicar. Besides, you're more use to us where you are,' the warden shouted.

Turning the corner into Down Street was like seeing normality where there has been none. Clement almost smiled. He looked at the group that had followed him out of no sense of purpose, like obedient children. Opening the church door, he ushered them in and down the stairs.

Helen Moore stood at the base of the stairs handing out slices of bread to the growing crowd. Clement glanced at James as he moved around the crypt checking on everyone. A woman was crying. 'We'll find him. I will come with you,' James was reassuring her. 'As soon as it is light enough for us to see.'

'Our Father which art in Heaven, hallowed be Thy Name,' he began, his voice echoing around the stone walls.

A chorus of people joined him. But James' words about his unexciting life flashed into Clement's mind. Was this what James and Helen Moore had to look forward to every night until either victory or the Germans came to England? It was just as valid a ministry as any clergyman on the battlefield, or any minister engaged in other, more covert, activities for that matter. He knew what had to be done. He closed his eyes. It could not happen.

Chapter Four

Friday 6th September 1940

By morning the sky was overcast again but nothing would be the same. A chill autumnal air greeted them when they surfaced. The vicarage was undamaged except for a few shattered window panes. James was dispatching those who still had homes to go to, and assisting the ARP Warden with the rehousing of those who didn't. Looking along Down Street, Clement could see an ambulance. Beside it, blankets covered low forms lined up along the pavement. A pair of lady's feet wearing high-heeled shoes protruded from under the blanket. 'Helen, do you think the people from the crypt could wait in the vicarage? James is needed,' he said, his head indicating the line of bodies.

'Dear Lord,' Helen whispered, and fetching the remaining group ushered them and the children into the house.

He checked his watch. If the plans made the day before were still to be followed, Johnny would be arriving within minutes. He pondered whether he should stay to help. It was the right thing to do. But he knew his war was elsewhere.

James joined him.

'There will be people you know there, James,' he said pointing to the line of corpses. 'Have courage. Remember, the grieving need you to be strong.'

The young vicar took a deep breath.

'And James, if I may offer a suggestion?'

'Of course.'

'Prepare the crypt for other such events. Blankets, food, a means of boiling water, beds if you have any spare, stretchers and some medical supplies.'

James Moore nodded. 'You think they will come again?'

'Yes,' he said, thinking of Gubbins.

'Quite a night, Clement,' Johnny said as he got into the car. 'And I am quite surprised this area was hit at all. Until now Jerry has been targeting the airfields and the North. Bombing London's residential streets is something new.'

He closed the car door. 'You think it was deliberate?'

'In the East, yes. But around here? It was possibly a left-over bomb or two they dropped randomly on leaving.'

He thought of the dead and homeless of Trebeck Street. One man's finger had determined their fate.

'I think Reverend Moore will manage.'

'He's a good man. And has a capable wife. He is fortunate that he is not the vicar of an East End parish,' Johnny remarked.

'Yes,' he replied, remembering the glow in the East. The car turned into Piccadilly. Other than the devastation around Trebeck Street, the West End appeared largely unaltered.

'Clement. I don't mean to sound hard or uncaring. The local vicar plays a huge role. Especially if we see more of what we had last night. But I think you can understand that what we are asking you to do is part of the bigger picture. Church matters are important. And grass-roots support is vital for morale as well as for body and soul. But that is for others now.'

He didn't answer. He felt like he was on the edge of an abyss, about to consciously take a step into oblivion. Staring through the window he watched as small rivulets of rain meandered their way down the pane.

'I see you survived last night well enough?' Gubbins said as Johnny closed the door to the inner office.

He wasn't sure if the Colonel meant the raid or the dinner at the Officers' Mess.

'Your decision?' Gubbins asked.

He could feel his throat tighten. There would be no going back. His gaze shifted from the grey skies beyond the window to the waiting Colonel. One thing amazed him about professional soldiers. When decisions had to be made, there was no small talk. Life. Death. Nourishment. Routine. Had life been reduced to these four elements? He thought on all the events of last night. It was certainly true for the families in Trebeck Street. Perhaps there were now only two elements.

'Yes,' he said.

'Good man!' Gubbins replied.

'But I may need help at the church. A retired minister or curate, perhaps?' he asked.

'John will arrange it,' Gubbins said. 'There are just a few other issues I need to raise with you. We would like you to prepare a list of around thirty names of suitable men to be in your cell. From these thirty you will need to short-list about six to eight men, based on consideration of their abilities, physical and mental, and also their characters and age. Ponder as well their circumstances, and remember that you must be self-sufficient. Farmers are good choices, landowners or gamekeepers if you have them, and also professional men. You should have a variety of skills but you should all be able to live off the land for some weeks.'

'Will there be any training?' asked Clement.

'Yes. Once you have chosen your cell, we will arrange for you to attend a course at Coleshill House in Wiltshire. They are usually weekend courses for people otherwise engaged in reserved occupations, but after last night I have decided to step up the intake. Members of these Auxiliary Units would ideally already be in the Home Guard. If your final list includes men not in the HG, John will arrange for them to be issued with uniforms. Then on Monday morning you can travel to Wiltshire where you will also be supplied with weapons.'

Gubbins looked up and stared him in the eye. 'You will be learning how to use explosives, Wisdom, and of course, how to kill.' Gubbins paused.

Here it comes, he thought.

'And there is one person who will be top of the list when the invasion comes,' Gubbins said. 'It is customary for you to have your local, senior police officer vet your chosen men.'

Inspector David Russell was not a man Clement cared for. And certainly not a man he trusted to interview men for such an enterprise. 'I have very great reservations, Colonel. Inspector Russell is not a man of character. I must protest about involving him. Is there not another way?'

'Perhaps Commander Winthorpe could visit you on Sunday,' Gubbins said. 'You and he could go over the final list of names and meet with the men. But your police chief must be informed, Clement. A sealed list would suffice.'

'With respect, Colonel, must Inspector Russell know at all?'

'The list is for your protection. Imagine if a local found your Operational Base, not to mention the weapons you would have at your disposal, they would surely notify your police and perhaps even Special Branch who would arrest you as a collaborator? How would you explain it?'

He pondered it for a minute. He did not like the thought of David Russell having top secret information.

'However, we are getting ahead of ourselves,' Gubbins continued. 'When you receive the "Cromwell" alert, your senior policeman is your first victim. He must be eliminated if your group is to be effective and if any of you are to survive long enough to thwart the German advance.'

He knew he was staring. He couldn't help it. He had wrestled with his conscience about killing the enemy. Now Gubbins was asking him to kill a man who, although he did not much like, he had known for years.

'Clement, if your police chief was taken prisoner by the invading Germans, your cell would be compromised and your entire group rounded up and shot. The Germans would then know all they had to do was seize the senior police officer in every town and they would have every cell in every county in England; our entire guerrilla network taken out by just one man. Unthinkable. There is no alternative, Wisdom. However distasteful, it must be done.'

What was happening to his world where good and decent men cut the throats of others because they knew too much? He had thought the Auxiliary Units a good idea. And during the previous night he had even been convinced of the need for such groups. Moreover, he believed that God was telling him to do it. His mind whirled.

'It is easier for our consciences if we kill someone dressed in an enemy's uniform,' continued Gubbins. 'But that enemy is still a man, with a mother and father and possibly a wife and family. Pull the trigger or use a blade, the result will be the same. If it helps, Clement, your police chief is one man, but if he talks, his loose lips could kill thousands of brave, decent men and women up and down the country.'

He nodded. It didn't help. Murder was still murder. But evil had to be repulsed. His friend Peter had told him about supposed ghettos in Poland where they were forcefully congregating those of the Jewish faith. Such brutality astounded him. There was no honour anymore, the first war had seen to that. It reconfirmed his opinion, though, about the second madness. He had killed soldiers in the first war, but never civilians. He thought of the family in Trebeck Street. What had they done to the Germans? The high moral ground is so easily taken in theory or in peacetime.

He thought of the verses in Ecclesiastes and Ephesians, the five loaves in Helen Moore's kitchen, and the glow in the east.

It had to be done.

'John will visit you on Sunday and you can go over the final list of names. You should invite your selected men to a special meeting of the Home Guard on Sunday afternoon. It doesn't give them much time to contemplate their decision, and perhaps that is a good thing. Either way, Clement, you will be different men when I see you next.'

The interview was over.

Outside, there was a hurried tension about London. The bombing of last night showed on the faces of the passing crowds. Shopping bags were full of all kinds of rationed foodstuffs. Even small children carried string bags containing bread and tinned food. He watched a red bus pass. On the outside written in gigantic letters was the statement; *Loose Lips Sink Ships.* He had seen the sign before but now it meant more. He felt his heart pounding. The period the newspapers had called the Phony War really was over. Europe had fallen.

'What about some lunch?' Johnny was saying. 'We could go to the Savoy. Special treat before the austerity begins in earnest.'

Special treats. For a moment he wondered what the famous hotels did offer travellers. He visualised French chefs weeping at the thought of serving meat loaf. But it was not what he wanted now. He felt hollow. The seriousness of it all had impacted hard. He felt drained, but above all, he wanted to see Mary. Not that he could discuss any of it with her. But he needed to see her face. 'No. Thank you, Johnny. I would like to go home. Could your driver drop me at Victoria Station?'

'Of course.' Johnny hailed the driver, who was waiting on the opposite side of Whitehall Place, and they drove past St James' Park and the Palace. He looked up at the Royal Standard fluttering high above Buckingham Palace. 'Will they leave London?'

'Unlikely. I can't tell you how relieved many of us are that we have the King and Queen we now do.'

'Divine intervention?'

'Indeed.'

The cab pulled up outside the station. 'See you Sunday, Johnny.'

They shook hands.

'I am pleased to have you with us, Clement.'

The next train south was not for another thirty minutes. He purchased a ticket then went to the tea room. Names started filtering through his mind and he took a small note book from his pocket.

As the train left the outskirts of London he stared at the passing scene. What he had witnessed in Down Street made his heart heavy. But he acknowledged that with his commitment to Gubbins, his life would never be the same. By the time he passed East Croydon there were two names already on the list; Peter Kempton and Reginald Naylor.

He stepped down onto the platform at Lewes, the bus for Fearnley Maughton not due for another twenty minutes. If the invasion took months, he and whoever he selected would have to work and survive through the winter. Underground and bitterly cold. Not his favourite combination. And only two days' training to transform law-abiding men into saboteurs and assassins. But it was Gubbins' parting information that had shocked him more than anything. Once activated, Gubbins had told him, the cell had a life expectancy of two weeks. If the invasion was at hand he may not need to worry about winter.

Everything he saw now in Fearnley Maughton looked different to him. He wanted to remember it just as it was, like a photograph for his memory and the hard times ahead.

Across the green was the *The Crown Inn*, where the face of a young Queen Bess was painted on a sign swinging above the door of the black and white Elizabethan building. Further up the High Street was the elegant Georgian building that was Peter Kempton's legal office. Beyond that was the doctor's home and surgery, as well as the police station, beside which was Church Lane, leading to the rectory and *All Saints*. As he walked through the village he smiled and was greeted by people he had known for years. A shop door opened and young George Evans, the local postman, stepped out.

'Afternoon, Vicar,' he said.

He smiled at the boy who hurried away on his rounds. *Afternoon, Vicar!* How many times had he heard that in twenty years? Village life; its familiar routine was like an old and cherished clock; a blessing when all its parts worked in harmony. And it had for the most part been a blessing.

He turned right into Church Lane.

Mary.

He almost ran to his cottage, the last of the flowering shrubs by the fence, the hanging basket of brightly coloured annuals lifting his heart.

Holding Mary in his arms, he breathed in her scent. He hoped never to forget it. He had always loved her. From the moment he saw her in St James' Park, there had never been anyone else. Sometimes he felt guilty for marrying her and reducing her life to one of church committees and peeling beans, childless. He thought of Helen Moore and her brood of children. Mary had wanted to be a mathematics teacher but her father had refused it. For his own part, he was glad of it for he knew he would never have met her in a classroom. His wife's life was one of care and devotion to him and his calling. And to her sister, Gwen. He couldn't do without her in the parish. She organised everything from counting the offertory and keeping the parish books to taking the minutes at the endless committee meetings.

'Well! Do tell me, Clement? Are you to be Archdeacon Wisdom?' Mary asked, breaking free of his embrace.

Clement shook his head. 'It was Home Guard business, Mary. Johnny has been made a regional commander and they want to increase the role of the Home Guard. Nothing very exciting.'

He saw her face fall.

'Never mind. We are happy here, aren't we?'

She smiled and picked up the knife. 'Well, we have had some excitement. And I was a bit concerned for you, Clement. The village is buzzing about the German planes seen flying north.'

'German planes?' he asked.

'The men on duty last night with the Observer Corps reported hundreds of German planes flying overhead. Did you see them in London?'

'You wouldn't recognise London, Mary. Sandbags, barricades and windows boarded up everywhere. There is such confusion. Johnny will be coming down on Sunday. He says he would like to meet some of the men from the Home Guard.'

The peeling stopped. She was staring at him but she said nothing.

There was a pause.

'I will arrange the sandwiches,' she said, the knife slicing into a carrot.

He heard the controlled disappointment. He knew he had evaded her question about the German planes. But he couldn't talk about them for fear that he would let something slip about the Auxiliary Units. As the seconds ticked by, he couldn't think of what to say and the need for an answer faded.

'Well, I'll just go and unpack my bag,' he said.

He heard the distinctive sound of the lock click as he closed his study door. Mary would not disturb him until supper time. He was glad of it. He needed time to consider the men and the attributes each would bring to the group. But more than that, he felt guilty for evading her question. Secrecy. It divided. And he didn't want any enmity, especially with Mary. Perhaps he was being overly cautious. He glanced out the window at the evening sky as he sat down. 'Time heals all wounds,' he muttered. But the proverb came to him in his mother's voice. He visualised the loving, gentle face of his late mother. He had not known his mother's life aspirations but he felt that she, like Mary, had probably not achieved them. He was sorry about that. Children never really know their parents' dreams and disappointments. He missed her, even now. Childhood had ended for him the day his mother died. He had been fourteen. After her death, his father, always a stern man, had become remote and more authoritarian until in the end he and his father had become strangers. Clement's mind returned to his mother and the few cherished memories he had of her. As a small child he had enjoyed long walks with his mother along Winchelsea Beach, collecting whatever the tide brought in. He had loved those times; her hair loose and caught in the wind, the laughter they had shared. Perhaps he would have seen less of his mother if he had had brothers and sisters. He frowned. He had no memory of his parents ever laughing together. There were no stories. No family outings. Meals were taken in silence with a leather strap sitting folded on the table beside his father's large hand. His enduring memory of his father was of the thrashing he had received not long after his mother had died. His stomach knotted at the memory. He had arrived home late having gone out on one of Rye's fishing trawlers. His father had forbidden him to associate with the fishermen, calling them all smugglers. Clement had always thought it odd that his father, who was the rector of St

Mary the Virgin Church, had hated fishermen. Yet Christ recruited such men as disciples. After the beating he avoided his father and at the age of sixteen he had accepted a position on Romney Farm. His father died while Clement was in France during the first war, but his father's passing had meant little to him. 'It could have all been so different,' he mused. He did not miss his father but he mourned the lost opportunity to have had a better relationship with the man. His thoughts returned to his mother. Her life should have been happier. He pondered the role of women. Was it solely to care for others? It was so for his wife and his mother, and no doubt for most, but thinking of all the women he had seen in London in uniform, Clement wondered if the future would be different. He wondered if his mother's reasoning behind the proverb was more to do with time diminishing disappointment. Life dealt harsh blows at times. He thought of Mary's tears, shed for want of a child. How he had wrangled with God about that. It was another mystery for which there were no answers. Yet life could also deliver such joy. He thought of Mary's ankles, her sense of humour, the delight he felt when he beat Peter at their weekly chess game, and all the people of Fearnley Maughton who at one time or another had sought his guidance. His mind returned to the sound of the door click. Strange how something so simple could symbolise so much. Everything he held dear was in that click.

He shook his head.

'No more philosophising!' he remonstrated. He swivelled the chair and turned to face his desk. Pulling his notebook from his jacket pocket he read the two names: Peter Kempton and Reginald Naylor.

Peter's calm, analytical mind would be an asset to the group. And although Clement's friend was now fifty-nine years old, he had kept fit from walking the South Downs Way with Boadicea, his black Labrador. Reginald was a landowner, not gentry but he had made his money from selling American sewing machines to British housewives. But unlike Peter, Reginald was not a member of the Home Guard. He was married, but other than his wife Geraldine and a son who had moved to Australia to run a sheep station, Reginald had no dependents.

He leaned back in the seat and gazed out the window. The list was proving harder to compile than he had imagined. He decided to make a start on his sermon, hoping that as he did so names would filter through from his subconscious mind. He reached for his lectionary and turned to Sunday, the Eighth of September, the fifteenth Sunday after Trinity, and read the suggested Biblical texts. He decided to focus on divine help in adversity through faith. As he wrote, names flowed in and out of his mind.

By supper he had his thirty.

An hour later it was a dozen.

And by bedtime he had a short-list of nine men.

Other than himself, Peter and Reginald, the list included Clive Wade the baker, young George Evans the postman, widower Ned Cooper who had a farm on the outskirts of the village, the village doctor Phillip Haswell, Inspector Russell's son Stanley, the local butcher, and John Knowles the bank manager.

How was he going to ask each man to be involved without saying too much? He was not good at deception. Mary had always seen through him when it came to hiding Christmas or birthday presents. He turned off the lights in his study and opened the curtains, staring through his study windows at the slice of moon which shone above them. The moonlight would increase each day from now on. He reached for his calendar and checked the moon's cycle. The full moon would be the sixteenth of September. That night and the nights either side of it, London would be lit up by the heavens. He stared up at the omnipresent moon, frowning. He had not heard the low drone of the bombers this evening, and he began to wonder if the previous night had been a rehearsal for something far more catastrophic.

Chapter Five

Saturday 7th September 1940

Reginald and Geraldine Naylor were not exactly reclusive, but Clement had been to their home only occasionally. It was a two-storey Georgian house, the epitome of its owners; conservative and ordered but with evident Protestant frugality.

He sat in the drawing room while Geraldine brought a tray of tea and fish paste sandwiches.

'Is that all we have?' Reginald looked up at his wife.

'And lucky to have anything what with the convoys being targeted the way they are. Remember Mister Wade's boy?'

Reginald appeared to be chastised.

'Damn Germans!' Reginald Naylor said.

Clive Wade, the village baker, was on Clement's list, for the very reason that he had lost both his sons during the year. The baker understandably had an entrenched and vocal dislike for the Germans and, in addition, had a van to make his home deliveries, and so knew his way better than most around the country lanes.

'Well, Vicar? I am guessing your visit is not entirely social?' Reginald said.

He placed his cup and saucer on the low table before him and shot a glance at Geraldine, then cleared his throat.

Reginald's teacup hit the edge of the saucer, spilling tea onto the rug.

'Reg!' Geraldine chided and ran from the room.

'Quickly, Vicar, you have about a minute.'

'I have been asked to form a sub group to the Home Guard which I would like you to be involved in. Can you come to a meeting in the vestry tomorrow after church?'

'I'll be there. Probably not the service. What time, Vicar?'

'Midday?'

Reginald Naylor nodded as his wife returned with a towel and a fresh pot of the palest tea Clement had yet seen.

They talked mostly about the bird life of the Downs. Geraldine raised the subject of the German planes sighted the night before last, but Clement said he knew nothing other than the rumours that everyone appeared to know. He drank his tea. Half an hour later, he left.

It surprised him to see the black car parked outside the vicarage. Standing in his opened doorway, he listened. He could hear Mary's voice. She was laughing. It was like a sudden burst of sunshine to his ears. He followed the sound of voices to the kitchen.

'Hello, Clement. Mary has asked me to stay. I do hope that is convenient with you also?'

'Johnny! We expected you tomorrow. Is everything alright?' he asked.

'Yes. I had some business in Brighton which concluded sooner than I had expected. I hope you don't mind me showing up earlier than anticipated?'

'Of course not.'

'Excellent. We can continue our chat about old times,' Johnny said smiling. 'And, of course, I was keen to meet your better half.'

Mary laughed. Sandwiches were being churned out. Fish paste. He made a mental note that if England won the war he would never eat fish paste again.

'Now, you two go into Clement's study. I'll bring the tea as soon as it is ready,' Mary said.

'Every vicar should have a wife. In fact, I do not know how I have managed without one all these years!' Johnny told them.

Clement left the kitchen without comment. Johnny had a way of charming people. It was a skill that he had never acquired. Pity. Charming people got church roofs fixed and organs repaired.

He closed the door to his study, the familiar click soothing his ear.

'Has anything happened?' he asked.

Johnny smiled. 'Do you have your team, Clement?'

He nodded. He realised Johnny hadn't answered his question but he ignored it. 'Nine. I've made a list,' he said. He glanced at Johnny who had seated himself in one of the winged armchairs before the fireplace. 'And my assistant?'

Johnny reached into his coat then handed a folded piece of paper to him. 'Reverend Herbert Battersby. Retired, but lives in Lewes. A good man. Knows how to be discreet and will only come when you call him. All he knows is that you have Home Guard duties which could call you away at a moment's notice.'

'Thank you,' he said, taking the name and telephone number. He took a small note-sized piece of paper from between the pages of his diary and handed it to Johnny. 'Everyone on the list has either knowledge or skill which, I believe, will be useful.' He told Johnny about his friend Peter Kempton and about Clive Wade, the village baker with the van. 'I spoke with the landowner, Reginald Naylor, earlier this morning. He will attend the meeting tomorrow after church. I have also selected our local postman, George Evans, a lad from Wales who is an accomplished Morse Code telegrapher. And because George delivers the post he knows most of the goings-on in the village. George does have a heart condition, so the army wouldn't take him but I know he has a personal reason for wanting to do his bit.'

'Which is?'

'I did say I wouldn't tell anyone, Johnny.'

'Sorry, Clement, no confessional privileges. Not for this. I must know everything about them. All our lives are in their hands.'

'He received a white feather. Don't know who sent it but it was a beastly thing to do to the lad.'

'And the heart condition?' Johnny asked.

'Irregular rhythm, apparently. Considered minor but enough for the services to refuse him.'

Johnny nodded. 'Next?'

'Ned Cooper is a farmer. His old dad, who died last year, fought in the first war and was gassed. Then recently, his son, an awkward boy, was killed when a Stuka fell from the sky over their fields. Some of the shrapnel hit him. Cut the lad in two.'

'Who will be running the farm in his absence?' Johnny asked.

'Ned is a widower, so he has three Land Army girls who do wonderful work.'

He paused. No emotion, he told himself. 'The sixth is Stanley Russell, our butcher. He is single and, of course, can use a knife,' he stopped. Beans and carrots. Perhaps he should have asked every married woman of twenty years or more to join. 'Then there is Doctor Phillip Haswell. Phillip lost his wife in childbirth around three years ago. The child also died. He has not remarried and has no dependents. And finally John Knowles, our bank manager. A good man,' he paused. 'But I cannot decide if he should be included or not?'

'Why?'

'His wife, Margaret, is expecting a child. This alone should be a reason to exclude John. However, John is what Mary would describe as "highly strung".'

Johnny raised his eyebrow. 'Why do you wish to include him?'

'He speaks German.'

Johnny nodded. 'You said that Knowles' wife's pregnancy alone should be reason to exclude the man. Do you have other reasons?'

'Our police chief, David Russell, to whom I must give the list of names, is very charming. Too charming. David, apparently, enjoys spending time with other men's wives. Margaret appears to be a favourite. It is probably innocent but it is not well received by the women's husbands.'

He watched Johnny processing the information.

'And, of course, myself,' Clement said. There was a light tap on the door.

'That will be our tea,' he said, opening the door.

Mary stood in the hallway but there was no tray. 'John Knowles was just at the door, Clement,' Mary told him in a low voice. 'He is very agitated and wanted to speak to you but I said you were with someone and that you would call him later.'

He nodded.

'I'll get the tea,' she said.

He watched her walk back along the corridor before closing his door again. He heard the click.

'Anything you need to look after urgently, Clement?' Johnny asked.

'It can wait,' he replied. But something troubled him about John Knowles' visit. He hadn't heard the doorbell. He glanced at the window. It was ajar. Had John overheard their conversation? He chastised himself for being so suspicious. Why would anyone stand under a window amongst the flower beds eavesdropping anyway?

'We will leave out the bank manager. Language skills aside, the man may not have the mental stamina. Imagine if he was interrogated by the Germans.'

He nodded. He could almost visualise John Knowles telling the Germans anything they wanted to know.

'And the doctor,' Johnny continued, 'we will exclude also because his skills would be required in the village. Are they both Home Guard?'

'John Knowles isn't. Phillip Haswell is and he is a church warden. I know he would be disappointed not to be included, if he knew about the Auxiliary Units.'

'That can't be helped,' Johnny said. 'This butcher, Stanley, he is a stable character?'

He nodded. 'Yes, I think so. Although his father treats him rather badly.'

'Father?'

'Stanley is Inspector Russell's son. But he is a decent young man.' Unlike his father, he thought. 'I'm sure he will be an asset to us. It could be the making of him.'

'And you don't foresee any problems when the time comes to eliminate the Inspector?'

'I know this will sound odd, but I do not believe Stanley will be too upset at his father's passing.'

Johnny nodded. 'You have chosen some interesting people, Clement. So what is your sermon for tomorrow about?'

They talked for an hour about everything and nothing; the old days at Oakhill, rationing, London. But the war, everyone's favourite subject, was not mentioned. Towards two o'clock Clement reached for his cassock and stole and dressed before leaving the vicarage to greet the bridal party at the church.

Johnny stood and walked with him to the doorway.

'Don't worry about me, Clement. I can amuse myself. Perhaps I can assist Mary with the sandwiches,' Johnny added.

'Sorry, it's such a busy day.' he said. 'And there is a baptism at half past three. But I should be back well before suppertime,' he added as he closed the gate to the vicarage and walked up the hill towards the church.

It was just on five o'clock when he returned. Johnny was reading in the study. Clement hung his clerical robes on the hook and placed the marriage and baptismal registers on his desk.

'Mary says dinner will be at seven,' Johnny told him.

'Can I interest you in a stroll on the Downs before dinner?' he asked.

As he closed the garden gate, Clement told Johnny about his lunar observations.

'An interesting theory,' Johnny said as they walked away from Church Lane. Within the hour they stood on a ridge and surveyed the expansive valley before them, watching it transform from verdant green dotted with the rustic colours of autumn to deep purple in the dwindling evening light. The sky turned a translucent blue and the occasional star twinkled above them. A crescent of golden moon was low in the sky. It was a breathtaking sight. But it made Clement think about the full moon and the nine days before the sixteenth. He glanced at Johnny who had followed his gaze to the heavenly realm.

'If your theory about the full moon and the rehearsal run is correct, Clement, then we have nine days before the sixteenth to ponder it. And it is true that last night there was no bombing in London. But,'

Clement reached out to grab Johnny's arm. 'Listen, Johnny.'

Silence.

'Listen,' he said again. He stared into the evening sky. Although the light was fading, it was not yet dark. He could feel Johnny's eyes on him, no doubt thinking him mad. He squinted, scanning the darkening sky, inch by inch. He couldn't yet see them but he knew they were there. 'Aeroplanes, Johnny. More than one and not fighters. I know the sound of fighters. We have heard little else for over a month.'

'Are you sure?' Johnny asked.

'No. But I'm certain the drone is different. It's lower.'

'There!' he pointed at the black specks in the sky which grew with every passing second. The low drone increased. Within minutes it was noise, too loud to ignore. As they passed overhead the sound was like thunder.

'I must get back to the vicarage. Can I use your telephone, Clement?'

He was out of breath as he opened the door. Johnny had run ahead and was standing in the hallway, the telephone receiver in his hand.

'Bombers, aren't they?' Mary said as Clement entered the house. 'Could you see them?'

He nodded.

'London?' she asked.

'It would be my guess,' he said.

Johnny was depressing the dial tone buttons on the telephone. He looked up as Clement entered. 'I can't get through. The lines must be down.'

There were multiple reasons for that, none of them good.

'Should we go into the shelter?' Mary asked.

'They are too high for us,' he said.

'No such thing anymore, Clement. It is unlikely they would target Fearnley Maughton. But there is no point giving them direction lights. Have you drawn the blackout curtains?'

'I'll check the bedrooms,' Mary said, disappearing up the stairs.

He went to his study and drew the curtains. He knew what must be happening in London.

They sat in the dimly-lit sitting room eating their dinner of tongue and vegetables. There was little conversation. They prayed for London, and for James and Helen Moore.

An hour later Clement opened the front door and peered out. Dusk had come and gone, and night had descended. No bombs had fallen on the village and no sirens had wailed. Every ten minutes Johnny tried the telephone but it was a further hour before he managed to contact the Admiralty. Only overhearing half the conversation did not make any of it intelligible. But he guessed what was being discussed. He listened for the word "Cromwell" but it had not been voiced.

'I should return to London,' Johnny said, entering the sitting room. 'There are things I need to do. It was my great pleasure to meet you, Mrs Wisdom. And thank you for the dinner,' Johnny said.

He walked with Johnny to his car. 'Is there anything you would like me to do?'

'Just get your team, Clement. The training will take a minimum of two days. As soon as you and your team have returned to the village, be in a state of readiness.' Johnny lowered his voice, his eyes glancing around. 'Gubbins believes it has begun.'

Chapter Six

Clement chose *O God, our Help in Ages Past* as the processional hymn. He had never seen morning service so well attended. Even the Naylors were in the front pew. Impending invasion was the cause. During the previous evening, over three hundred German planes had dropped bombs in two successive raids over London. According to the morning newspaper and wireless reports, the whole city, especially the East End, had been targeted. Fires raged, buildings collapsed and people, children included, were homeless or dead. Clement and his congregation sang the twenty-third Psalm, he read from the Bible on God's help in adversity, he even quoted Mr Churchill about preparation, duty and confidence. It applied as much to him as it did to the villagers. Possibly more. He finished his sermon with his favourite line from Shakespeare. It seemed to help. People said they were encouraged. But he could see on their faces the effect of recent events. While some displayed inner fortitude, others were wide-eyed with fear at what lay ahead.

'Excellent sermon, Clement,' Peter said.

He shook Peter's hand. He noted that his friend's eyes had glazed. The reaction surprised him. But then, none of them, including him, really knew what the future held.

Reginald Naylor nodded to him as he escorted Geraldine from the church. The woman was crying, and several of his regular congregation held handkerchiefs in their hands. Their anxiety was palpable and barely suppressed. He expected that when the time came, many would crumble in fear. But for now the fragile tie of the unknown bound the villagers together.

He checked his watch. In fifteen minutes he would be meeting with his chosen men. But the well-proportioned Mrs Greenwood, who was always the last to leave, hovered in front of him. As the village postmistress and telephone exchange operator she knew more than she should about the village, and invariably had some confidential piece of gossip she believed that Clement, as vicar, should know. Today it concerned Margaret Knowles and something about where the woman's bicycle had been seen. He sighed, dismissing it from his thoughts, glad that Johnny had excluded John Knowles from the group. He wondered if every parish had a Mrs Greenwood.

Clement closed the door to the church and went into the vestry to remove his cassock. He also removed his clerical collar. The small article of apparel symbolized everything his Christian faith meant to him, and it didn't seem right wearing it to discuss sabotage and assassination. He opened the small door to the churchyard. Six men stood waiting, brief smiles the only communication between them. As yet there was no semblance of a team about the group. He hoped that would not last long.

'What would you like us to do, Vicar?' Stanley Russell asked as they filed in.

'If you give the man a chance you will find out,' Peter chided.

He smiled. Leaders and followers. He had seen it during his training for the last war. Some would naturally exhibit what his former commanding officer had called "leader's legs". Others would follow. And some may fail. Only time would tell. But all had to make a decision and all had to know the worst.

He stood before them. But it was different to standing in church to deliver a sermon. In the pulpit there was a separation of sorts; clergyman and flock. But as a member of an Auxiliary Unit there could be no division. Somehow he had to make them a team; individually independent yet integral members of the whole. He ran his eye along the row of faces he had known for many years. 'Commander Winthorpe intended to be here today to meet you, but with the bombing last night he was needed in London. And he will keep us informed as to what is happening on a wider scale.' He glanced down at his notes. 'I have been asked to form a special group, and what I am asking you to do is not for the faint-hearted. It will be tough, physically and mentally. We have all witnessed the planes in the skies this last month and now they are bombing our homes, not just our factories. Invasion is no longer probable but imminent. If the Germans land along the Sussex coastline, it would be our job to stay behind enemy lines and do as much damage to their advance as possible.'

'Like guerrilla fighters?' George said.

'Yes,' he said, aware of George's excitement.

'More than Home Guard duties, then?' Ned Cooper added.

'Yes,' he replied. He looked into each face. 'I cannot force you to volunteer for this. It is dangerous and you will most probably not survive. Should you agree, there will be some extra training involved.' He stared at the men.

'How much time do we have to think about it?' Reginald asked, breaking the silence.

'Not much. In fact, I need your answer before you leave here today,' he said.

The men stared at him for what seemed like hours.

'Where is this training?' Clive asked.

'Wiltshire.'

'How long, Clement?' Peter asked.

'You will be back on Thursday. As far as your family and anyone else are concerned, you are doing exercises with the Home Guard. I wish to stress that this is top secret and cannot be discussed with anyone. You will be asked to sign The Official Secrets Act. Our safety lies in our coherence as a group and our loyalty to each other.'

'It doesn't give us much time to rearrange things. I've got meat that needs portioning for the rations,' Stanley said.

'I'm sorry about it,' he said, looking along the row of faces. 'But time isn't exactly on our side.' He had expected some degree of apprehension or even excitement, but given what was happening around them, he had not anticipated that chopping up meat would usurp the Prime Minister's plans to thwart the invading enemy.

'No, we apologise, Clement. I don't think any of us really believed the invasion would happen this quickly. Of course we will reschedule things,' Peter added, glaring at Stanley.

'I suppose Gladys can do it,' Stanley added in a low voice.

Clement saw the pink flushes in Stanley's pale cheeks. The man would feel silly enough without further comment from him. At least, he hoped so.

But courage is a curious human trait. It has no signs or symptoms until displayed. Every man among them joined the team without further hesitation. He almost thanked the Germans for the bombing of the previous evening. And Peter for his steadying influence.

'You need to be at Lewes Station tomorrow morning at six o'clock. Wear your Home Guard uniform if you have one and bring only the personal items you need. Everything else, including weapons, will be provided.'

It was a mixed group who left the vestry. But Clement believed he discerned a growing cohesion between them, even at such an early stage. The younger men saw their task as an adventure; he had to remind them of the group's secret nature and not to show their ebullience. The older men were more sober. They saw it as the duty of decent men to country and loved ones. He checked his watch and replaced his clergyman's collar. It was not only the responsibility of leading the group that was weighing on him... The sealed list of names, and what had to be done once the group was active, burdened him too.

Closing the door to the vestry he walked back to the vicarage. He was expecting his new assistant at three o'clock. He closed the gate and opened his front door, going straight to the kitchen. A meal of cottage pie with beans and carrots was already on the table. He thought Mary seemed to have an energy that he had not seen in a while. He smiled. He knew why. On his return from London he had asked her to arrange and manage the exercises for "invasion day", as they were calling it. She had already compiled a roll of all the villagers' names. And she had chosen *The Crown* as the emergency assembly point. She had also planned a meeting with the villagers for Monday evening to discuss the arrangements. Furthermore, she had arranged with Doctor Haswell to have emergency medical supplies located at the public house. And it had not been difficult to convince her that he would be absent due to his need to be with the Home Guard when the invasion actually began.

Clement said Grace and picked up his knife and fork. From the corner of his eye he watched Mary. He loved her so much; her capability, her practical nature and calm efficiency. He wanted to tell her how much he loved her but he thought it may alarm her. He felt his left eyebrow rise. He wasn't sure much would perturb his indomitable, pragmatic wife. He envisaged her telling some German General that they had no right to enter her house. He prayed that when the time came, she would indeed be as strong as he believed. He also prayed for himself and for the strength he would need once the invasion was announced.

Reverend Hubert Battersby was, Clement learned, nearly eighty years of age, but the man had a gentle, softly-spoken, winning manner which he believed the villagers would warm to.

'I had my own parish in Gloucester, Reverend Wisdom. There isn't much about village life that would surprise me,' he laughed.

Twenty minutes later Mary joined them and they went over Mary's plan for invasion day. He was pleased to see there was an immediate rapport between Battersby and Mary. Pleased not just because he knew the village would be in good hands, but also because in all the activity to which he, alone, was privy, he could visit Inspector Russell covertly, when the time came.

Chapter Seven

Monday 9th September 1940

Lewes Railway Station was cold and windy in the early light. Stamping his numb feet, Clement drew his overcoat around him and stared at the cool, damp fog hanging like a shroud over the valley. Poking through the mist were the buildings of the Lewes High Street and above them, on the hill, the Norman Keep of Lewes Castle. He had always thought the old ruin romantic, but now he saw it as a reminder of the last time a foreign power successfully invaded. A thousand years of keeping invaders at bay. It was a proud history, and one to cling to when fear and hopelessness tried to conquer. He pushed the thought from his mind with a silent verse of *Onward Christian Soldiers*.

He saw the smoke of the approaching train. Hurrying through the small crowd gathered on the platform, Stanley Russell ran up to them, his face flushed.

'Sorry I'm late, Vicar.'

Clement felt a frown crease his forehead.

'He'll be late for his own funeral, that one,' Ned said under his breath.

Clement smiled. But he wasn't happy.

They sat in one of the few empty compartments. Spirits were buoyant and excitement kept the men chatting. They stowed their few possessions and sat as the train pulled away from Lewes Station.

It was late afternoon when they walked down the road, away from Swindon station. He checked his watch. Six o'clock. The transport was due any minute. He heard the grind of gears and looked up. A three-ton truck bearing the GHQ Home Forces insignia, a lion rampant and the unit identification number 490 came rumbling towards them. The truck drew up beside him and a man jumped down from the truck's cabin.

'Captain Wisdom?' the man asked.

Clement nodded. The Corporal's use of his rank surprised him. He had been Reverend Wisdom for so long he couldn't imagine going by any other title.

'I am to take you directly to Coleshill House, Sir. Major Bannon is expecting you,' the Corporal said, opening the passenger door for him.

The men threw their packs into the rear of the truck and climbed in. Clement took the front seat beside the driver. He felt awkward about the distinction, but he wanted a chance to question the driver.

'Are there any activities planned for this evening, Corporal?' he asked, recalling his military training prior to the first war. In his mind he could hear the gravelly voiced Drill Sergeant of long ago telling the new recruits to form a circle of equal sides. He smiled at the recollection.

'Major Bannon's the one to speak to, Captain.'

The truck left the main road and they entered the estate through a pair of tall ironwork gates. He had hoped to have forewarning about any activities planned for the remainder of the day. The Army had a habit of springing exercises on the unwary. He glanced at the passing meadows. On both sides of the drive were fields with stands of mature trees. Off to the east was the dense foliage of a forest. A few minutes later Clement saw Coleshill House, a beautifully proportioned four-storey mansion.

'The big house is for the officers. And the two old girls who live there,' the Corporal told him.

'The owners are still in residence?' he asked.

'Elderly sisters, Sir. And their dogs. All other ranks are in the stables. Major Bannon regrets that due to you coming mid-week, there is no room for you in the big house.'

'It suits me,' he said. 'Actually, I'm a vicar. My boss was born in a stable. And his parents encountered the same fate.'

The driver smiled. 'Let's hope the Lord didn't have to worry about rats.'

Rats. He hated them. Their furry little bodies and their smell were instant reminders of the trenches. As the truck pulled up in a courtyard at the side of the big house a man in a major's uniform approached them.

'Sorry I wasn't there to meet you, Wisdom,' the Major said. 'Bannon is my name. The Corporal will show your men where to put their things and we will assemble at 1930 hours in the house.'

He checked his watch. They had about forty minutes to acquaint themselves with the stables and the rats.

'I understand I am also in the stables, Major?'

'Sorry about that, Wisdom. Full up this week,' Bannon said. But there was no reason provided.

It didn't matter to him. Actually he was grateful. His men were not only people he had known for twenty years, but if he was about to spend the rest of his – possibly short – life with them, he wanted to know as much as possible about them. 'Will there be any training this evening, Major?' he asked.

'We will have dinner at 2000 hours,' Bannon said. 'And tonight there will be an address by the Colonel followed by a lecture on intercommunication. Tomorrow we begin in earnest. It's a full programme, Wisdom. Usually we see recruits on weekends but your group is a bit of an exception. Colonel Gubbins has given your sector top priority. You're from Sussex, I understand?'

He nodded. 'What we will be learning?'

'Explosives in the morning. Unarmed combat in the afternoon, then a lecture on guerrilla tactics, and after dinner a lecture on the Jerry army. Then it's a night patrol, I'm afraid.'

He watched as the Corporal herded his men from the truck. They disappeared into the two-storey stable buildings.

'And Wednesday?'

Major Bannon turned to face him. 'On your second day we teach you about your Operational Bases, where you will be living. And then you'll start putting the theory into practice. Normally the groups leave in the afternoon, but Gubbins wants your group to learn a bit more about our clandestine enemy.'

'Is there a reason for that?' he asked.

'You are pretty close to the coast there, Wisdom. It could be that you will encounter enemy spies. Interrogation is easier and produces greater results if you understand what motivates them. Your lecturer for that session is a civilian. And a woman. Comes from a family in your line of work, actually. Then there will be your assessments in the evening. So you will be leaving us on Thursday morning.' The Major smiled. 'Remember Wisdom, you never know who you are talking to. We have a slogan for that, *The Enemy is Always Listening*. Well, I'll leave you to settle in. See you in the house in half an hour.'

Sir,' he replied, saluting.

'We don't salute here, Wisdom. Not a habit we encourage in our line of work. Remember Nelson.'

Clement watched Major Bannon walk away, then followed the team to the stables and the waiting rats.

Inside were rows of timber bunks. Each was topped with a rolled-up mattress and between each structure were a small cabinet and shelf. No other adornment of any kind graced the walls or floors. Peter already had the men stowing their few possessions.

Clement told them what he had learned about the training. 'Doesn't appear as though there will be much time for sleep. And a word of warning. Expect the unexpected. The Army has a habit of arranging surprises for the unwary. Especially after a large dinner. Have you encountered any rats?'

He saw the apprehensive expressions.

'I think they will be the least of our concerns,' Reginald said, stowing his razor and soap in a cup on the shelf.

He was inclined to agree but he didn't say so. Experience had taught him that the Army tested men's resolve at every opportunity. And it was as much a test of the man as it was the team. 'Leader's legs,' he muttered.

A whistle was shattering the silence. He swung his legs over the bunk and stood up. In the pre-dawn light, the Corporal was standing in the stable doorway. 'What is it, Corporal?'

'You need to locate a truck on the grounds. About a mile south of here. Once you find it, climb aboard and drive it back here. You have one hour.' The Corporal vanished.

Clement checked his watch as he pushed his feet into his boots. Half past five. Tying his boots, he stepped outside.

A grey-blue light filled the courtyard, but the Corporal was nowhere to be seen. In fact, nothing stirred. Peter and Reginald were beside him.

'How do you want to do this, Clement?' Reginald asked.

He pulled a compass from his pocket, a last-minute inclusion as he left the vicarage. 'Due south is back down the drive we came in by,' he said. 'Peter, will you make sure everyone is up and that their boots are comfortable. We leave in one minute.

'What do we bring with us?' Reginald asked.

'As we haven't yet been issued with weapons, I can only surmise that this is a fitness exercise,' he said as the men strolled out of the stable.

'Look lively. And form two lines. Hurry up, Stanley!' Peter called.

Clement stared at the group. Other than Reginald, the team didn't seem to be showing much enthusiasm for the task. From the corner of his eye he thought he saw a curtain move in an upstairs window. He couldn't see anyone but he felt that the Major's eyes were probably on them. They broke into a slow run heading south.

Twenty minutes later he signalled for the group to squat in the long grass. He could see the parked truck under a tree about fifty yards ahead. There was no-one around it.

'Thank goodness for that,' Stanley said, flopping down into the grass beside him.

'Quit your whinging, Stanley, or I'll put you on the bus for Sussex myself,' Reginald whispered between clenched teeth.

Stanley's face was flushed.

Whilst he thought Reginald's comment was harsh, it had achieved the desired result. Clement looked back at the lorry. He was about to speak when he heard the truck's motor start. The vehicle drove onto the drive and disappeared among the trees on the right. It was an old trick. And one the Army used to test stamina, physical as well as mental.

'Gather round,' he whispered. 'We know approximately where it is now, but from now on there is no talking, only hand signals. We will divide into two groups and approach it from both sides. Clive, Stanley and Reginald, you come with me, George, you and Ned go with Peter. And stay low and off the road.'

He knew the twofold purpose of the exercise and he was pleased that none of his team had succumbed. Although he kept his eye on Stanley.

'Well done this morning, Wisdom. You only fell into our trap once,' Bannon was saying as they walked towards a low outbuilding.

He grinned. But it had been a salutary lesson. Nothing could be taken at face value.

They walked into a long wooden hut and the Corporal shut the door. In the centre was a long table and on it were various objects, some of which he recognised.

'This morning we will be handling explosives and learning how to avoid blowing ourselves up,' Bannon was saying. 'This is a detonator.' Bannon picked up a short aluminium tube about two inches long. 'Open at one end, they contain a very powerful explosive and can be used to explode charges of high explosive using Safety or Orange line. The fuse is inserted into the detonator and crimped in place. Orange Line contains more gunpowder, and burns at a rate of ninety feet per second.'

Clement looked along the line of men. Every eye was on the Major.

'This makes sense to me, Clement,' Clive whispered. 'Not all that running around in the dark we did this morning. I understand why we did it, but it still annoyed me. But this!' Clive said, grinning. 'This is how we will kill the bloody Germans. As long as I get just two of them I'll be happy.'

'Pay attention, Clive,' Peter chided.

But he knew what Clive meant. Revenge was a powerful motivator. He smiled at Peter. His friend felt like his right-hand man. Always there, at his elbow, correcting and encouraging. He glanced at Ned, who along with Clive had the strongest reasons for despising the Germans, in Clement's opinion. But if Ned hated Germans, the man didn't show it. But perhaps that was the difference between the mature man and youth. The man's concentration was absolute. Clement felt a smile cross his lips. Peter and Ned had been good choices. Rational and thorough. About as perfect a combination as there could be.

By lunchtime, George too had shown his abilities. In fact, the boy seemed to have found his calling with wires and plastic explosive in his hands. Clement pondered the heart condition. He didn't know much about irregular rhythms, but he resolved to question Doctor Haswell on his return to the village.

The early afternoon was spent using and becoming familiar with their new weapons. Reg, as he now liked to be called, had proven to be an extraordinary marksman. The man held the Sten gun as though he was holding a pedigree cat. But the one he wasn't sure about was Stanley. The lad was a little overweight, always had a comment to make and was always the last one to join the team.

'Where's Stanley?' he asked Peter as they walked to the unarmed combat lessons on the front lawn.

'Lavatory.'

He heard the crunching of gravel under running feet as Stanley joined them. 'Stanley, you really must be more punctual.'

'Sorry, Vicar. It won't happen again,' Stanley said, his flushed pink face shiny with sweat.

He had heard the excuse before and he was having regrets. 'You really shouldn't eat so much.'

A whistle blew. He turned around. The Corporal, who was taking the unarmed combat lesson, was waiting for them. Beside the corporal were several straw-filled dummies in German military uniform. After teaching them how to dispatch a victim silently from behind, the corporal issued them with their commando knives.

He knew that Stanley, as a butcher, could use a blade. But the force with which Stanley plunged the dagger astounded him. He couldn't tear his eyes away from the lad. Stanley stood with his feet spread wide, the Fairbairn Sykes double-edged blade clenched in a tight fist, stabbing and punching the dummies with incredible force. A stab wound aside, no man would survive Stanley's powerful swing.

'Did you see Stanley with that knife?' Peter whispered to him.

'I did,' Clement replied.

'I think I am pleased he is on our side.'

He had to agree with Peter. The lad had been a revelation. But he wondered what was motivating Stanley. Had the lad just found a skill he was good at? Or was there another reason behind that force?

Clement lay back on his bunk bed. Some of the men were asleep already. He checked his watch. It was a few minutes before seven o'clock. The lecture on Gubbins' own Nine Points of Guerrilla Tactics had been short. Every muscle in his body ached. But the night patrol loomed and he knew they would have to embrace the skills.

At nineteen hundred hours, he roused the men, starting with Stanley. Dinner was at nineteen thirty sharp. And lateness and slovenliness were not well regarded. During dessert he received a sealed envelope. It contained a note and a map. The aim of the night patrol was to locate a specific road and blow up a German vehicle which would be carrying high-ranking German officers. The vehicle was expected to be on a specific road between midnight and one o'clock. He folded the note and placed it and the map into his pocket. He checked the time; nineteen fifty hours. The sun had not long set and the forest would be cold and dark. He calculated that it would take them about two hours to reach the designated road.

The evening lecture on the German Army might have been interesting, but Clement's eyes closed at odd moments and he struggled to stay awake.

At twenty one hundred hours they returned to the stables.

'I have the map and target for tonight's patrol,' he said and told them his plan for the exercise. 'Get some sleep now. I'll rouse you in forty minutes.'

The men hadn't spoken. Everyone was in his own space and exhaustion had taken hold. If he shared his bed with a rat or several, he didn't much care.

Clement closed his eyes and spent a few minutes in silent prayer. There had been almost no time for reflection during the day. He went over the men of his team one more time. He was happy with his selection, especially Peter and Ned. But the others had individual abilities that made for a cohesive team. He put his hand to where his clerical collar should have been. He felt less and less like a vicar. But then, his men, no doubt, would be feeling the same about their vocations.

At twenty minutes to ten o'clock Clement woke the men. Checking that they had sufficient water, ammunition, explosives and detonators they lifted their packs and Sten guns onto their backs and headed out in silence. They fell into a mute column with himself in the lead, then Stanley, George, Reg, Ned, Clive and Peter. Leaving the house on their left, they headed east for the tree line. He had decided to wear his Fairbairn Sykes knife strapped to his inner left calf. As he walked he could feel it rubbing against his flesh. But he didn't remove it. Neither did he adjust it. He would get used to it.

The men had walked in total silence for over an hour. He reflected on the six disparate men he had seen outside the vestry only a few days ago. They hardly seemed the same men. Even though not a word had been spoken, there was a silent camaraderie developing.

Just before midnight they arrived at the road. He selected a section with a long curve for the ambush. Adjacent to the road was a depression surrounded by fallen timbers. Checking the site, he squatted by a hollowed log and studied the map.

'George, run a tripwire at head height at this point,' he whispered.

'Stanley, you and Clive place the charges. Use pressure switches and put two on the road in the tyre tracks about five feet apart.

George ran the wire across the road as Clive and Stanley attended to the explosives. Each man then took up a position around him in a circle to wait for the target. He and George occupied the middle ground. In front of him, Peter, as second in charge, sat beside Ned whose finger rested on the trigger of his Sten gun. Off to his left was Stanley. To his right was Clive and behind him was Reg. It was cold and he worried that the men, being tired, would lose concentration. Peter moved silently between them, making sure the men were still awake and alert. But one o'clock came and went, and still no vehicles appeared on the road. Clement signalled to Peter to do a solo patrol around the area. Ten minutes later, Peter emerged from the trees off to his right, shaking his head.

They waited.

Grey light from the half moon penetrated to the forest floor at odd angles, casting deep shadows across the sector. But nothing moved. He had expected the forest to have some noise. Small animals, something. Badgers, at least. The silence was unsettling. But given the number and frequency of explosions at Coleshill, the badgers had probably left long ago. He looked over the fallen log. He could see Peter and Ned in front of him. Tucking his head under his arm, he checked on the others to his rear. Perhaps the timing had been deliberately wrong, designed to put them on edge.

'Hurry up and wait', he repeated. It was an army motto the men had coined in the first war. The cold and damp were taking hold and as the time passed, he could hear Reg shifting position in the shallow dugout behind him.

He heard the motor and checked his watch.

Two o'clock; the approaching sound of a vehicle motor. He sat up and signalled the men to take up their positions. Peter and George crossed the road and lay under the shrubs opposite, their Sten guns aimed at the point where any single rider would encounter the tripwire. But the noise was not distinct, and Clement decided there were two vehicles. Sending Reg and Stanley further up the track to attend to any other vehicles, he lay in the foliage with Ned. Clive lay off to his right, behind a fallen tree trunk, three grenades lined up beside him.

As the vehicle approached, he saw a figure jump out and run into the bushes at the side of the road. Behind the vehicle, further back on the track, he saw Reg rush forward. In one movement Reg had the man on the ground, pinning him to the track as the vehicle with three straw-filled dummies dressed as German officers ran over the pressure switches. A small explosion, much less than the real targets would ever feel, lit up the dark forest floor. Machine-gun fire strafed the upturned vehicle. Peter came out of the shrubs beside the road, his Sten in his grip, pointing at the driver of the second car.

'Okay,' Major Bannon called, stepping from the second vehicle and blowing a whistle. 'Well done. Remove any unexploded devices, then make your way back to the house.' Bannon climbed back into the car and, collecting the prostrate Corporal, drove away.

Clement looked around at the men. 'Well done, everyone.'

He looked into the faces. He saw elation. It was deserved.

'No talking on our return,' he said. 'George, will you retrieve the trip wire?'

Ten minutes later, they headed off silently, crossing the forest. Within the hour they were in the fields, the chimneys of Coleshill House poking through the treetops.

Chapter Eight

Thursday 12th September 1940

When they saw Swindon Railway Station again, they were different men. What they had learned in three days could be condensed into one word: sabotage. What they had become also came down to one word: assassins. He believed none of them would ever be the same after Coleshill House.

They climbed aboard the train and settled quickly into one of the compartments. It would be some hours before they saw Lewes. Ned and George were asleep almost immediately. Clement took the corner seat and rested his head against the window, reflecting on their time at Coleshill. But it had not been until after the lecture on human psychology that he understood what he had witnessed in the course of the training. Beverley, the woman who had taken the lecture, if that was her name, had asked them to analyse what motivated them. Killing Germans had figured high on the men's list. For his own part, he had accepted the role Gubbins and Johnny had asked of him because he believed it was his duty. But were there more fundamental reasons? Beverley had condensed human behaviour into two prime motivators: the need to be loved, and approval. Reg had led a chorus of contemptuous remarks, saying that he was there to kill Germans not understand them. But Clement wasn't so sure. If you understood what motivated a person, you could manipulate them. It was almost sinister. He thought of his own childhood. He had never believed that his father wanted or loved him. Furthermore, he believed his father had never approved of anything he did. Was that true? Or was it just never discussed? Was it the same with his men? Many men of his acquaintance had had strained relationships with their fathers. Was indifference to each other the only outcome? Could it be more accurately described as rivalry? Did it manifest itself in anger?

He began to go through all his team and list what he had learned about them. Peter Kempton, although a widower, had a Jewish mother-in-law who had moved to Germany after Muriel's death and from whom Peter had heard nothing in over a year. Peter had reacted to photographs Beverley had shown them of German reprisals on members of the French resistance. His friend had said that the photographs were designed to arouse anger. And perhaps he was correct. Reg certainly had reacted with an angry outburst about German cruelty. But Peter's reaction differed from that of the other men. Peter, always a proud man, had become withdrawn, even sullen, saying that the photographs weren't true and that Beverley and her kind were using the group as guinea pigs. But perhaps Peter's indignation was not so much hatred for the Germans as anger towards himself for allowing Muriel to journey alone to Switzerland. Or perhaps the photographs were indeed faked. He knew the Army used arousal to insensate men's emotions. He shook his head, remembering what they had learned at Coleshill about the Nazi policy towards the Jewish people. Thousands had been displaced, their homes and possessions seized and for no other reason than that they were Jewish. How could any country treat its own people with such barbarism? He had tried to engage Peter in conversation about his quite reasonable fears concerning his wife's mother, but his friend had quite emphatically said he didn't wish to talk about it. Peter had avoided him after that and had not spoken a word to him since. Clement wasn't sure what he had said to occasion such a reaction but he prayed it wouldn't last.

But Beverley's lecture had made him appreciate one thing. Anger, in all its various forms, was a powerful motivator and in one way bound the group together. Peter, over allowing Muriel to go to Switzerland, Reg for what the Germans would do to his home, Ned for the gas which had made his father's life a living hell, not to mention his boy's tragic death; Clive for his lost sons, George to regain his honour, and even himself – the long-suppressed anger he felt towards his father. But the one that worried him the most was Stanley. He envisaged again the feet spread wide, the powerful lunge, the force of the knife as it ripped the straw soldiers. But was that swing the unleashing of years of hatred? Stanley's anger towards his father was embedded and long established; on the walk back to Coleshill House after the night patrol the lad had confided to Clement about his father's abuse during his childhood. But were the mental scars more worrying?

He closed his eyes but he did not sleep. David Russell. He had never liked the man; now he despised him. And he did not relish the thought of having to take the list to the Inspector. He had fought against it, but Gubbins had insisted. Not that Russell would know the contents of the sealed letter. Yet Clement harboured so many doubts about the man. And it was not inconceivable that Russell would open the letter. He had not yet compiled the list, but was waiting to see if his men were willing and able to continue after the days at Coleshill.

An hour out of Lewes and while the others still slept, he wrote out the list and sealed it within the envelope Gubbins had supplied for the purpose, with the Ministry of Home Security official stamp on the top left corner. He placed the envelope into his top pocket. He could feel it, the names burning into his chest. If the operation went ahead, every man on the list would die. Including himself. It was just a matter of when.

Even though they all lived within a mile radius of each other, their parting at Lewes station had a sense of finality about it. Was it lost naivety? Was it acceptance that with the Germans invading, simple life was no more? He stared at the faces of his team. Men he would know even more as the weeks passed, if they were alive in a few weeks' time. Life on the edge forged a union between men, rivalled only by the marriage bed for closeness. They had been away only three days, but those days had changed them all. He was glad of the camaraderie, for what had surfaced at Coleshill had been shared.

He watched Peter walk away, up the hill towards Lewes High Street. His friend had expressed a desire to purchase some books from the antiquarian bookshop in town. He wasn't sure the reason was genuine. But Peter's sullenness had softened to some extent. They had talked about the first aid class he and Peter, as second-in-charge had had to attend. They had studied photographs of stab and gunshot wounds. He had even learned how to amputate a limb if his team incurred such injuries in the field. No member of the team was ever left behind, dead or alive, and all traces of their presence were to be removed in the event of an aborted mission. But the subject of Peter's deceased wife and mother-in-law was not raised again. Reg had been met by his wife. Ned, Clive, Stanley and George walked ahead of him towards the bus shelter. They were a mixed group, as different as any group could be in age and background, yet he was proud of them. His choice of these men had been vindicated. He pondered the one emotion that they all shared and which, in a strange way, bound them together. Anger. Yet, whether between nations or men, anger and hatred were destructive forces. It was his job to transform that or, at the very least, harness it. As he often did when walking alone, his mind played with biblical verses. *Anger lies in the lap of fools*, so

Ecclesiastes stated. He hoped he was neither the fooled nor the foolish.

Thursday was usually his day with Mary. And now he had missed two, he felt the cool wind of disappointment.

'Would you like to go to Brighton tomorrow?' he asked as he entered the scullery.

The spoon stopped.

'We could take that Victoria sponge with us and have tea on the esplanade, if you would like?'

'What are you up to, Clement?'

'Nothing! I just thought that as I missed taking you out last week and today, I thought you might like a trip to the seaside tomorrow.'

'What about your chess morning with Peter? To say nothing of your sermon for Sunday?'

'It would be nice to see the sea birds and smell the salt air again.'

She was watching him, the hazel eyes missed little.

'A nice thought, Clement. But I think your war games have tired you out, and you're not as young as you used to be. Tea in Lewes will suit me just as well. Besides, I need to pick up some flour from the shops there. Mr Black is completely out,' she said.

It was a blissfully quiet evening. The radio was full of news about London and journalists speculating about invasion. It was a topic he did not wish to discuss.

The telephone rang.

'I'll go,' he said.

'Clement? It's Johnny. Can you talk?'

'A little.'

'No invasion as yet but your group is on high alert. How was Coleshill?'

'Exhausting,' he said.

'Good. Clement, you will be contacted by the Royal Engineers who are to build your Operational Base starting tomorrow. Could you select an appropriate site?'

'Yes,' he said. He glanced along the hallway. 'But could they work with my second in command?'

'That should be alright,' Johnny said.

The line went dead.

He held the receiver in his hand then dialled Peter's number. He was about to hang up when Peter answered.

'Sorry to disturb you, Peter,' he whispered. 'I do hope you were not in bed already. I wanted to alert you to a call you will receive tomorrow from the Engineers. I have suggested that they liaise with you about selecting the place for the Operational Base. And if you have no objections, I could use the morning to spend some time with Mary.'

'Of course, Clement. Happy to help. And Clement, don't worry about me.'

He smiled. 'Thank you, Peter. Good night.'

An hour later they lay in bed. He knew Mary was not asleep but they didn't speak. He was weary. But it was the unknown that drained him the most. Johnny had said they were on high alert. Any day. He felt a surge of acid churn his stomach. He was also pleased to have sorted any unresolved issue with Peter. The building of the operational base had been a blessing all around. He said a short prayer, asking the Lord for forgiveness for its brevity and turned on his side. In the darkness he stared at Mary. He loved her. He wanted to tell her how much. But he couldn't. Everything must seem as usual. As usual as it can be before relinquishing his clergyman's collar for an assassin's jacket. Another wave of droning increased and decreased overhead.

'London?' she whispered, turning over in the bed.

'Probably,' he replied.

He felt her nestle into his side and he drew her close.

Chapter Nine

Friday 13th September 1940

They walked towards the bus stop adjacent to Fearnley Maughton village green, and within the hour they were in the Lewes High Street. Mary slipped her arm through his. As they walked the street one unfamiliar face followed another, but his mind pondered the men of his cell and the faces he was beginning to know well. Private lives. Secrets. And skeletons. Asking Peter to liaise with the Royal Engineers had given him the opportunity to mend any rift. It appeared to have worked. The other older men of the group had returned to their usual lives, and to the casual observer nothing had occurred to change these men. But it was not the case for the two young villagers, Stanley and George. While in the village waiting for the Lewes bus he had seen them both. They looked at him differently. George had winked. It was foolish. Nothing about their activities at Coleshill could even be hinted at in the village and he intended to raise it with them the next time they were all together. He hoped that no-one else had noticed the gesture. Mary, who possessed extraordinary intuition, had not said anything.

But Stanley was a special case. He would never forget what Stanley had confided about his father and he couldn't eradicate the image of Stanley's powerful swing. Swift and deadly. Stanley had thrust the blade with such force that it shocked him. But, as he had discovered, each one of them had their Achilles heel. Anger, in all its forms, lurked within the human breast. They left the grocery shop, a brown paper bag of flour in Mary's basket, and made their way to the tea room.

Forty minutes later they finished their afternoon tea. He and Mary had discussed the meeting held in his absence on Monday night at *The Crown* and the plans for invasion day that she and the villagers had put in place. He wanted and needed to hear about it. But it also provided him with a reason to avoid discussing what he had been doing. It struck him as incongruous that today he sipped tea and ate Victoria sponge while two days previously he had held a commando knife at Major Bannon's throat and blown up a German staff car complete with three high-ranking German dummies. 'Not as good as your Victoria sponge, Mary,' he told her as they walked back to the bus stop.

Mary squeezed his arm.

'Do you ever think about all the people who have walked this High Street since the castle was first built?' he asked.

'You believe the invasion is imminent?' she asked.

He did not answer. Not that he intended to avoid her clairvoyant question this time, but they had reached the bus stop and a young woman was seated in the shelter.

'Are you going to Fearnley Maughton?' the young woman asked.

For a moment he could not answer, struck by her astonishing beauty. 'Yes. I am Reverend Clement Wisdom and this is my wife, Mary,' he said, his hand reaching for his hat.

'Pleased to meet you, Reverend. I'm Elizabeth Wainwright. But everyone calls me Elsie.'

'Do you have family in Fearnley Maughton?' Mary asked.

The girl shook her head. 'No. I'm the new nurse and midwife. I have to report to a Doctor Haswell tomorrow. Do you know him?'

'It is a small village, Elsie,' Mary said. 'We all know each other. Where are you staying in the village?'

'At *The Crown*. Is it all right? Decent, I mean?'

'It will suit you well enough,' Mary said. 'I didn't know Doctor Haswell required a nurse?'

'I answered the advertisement in *The Times*,' the girl said.

'Where have you come from?' he asked.

'London,' Elsie said. 'Actually, I am so pleased to find employment outside London. What with the bombing since Thursday night.'

'Is your family still in London, Elsie?' Mary asked.

'My parents lived in Eastbourne but they died some years ago. They were quite old when they had me. But I like what I do and I am looking forward to meeting some of the people in the village and who knows, perhaps I will meet someone special.'

The girl beamed her flawless, wide smile, her intense blue eyes sparkling.

The arrival of the bus halted the conversation and Clement watched as Elsie reached for a battered, red tapestry valise. He glanced at the size of the girl's baggage. It was not much bigger than Mary's shopping basket and he wondered if the girl had lost everything in the raids.

He noted that Mary did not chat on the return journey. That was unusual. And he knew the cause. Mary's eyes had not shifted from the disarming Elsie Wainwright, and he saw the evidence of disapproval in the corners of his wife's mouth. As intrigued as he was to learn why the girl should be the object of such scrutiny, he knew better than to ask.

'There is *The Crown*,' he said as they drew into the village. He bent to pick up the girl's odd, red bag.

'I can manage, really,' Elsie said grasping the tote.

'Will we see you in church on Sunday?' Mary asked.

'Yes,' the girl said. 'That is, if there are no babies to deliver.'

They watched the girl walk away, carrying her limited possessions. With several unattached young men in the village, he did not believe she would have to carry her valise for long.

They sat at the kitchen table, sipping tea and listening to the wireless. Neither of them spoke. London was ablaze, especially in the east. Bombs and burning aircraft fell from the sky. People everywhere were homeless. Hundreds of previously evacuated children who had returned to London had died or been orphaned. The fire brigade worked around the clock battling the overwhelming flames from incendiary bombs. Even the Palace and St Paul's Cathedral had taken a hit. And there was no indication that it would cease any time soon. He stood and switched off the radio, a gloomy pall descending.

'Clement, I think I should visit Gwen. She will be frightened,' Mary said.

'Do you think it wise?'

'Wise or not, Clement, she is my sister and Windsor is not that far away. I could catch this evening's train and be back tomorrow.'

He didn't like it, but there was little use protesting. Once Mary had decided, there was no stopping her. He glanced at his watch. It was not yet five o'clock. And even though he would worry about her safety, her absence would give him the opportunity to see David Russell.

While Mary went to pack a few possessions, Clement walked along the corridor to his study, thinking about what he intended to say to Inspector Russell. He closed the door and listened for the click. Sitting at his desk he reached for the envelope. He carried it on his person at all times, and never took it out anywhere but in his study. He ran his finger over the Ministry of Home Security crest and pondered the names on the list one more time. As much as he hated the idea of Inspector Russell's involvement, with the bombing London and other major cities were receiving, he knew Gubbins expected the German invasion any day.

He convinced himself that it would only be a matter of days at the most that Russell would have the list anyway. But then, that led to another unsavoury duty.

Within the hour he walked with Mary to the bus shelter.

'I've left some sandwiches for you in the meat safe for your supper. And don't worry about me. I'll be back tomorrow. Probably the evening train.'

He kissed her on the cheek and waited only long enough for the bus to leave the village. 'Always do the hard jobs first,' he muttered to himself.

He strode away from the village green towards the police station, tapping his fingers against his top pocket, feeling for the envelope. Fearnley Maughton Police Station was a building he passed daily, many times, but it was also a place he rarely frequented. Today was the day. There was still time. Besides, he needed to familiarise himself with its layout.

He pushed open the door and walked towards the desk.

'Good evening, Constable Matthews.'

'Good evening, Reverend. How can we help you today?'

'I would like to see Inspector Russell, if he is still on duty.'

'You are lucky to catch him in, Sir,' Constable Matthews said, glancing at the clock on the wall. The Constable entered Clement's name in the daily log and noted the time. He saw the entry: five forty-five pm. 'Will you take a seat and I'll let him know you're here.'

He sat in the upright chairs that lined the walls of the public area and slipped the envelope from his pocket. The sealed list felt warm and it had developed a curvature from contact with his chest. He replaced the envelope, pushing it down into his inside coat pocket. He could feel his breathing had increased and he felt like a child again outside the headmaster's office. What he was about to do was inherently wrong. He knew it. Even if Gubbins didn't.

He heard the slow but deliberate stride, and Constable Matthews reappeared. 'If you would like to come this way, Vicar?'

Constable Matthews held open the glass partition door to the rear hallway, and Clement crossed the waiting room. He had never been on the business side of that door. He looked around. The station appeared deserted. Constable Matthews' heavy boots echoed on the tiled floor.

'Just the Inspector and myself here at present, Sir, it being late,' said Constable Matthews.

'This won't take long, Constable,' he said.

Matthews smiled. 'I was just off home, Sir.'

In front of him, at the end of the corridor was a door and written in gold letters on it was the occupants name; Inspector D. Russell.

Constable Matthews tapped on the door, pushing it wide.

David Russell was a small man in his mid-forties, red-faced, red-haired and with piercing blue eyes. Clement had never considered the man's age before, but now that he knew Stanley's exact age and about Stanley's young life, he realised that David Russell must have been in his mid-teenage years when Stanley was born. It explained a few things. Russell remained behind his wooden desk, making no attempt to stand or greet him.

The Inspector gestured towards a leather-covered chair before the desk. 'Well, Reverend, what can I do for you? I hope you haven't come begging for money?'

He felt himself groan, although it was not audible. He furrowed his brow, visualising the day, which could be soon, when he would have to eliminate the man. 'I have come on the most secret of issues,' he said, his voice low.

He saw the Inspector slouch in the chair. There was something condescending about Russell's posture, as if he were saying, what could you possibly know that would be deemed secret? He saw a curl spread over the man's lips. It was a derisive gesture and he sensed that Russell intended it to be.

'Last week I met with Colonel Colin Gubbins in London,' he began. 'Under direction from the Prime Minister, he has formed an elite sub branch of the Home Guard known as Auxiliary Units.' He reached into his coat and withdrew the letter, his fingers pinching the paper. 'This contains a list of names of men who have been trained to kill the enemy once they land on our shores. Only you and I know of the existence of this list. And it is to stay that way. You are involved only so that when the invasion is announced you will not impede these men in any way nor interfere with their decisions. The men on this list have authority far beyond your own.' Reaching across the desk, he handed the envelope to Russell who leaned forward to take it.

Russell turned the envelope over in his hand, his eyes taking in the official envelope of the Ministry of Home Security.

'You will notice that the letter is sealed. I cannot express to you enough the seriousness of this. This letter is both a protection for these men and a death warrant should it ever fall into the wrong hands,' he paused. 'When I receive notification that the invasion has occurred, I will come here directly and you can open the letter in my presence. Until then, it must remain sealed and locked in your safe, and I am to witness it being placed there.'

'What's this all about, Reverend?' Russell said, the pink lips curling at the corners.

'I have told you all you need to know. If you wish to confirm anything I have said, you should call Colonel Gubbins on this number for verification.' He handed the Inspector a folded piece of paper with Gubbins' London telephone number on it.

'You're serious, aren't you?'

'Very,' he said.

Russell hadn't moved from his reclining position in the chair.

'I will not leave until I see that envelope in your safe.'

Russell leaned forward and picked up the receiver to the telephone on his desk. Constable Matthews' voice responded.

'Bring the keys to my safe, Constable,' Russell growled.

A minute later the door opened and Matthews walked towards Russell's desk with a set of keys.

'That will be all, Constable,' Russell bellowed.

Clement noted that Russell blocked his view of the safe, a contemptible gesture. Young Stanley flashed into his mind. He would have liked to chide Russell about the abusive treatment the man had served up to his son over the years. As it was, he was pleased to see the man reset the locks. Now he could leave.

'Satisfied?' Russell asked.

He stood. 'Call Gubbins,' he said, 'and safeguard that letter with your life,' he added, his eyes flicking to the safe.

He left Russell's office. Just being in the man's presence made him bristle. 'In the Lap of Fools,' he muttered, struggling to suppress his indignation at the man's cynical complacence.

He stood on the doorstep to the police station, feeling vulnerable for both himself and the men. He wondered if the Inspector could be trusted not to open the letter. Gubbins had insisted. But if Russell learned the names on the list, Clement's life and the lives of his men, including Stanley, would count for nothing. Their lives were in Russell's hands now.

Looking up, he saw the front door to the doctor's surgery open and Elsie Wainwright came out. The girl descended the steps and reached for Doctor Haswell's old battered bicycle, which was leaning against the wall adjacent to the surgery door. He lifted his hat in greeting.

'Hello Reverend,' she said.

The crisp, light voice was a stark contrast to the growl of David Russell.

'How are you settling in?' he asked.

'Very well, thank you,' Elsie replied. 'I have just finished my rounds in the village. It is hard with all the sign posts removed. But I suppose I'll soon learn the way.' Elsie beamed her angelic smile.

'I expect it is because they want to confuse the Germans, if they come,' he said. 'Well, I must not keep you. It's getting late.' He lifted his hat in farewell. His gaze followed her as she cycled down the street past the police station and disappeared from view.

He walked back to the vicarage, pondering the events of the day. It was a pity the doctor's house was opposite the police station. He hoped the pretty young nurse wouldn't meet the lewd David Russell for some time to come.

He opened the door to his home. David Russell had occupied his thought so entirely that he had forgotten Mary had gone to her sister's. He stooped to open the meat safe and saw the two sandwiches wrapped in brown paper. He wished she was there. He wanted to share his misgivings about Russell. But he couldn't share this anyway. It was as well she was at Gwen's. He unwrapped his sandwiches.

Chapter Ten

Sunday 15th September 1940

He should never have agreed. Clement reached for his cassock and placed his stole around his neck. He had no wish to disobey orders, but he had worried about it all the previous day and his instinct told him it had been a mistake. Collecting his Bible from his desk, he closed the front door to the vicarage and strode up the hill. By the time he reached the vestry he had resolved to telephone Gubbins first thing tomorrow, and then visit Russell to retrieve the list. Gubbins would just have to understand.

There were more people in church this morning than even the previous week. Fear of invasion was the most likely cause, but the number of young single men led him to believe there was another reason. Half way back on the left hand side of the church sat Elsie Wainwright. On one side of the girl was George Evans and on the other was Stanley Russell. As he stepped into the pulpit he cast his eye along the rows of his parishioners. Behind Elsie were several other single men who seemed very keen to pass her a hymn book already open at the correct page. The matrons were on the right side and he thought he discerned the thin pursed lips of disapproval.

His sermon was on trust and betrayal. Not that the one person he had in mind for his instruction was actually there. In the twenty years he had been at *All Saints*, he had never seen David Russell in church.

He stood by the old door to his church and shook the hands of his parishioners as they left.

'I see you have met our new nurse, Stanley,' he said.

Stanley blushed. 'Elsie told me she met you and Mrs Wisdom in Lewes.'

'She is coming with me to Brighton next week,' George interrupted. 'We are seeing the new flick at the Palace Theatre.'

He glanced at Stanley. Then George. He saw the rivalry. Beautiful girls, lovely though they were, and Elsie was more lovely than most, caused trouble. And trouble between his men he could not have.

'Have you found somewhere more permanent to live yet, Elsie?' he asked.

The girl shook her head. It seemed to sway side to side, the corn-blonde hair falling and floating over her shoulders. On duty, Elsie wore her hair pinned up and under her neat nurse's hat, but not today. It was loose and curled and it glittered in the morning sunshine.

'We mustn't keep you, Elsie,' Mary said, standing beside him. 'Mrs Faulkner! Good morning to you. And don't the flowers look lovely today.'

Elsie and her entourage wandered away.

Among the congregation was another new arrival. Not new to the village, like Elsie, but new among his flock. Reg Naylor had joined the congregation. Coleshill may have shifted things for Reg but Clement did not believe Reg had had an epiphany. Attending church, or so it appeared to him from where he stood in the pulpit, kept Reg involved and informed. The man had taken a seat in the back of the church. During his sermon Clement could see Reg's eyes scanning the assembled group, waiting and watching for trouble. It was unnerving. The penetrative gaze had even sent Mrs Greenwood hurrying from the church. He decided that back row dwellers fell into two camps: shy and retiring, or misfits and rebels. He remembered his school days and the boys who claimed the back row. Without fail that second group of boys ended up in the headmaster's office every Friday morning.

'A word, Clement?' Reg demanded.

Reg's pragmatic voice brought him back to the present.

'That needs to be nipped in the bud,' Reg said his eye shifting to Elsie flanked by George and Stanley. 'I'll do it. You will be too soft. Besides, they know not to mess with me.'

He watched Reg walk away. He hadn't actually said anything. Yet Reg had taken it upon himself to sort out what Reg evidently saw as a breach of discipline. It concerned him that the man was becoming obsessive about their clandestine mission. Major Bannon had said that Reg was a born sniper. He knew Bannon was not only referring to Reg's weapons handling. It was the psychological profile that fitted, and that worried him.

'Reverend?'

He heard the shrill voice coming to him from the lych gate.

Ilene Greenwood was calling to him. 'Do you know where Nurse Wainwright is?'

'I last saw her walking towards *The Crown*, Mrs Greenwood,' he said. 'Is something amiss?'

'No,' the woman replied. 'I have a message from Mister Knowles. His wife has gone into labour.'

'Well, you best hurry, Mrs Greenwood,' he replied. Babies. He knew nothing about them. James Moore's urchins flashed into his minds. Humans in miniature. Everything about them was foreign.

Checking to see that no-one was still at private prayer, he reached for his key and locked the door. He did not like having to lock the church. There was something inherently wrong about closing a house of God. Yet he would never challenge a directive from the Archbishop of Canterbury who had sent out the circular requiring the closures. Still, it did not sit comfortably. Apparently churches had been used by German spies as dead letter drops. Until his visit to Coleshill, he hadn't known what a dead letter drop was.

He thought of George Evans. He had chosen George to be their runner because of his knowledge of all things to do with the post and telegraph. George collected his report for General Headquarters which commented on happenings around Fearnley Maughton, and took it to the dead letter drop for collection by persons unknown. Amateur radio operators then forwarded the messages to London. The reports should have been simple enough, except Johnny had decided that his fifteen-mile-radius sector should also include the country adjacent to the coastline from Eastbourne to Brighton. Cuckmere Haven, just west of Beachy Head, had been added to the list of sites possibly vulnerable to German amphibious invasion, so his reports of the coastline had to be received and transmitted daily, without exception. George, as the village postman, was the perfect choice. But Johnny had been explicit that none of his team should ever actually go to any of the beaches, especially Cuckmere Haven. Clement did not know why and he did not care to know. Besides, the beaches were off-limits and most were festooned in barbed wire and, reputedly, mined.

'You know what they are saying about Margaret Knowles?' Mary whispered into his ear.

The question jolted him back to village reality. 'Mary, I have never taken you for a gossip.'

'You need to be prepared if John Knowles comes back. That is all I am saying.'

He stopped dead in his tracks. He had forgotten that John Knowles had come over a week ago to the vicarage, wanting to see him.

'Oh dear! In all that's happened I forgot him.'

'You know that they are saying the baby is not his,' Mary told him. 'She never deserved a husband like John. And that David Russell, he is a predator of the worst kind. They also say he takes bribes. They deserve each other!'

'I have never asked you to remain silent in the twenty years we have been married. But I must ask you, Mary, no more. John Knowles has enough to worry about, especially if what you say is true, without being the victim of village gossip.'

He pushed open the vicarage door and went straight to the telephone. Lifting the receiver, he dialled John Knowles' number.

Mary had not spoken another word during lunch. It was so unusual. And John Knowles had refused to speak to him. He felt responsible and guilty. But what worried him most was the revelation that David Russell took bribes. If David Russell was corrupt with his own, how quickly would he tell the Germans about the list, especially if he thought it would save his life? His mind was made up.

An hour later he closed the door to his study and reached for his coat and hat. Standing in the hallway he called to her. 'I'm going for a walk, Mary. I'll be back in a couple of hours.'

She had not responded but he knew she had heard.

The hour after lunch in his study had only eroded his resolve, and again he felt hesitant about calling Gubbins. But with or without the list, men's lives were at stake. He would have to bear the responsibility of whichever decision he chose. He hoped the fresh air of the Downs would clear his mind.

Despite his ambivalence, he knew what had to be done. He sighed hard and long. Disobeying orders, no matter what the reason, was a serious offence. Yet as far as David Russell was concerned, his end was predetermined. As, indeed, was Clement's own. But he did not feel any better about it. Closing the gate, he walked down Church Lane. As he turned the corner into the High Street he hoped he might meet Peter walking Boadicea, and then they could chat about the Operational Base while walking the Downs.

He had not yet seen the base but Peter said it was exactly the same as the demonstration base used for training at Coleshill, and that they had chosen a site about half a mile into Maughton Forest from the western side of the woodland.

He walked towards the village green, intending to take the bridle path to the South Downs Way. Even from some distance he could hear the laughter. He paused. The front windows of *The Crown* were open and he could hear the jollity flowing into the street.

Laughter. It is a wonderful sound; full of fun and happy expectation. He smiled just listening to its joyous sound. The bombings and chaos of London seemed worlds away, and for a moment the village had taken on its pre-war isolation. Or so it felt to him. He walked towards the inn, and opening the door stepped inside. He felt the warmth of the fire even though he could not see it for the men standing around. The pungent aroma of tobacco smoke filled the small, low-beamed front room. As the men jostled about he caught a glimpse of someone sitting on the bar itself. It was Elsie. He could see her clearly now. The slender, crossed legs were swinging, the skirt pulled high over her knees and one high-heeled shoe was dangling from her toes. She was holding their attention so completely that no one had even noticed him.

'You'd better drink up, gents,' the barmaid called. 'We'll be closing in fifteen minutes.'

There was a chorus of groans. 'Go on, Elsie. Don't mind her,' one man said, eyeing the barmaid.

'You should have heard him scream,' Elsie was saying. 'She is grunting like a stuck pig, the baby's head just visible between her legs and he starts yelling, "Whose is it, you whore!"'

'Well?' said one of the men. 'Is it his?'

'Unless he had red hair as a kid,' she said. 'I'm guessing you probably know who.'

All heads turned. As the noise settled the crowd hushed and he could see Stanley sitting beside the fireplace. Stanley placed the glass on the hearth, his movements slow and deliberate.

'You've got a brother, it seems, Stanley,' one said.

Stanley stood and moved through the crowd, stopping beside Elsie.

Clement wasn't sure what Stanley intended to do, but as he watched, the door to the street opened and John Knowles staggered in.

No one moved.

'Have a drink, John,' someone said. 'To wet the baby's red head!'

Laughter ricocheted around the small room.

For a few seconds John Knowles stood shaking, his thick spectacles askew on his nose. Knowles was only a slightly-built man, but the facial tic that manifested under stress caused the man's whole body to twitch, and an unsightly red skin rash flamed across the pale cheeks. For one second the man seemed to be attempting to show bravado, even defiance, but he stumbled backwards, hitting his back against the bar.

The crowd laughed aloud.

Knowles' shoulders drooped in defeat. 'I want a whisky!' Knowles demanded, grasping the counter.

'You must be drunk. We haven't had whisky for over a month,' the barmaid scoffed and pulled a beer, placing the glass on the counter.

John Knowles drank it back.

No one spoke.

But he knew every one of them wanted to ask.

All eyes were still on John Knowles.

'I'll kill that bastard! Do you want to help me, Stanley? Or perhaps one of your special army friends could do it?' John slurred.

Clement felt his eyes widen. He stared at Stanley. What John had just said sent alarm bells clanging. He glanced around the room. All eyes were on either John or Stanley who were staring at each other. He recognised his own reaction on Stanley's face. He swallowed. Had it been a throwaway line? A derisive, even sarcastic remark about the Home Guard... or did John Knowles know something? He frowned, remembering the telephone conversation with John Knowles. The man had been dismissive of him and of God. He knew it was because the man felt forgotten. Which, sadly, was the case. But had John overheard anything? The man had come to the vicarage the day he and Johnny had selected the members of the team. Clement glanced again at the crowd. It seemed to him that they had not paid much heed to the remark. Their interest lay in knowing the paternity of the child. Stanley seemed transfixed, but Clement could not tell if it was due to the remark or for another reason. John Knowles slumped onto the bar, his head in his arms. The man seemed to be sobbing.

Stanley moved forward, towards John Knowles. But then stopped and put his arm around Elsie. As the big man swept the girl from the counter their eyes met. Everyone in the pub followed Stanley's gaze, their eyes settling on Clement, standing by the doorway.

'You want a drink, Vicar?' the barmaid asked. 'You'll have to hurry if you do. I got to close in a few minutes.'

'No, thank you.' He turned to leave. 'John, go home. You have had enough alcohol. That applies to you too, Stanley.' He paused. He wanted the whole room to hear. 'The child is innocent. Just remember that when you cast your judgement.' As he turned he stared at Elsie. The wide blue eyes flared back. She had bewitched them all. Even him. Mary had had the girl's measure from the start.

Leaving the bar, he closed the door on all he had just witnessed and stood on the opposite side of the street. He felt for John Knowles. He had let the man down when he was most needed. For that he would be eternally sorry. But John's remark about "special army friends" worried him. There was nothing to be done. In fact, investigating it further would only increase speculation. He no longer wanted to walk on the Downs. He just wanted to be with Mary. From where he was standing, he saw the door to the public house open and John Knowles staggered out, ahead of the other patrons who no doubt would return to the pub when it reopened in the evening. There was no point remonstrating with the man about his condition or anything he had said in the heat of the moment. Whatever John may or may not have overheard, the man knew nothing. John's head and heart were consumed with bitterness and the lifelong consequences of the day's event. Such things were all-pervading. He tried to imagine the public humiliation the man must be suffering. Small villages are unforgiving places. Yet forgiveness was the price John Knowles had to pay; for his wife and for David Russell, and for his own sanity. Not easily done. Anger and its brooding by-products were the likely outcome if John Knowles could not or would not forgive. Clement stood in the street and watched the inebriated John Knowles stagger away from the public house. For one moment he wondered if he should make sure the man went home. He couldn't. The man had too many issues to deal with. Home for John Knowles would never be the same again. Clement started up the hill but after only a few paces he stopped. Overhead he heard it beginning. The unmistakable low drone. He looked up. He knew from the radio that planes had been dropping bombs all day in London. In the afternoon light and with his eyes lifted, he watched, mesmerised. Wing tip to wing tip, planes occupied the skies. Bombers and Fighters. As the minutes passed, hundreds and hundreds of planes passed above him. He felt his heart sinking. Planes of every size and type were heading for the capital. People came out of the buildings and were standing in the street, struck dumb by the clamorous noise and number of aircraft. He looked around him and saw the young grocer's wife crying, the tears falling unrestrained from her eyes. He felt dizzy with the volume of aircraft.

'What do we do, Vicar?' the young woman sobbed.

He heard the panic in her voice.

'Stay calm. It is unlikely we will be affected, Mrs Black. Just make sure your black-out curtains are in place. Now go home and look after your little one,' he said. But he was praying as he turned and hurried back to the vicarage. Surely this was it!

Chapter Eleven

Monday 16th September 1940

George was at the front door, ashen-faced.

'It's come?'

The boy handed him the sealed envelope. Clement's heart was pounding as he opened the telegram. '*Cromwell*'.

'George, go home and collect your bag, and I will meet you at the Operation Base in...' he checked his watch. 'Two hours. Walk half a mile into the forest on the western side. Peter will be there.'

As soon as George left, Clement rang Peter. 'Cromwell,' he said. 'If you don't mind, Peter, I'll call Reverend Battersby, then collect my kit and come to your office.'

He rang off, then telephoned Battersby.

Ten minutes later he took the church keys from his desk drawer and left the house. Unlocking the door to the vestry, he walked into the quiet little room with tall stone walls and ancient windows. He glanced at the stained glass. The familiar scene of St George stared down at him. He reached into the desk drawer and withdrew another set of keys. Opening the cabinet that held the altar vestments, he reached for his pack. He had hidden it in a cupboard to which he had sole access. Lifting the bag onto the desk, he checked the contents. The Sten gun and its silencer sat on the top of the arsenal of weaponry beneath. He took the Fairbairn Sykes knife from the bag and strapped it to his inner left calf. Replacing his trousers over the blade, he glanced around the vestry. All looked exactly like it always had, except now Reverend Battersby's robes hung on the hook behind the door. Five minutes later Clement was standing in the front hall of his home, the pack in his right hand. He could hear the sounds of running water coming from the wash house at the rear of the house.

'Mary,' he said.

His wife turned around. Her eyes took in his pack.

'It's come then?' she whispered.

He didn't know how she did it. 'I want you to go to the West Country. To your late Aunt's place in Combe Martin. Take Gwen if she'll go.'

'I'll leave for Windsor this afternoon.'

Mary said something about being careful and that she would always love him. But he didn't reply. It was hard enough just embracing her for what could be the last time. He left her in the wash house, promising to contact her when he could.

He stood in the hallway and stared at his home, his eye tracing every corner. He breathed in its smell. Swallowing, he placed his hand on the handle of the front door and called to her. 'I love you!'

The water ceased.

Time stood still in that second. He paused on the front doorstep before closing the door.

Walking the short garden path he reached for his bicycle that rested against the fence. It was the habit of decades; so unconscious an action. He lifted the pack onto his shoulders and swung his leg over the bicycle. Passing Phillip Haswell's house and the police station, he headed for Peter's office.

Everything he had learned at Coleshill he put into action. 'Peter, would you call Reg and Ned? Tell them how to get to the Operational Base. They must be there by midday. Perhaps you could be there a little earlier, in case anyone gets lost.'

'And you?' Peter asked.

'I'll go and see Clive and Stanley now. I'll see you at the *OB* at twelve. Could you take my pack with you?'

Peter nodded. 'You're sure about it, Clement?'

'I am.'

'Right.'

There was no further discussion. Anything else seemed pointless. He closed the door to Peter's office behind him and walked towards his bicycle. The file on Peter's desk occupied his thoughts; the neatly-tied pink ribbon of the legal profession. He had no knowledge of what the file contained, but someone's affairs would have to wait. Perhaps everything would be different if and when the Germans were in charge. Things that seemed so important in everyday life took on a different perspective in the light of invasion. A child had been born not twenty-four hours ago and would now wake to a very different world.

He cycled through the village, heading towards Clive Wade's shop on the far side of the village green. As he opened the door to the bakery he saw Clive look up, the grey eyes resting on him. He knew that look. The expression of something expected but dreaded.

Clive removed his apron and stepped into the rear of his shop.

Pushing back the dividing curtain, Clement followed. 'Midday, Clive.'

'I'll be there.'

On leaving the bakery, he said good morning to two ladies he knew. He found that hard, knowing that he may never see them again. Reaching for the bicycle's handlebar he pedalled towards Stanley's butchery, repeating his favourite line from *Henry V*.

The bells on the door announced his presence but it was Stanley's shop girl, Gladys, who greeted him.

'Could I have a word with Stanley?' he said.

'He isn't here, Reverend. Hasn't been in all morning. It is most unlike him. But,' the girl shrugged her shoulders, a

96

coy, knowing expression on her face. 'I did see him leave the pub last night with Elsie. They are sweet on each other, those two.'

He knew he was staring but he didn't know what else to do. It had not occurred to him that when the time came, one or more of his team might be elsewhere. Of all the times for Stanley to fall in love!

He left the butchery and cycled towards Stanley's thatched cottage. It had always amused him that Stanley, who was over six feet in height, should choose to live in a place where he had to stoop to move from room to room. It wasn't amusing him now.

He saw the cottage ahead. The curtains on the upstairs windows were still closed, and he wondered if Stanley and the girl had allowed their physical desires to overtake their common sense.

He knocked at the door and waited.

A full minute passed and still no one opened the door.

Clenching his fist, he pounded on the door.

No one.

With his temper rising he cycled away. If Stanley had not been in his shop and was not at home, he could only imagine that the silly boy would be at the public house. Didn't Fearnley Maughton have enough immoral behaviour? The pretty Elsie Wainwright with the long slender legs and provocative ways flashed into his mind. He pedalled as fast as he could without attracting attention. He knocked on the pub door until the barmaid opened it. The woman stood in the doorway, a towel over her shoulder.

'Is Stanley Russell here?' he asked, before the woman could make any comment about the time.

'No, Reverend. Not here,' the barmaid told him.

He hated the smell of bars. Airless places; the odour of stale beer and even staler tobacco wafted through the half-open door.

'What number room is Elsie Wainwright in?' he demanded.

'Six,' the barmaid replied.

Without waiting, he pushed past the woman and went straight to the staircase to the first floor.

'You can't just go up there!' the woman was screaming behind him.

He climbed the uneven steps to the upper floor. The floorboards of the old inn creaked under his tread but he had no time to waste. He knocked.

Again, no answer.

'Do you have a key to this room?' he asked as the barmaid appeared beside him.

'You can't just barge in!' the woman said.

'Give me the key,' he snapped.

He didn't stop. He almost closed his eyes as he burst into the room. What he found was an empty but perfectly made bed. He threw open the wardrobe. Coat hangers swung on the rail.

He turned around staring at the deserted room, his mind racing.

'Why that little fiend!' the barmaid was screeching. 'She's done a runner. She owes five shillings!'

He didn't know if he was relieved or annoyed at not finding Stanley.

There was only one other recourse. He needed to see David Russell anyway. He swallowed hard. The time had come. He needed to stay focused on his duty, no matter how unsavoury. But first he had to find Stanley. He moved his foot in his shoe and felt the hard blade of the Fairbairn Sykes knife strapped to his leg digging into his left ankle. He left the room and bolted down the stairs. Leaving the public house by the rear lane, he returned to the village green and strode towards the police station.

Not four minutes later he entered the red brick Victorian building. He glanced at the police station clock. It was just after eleven o'clock.

'Constable Matthews?' he called.

The Constable wasn't at the front desk. Clement went to the glass-partitioned door and looked into the hallway beyond. He waited only a few seconds before he saw the Constable walking along the corridor, a dustpan and brush in his hand.

'Reverend? And what can I do for you today?'

'Is the Inspector in?'

The man nodded. 'Once again it is just him and me. Skeleton staff, what with the pounding London copped last night. They say the invasion is imminent. What do you think, Vicar?'

He smiled. 'I just need to see the Inspector.'

'Of course, everyone's in a hurry today,' Constable Matthews said, and glancing at the clock on the wall, entered the time of his visit in the daily log. 'There was quite a to-do here this morning, Vicar. I'm surprised you and your good lady didn't hear it in the vicarage.'

'What was that, Constable?'

'Mister Knowles, Sir. He came here earlier this morning. Nine thirty-five to be precise. Accusations were flying all over the place. Harsh words, vicar. All kinds of threats,' the Constable turned to face him. 'I shouldn't say it,' Constable Matthews whispered, 'but Inspector Russell is too fond of the ladies. I knew one day it would get him into trouble. Only from what I understand it is Mrs Knowles who is the one in trouble. Red hair. And a big baby I'm told. Just like young Stanley when he was a little one.'

'Have you seen Stanley, Constable?'

'He was here too this morning.' The Constable shook his head. 'More shouting. Only this time about money. Stanley came for his late mother's inheritance, saying he wanted to start life afresh, but his father was having none of it. In my opinion, and I suppose I shouldn't say this either, but I don't believe there is any money left, Vicar.'

'Well perhaps you should keep that to yourself, Constable. Do you know where Stanley is now?'

The Constable shook his head. 'Left here about half an hour ago threatening all sorts of violences against his father.'

The Constable moved to the partitioning door and held it open for him. They walked along the corridor to the rear office. He could see that Russell's door was slightly ajar. Constable Matthews knocked at the door and pushed it open, then turned and walked away.

From the doorway Clement could see the empty chair behind the desk. The window to the rear lane was open and a light breeze was lifting the loose weave curtain. Through the window he saw the dark shape of the Inspector's car in its usual place.

He scanned the room. He was about to call out to Constable Matthews, to say that the Inspector was not in his office, when he saw the shoe. He ran around the desk.

'Dear Lord!' he exclaimed. He drew in his breath as he stared at the prostrate Russell. The man was lying on the floor, the eyes open and wide, the head tilted to the left. Congealed blood surrounded the man's head like a macabre halo. It had poured from the long, gaping cut to the neck that extended from one ear to the other.

From the corner of his eye he saw the safe. The door was open. He could hear the Constable's tread disappearing along the corridor. Standing, he stared into the safe, his eye searching for the sealed envelope. There wasn't much in the safe, some papers and a few five-pound notes. But the envelope was not there.

'Constable Matthews!' he bellowed.

He heard the tread stop, then return with haste along the corridor.

Matthews rushed through the open door.

'Call Doctor Haswell, Matthews! Hurry!'

The Constable came into the room. 'Dear God!'

'The Doctor, Constable!'

Constable Matthews turned and ran from the room.

For one second Clement prayed the doctor was in his surgery. He went to the window and looked further along the rear lane to where Doctor Haswell parked his car. He felt the wave of relief on seeing the vehicle. Returning to the Inspector's side, he knelt and placed his fingertips under what was left of David Russell's jaw, trying to feel for the pulse in the neck. But he knew it was useless. He had seen enough death to know its pale, rigid stare. He withdrew his hand and, turning it over, he stared at the dark red stain.

Blood. It sat like a thick maroon scarf around Russell's neck. A dark curtain of the stuff ran from the man's throat to the floor. Clement felt light-headed. It had been more than twenty years since he had seen such a sight. Not easily forgotten. But still just as shocking. Taking his handkerchief from his pocket, he used it to wipe his fingers, the man's blood staining the freshly ironed and neatly folded linen cloth. Mary. He had left her doing the laundry. Soon she would be on the bus for Lewes to catch the early afternoon train. He felt the pulse in his temple thumping. He ran his hand over Russell's trouser pockets and checked the inside of the man's coat, waistcoat and shirt pockets. He found a long, unmarked key but the envelope was not there. He pushed the key back into Russell's pocket.

He scanned the papers on the Inspector's desk. Using his elbows he pushed the papers around in case the envelope was beneath the disorganised chaos. Nothing. He heard the sound of running feet: the Constable and presumably the Doctor.

The Doctor went straight to the Inspector, dropping his medical bag on one side of the body and kneeling beside Russell's head. He remained hunched over Inspector Russell for a few seconds before leaning back on his haunches. 'Nothing I can do for him. He's yours now, Clement,' Haswell said, opening his medical bag and withdrawing a large rectal thermometer.

The Doctor went about his duty of determining the time of death with the detached precision of his profession.

'How long?' he asked.

'Not long at all,' Phillip said, staring at the thermometer. 'There is no sign of rigor mortis yet. But his temperature has dropped a little.' Haswell studied the room. 'Was the window open when you came in?'

'Yes.'

'I put it at about an hour.'

He watched the Doctor turn Russell's head. The cut extended almost from one ear to the other and had severed his windpipe. Clement was trying to see the extent of the injury. He did not wish to appear macabre but he knew he had seen such wounds before. In pictures. At Coleshill.

The Doctor glanced up at him. 'It was a knife. It was pushed into the neck just under the right ear, then forward. You can see the point of entry here,' Haswell pointed. 'The force of entry caused the bruise. It was done by a strong person and one who knew what they were doing, by the look of it. No hesitation, Clement. Swift and lethal.'

Clement stared at the bruised entry point, his mind reeling. 'He was murdered?'

Phillip Haswell looked up at him. 'No question about that. I could take him to my surgery but I have no way of keeping him cool. They will want a post-mortem.'

'We should call Lewes for an ambulance,' he said.

'I expect they will have been seconded to London, given the bombing up there,' the Doctor answered. 'I could take him, if you would give me a hand to get him into my car?'

'Yes, of course. Thank you, Phillip, if you don't mind?'

Haswell shook his head. 'Perhaps a report should be made about this room and how you found it?'

He nodded. It was just as well someone was thinking logically.

'Constable Matthews,' he said, 'can you make sure nothing is disturbed in the Inspector's office? You had better close that window, but you should note in your report that we found it open. Then we should notify Lewes Police. No disrespect, Constable, but you will need someone more senior for this.'

Constable Matthews stared at his dead Inspector. Clement knew Matthews had little respect for Russell, but as he was the only other person in the police station, and held the keys of Russell's safe, he would at the very least be called to give evidence at the inquest.

Clement checked his watch. It was already half past eleven and he needed to locate and be at the Operational Base by midday.

'Constable, can you get a blanket from one of the cells? We don't want to frighten anyone who may be in the rear lane,' Haswell asked.

Matthews nodded.

Clement stared at Russell's corpse, the list dominating his thoughts. He was pleased he had been spared the duty of taking Russell's life. But the murder raised so many questions, and he needed time to think it through. But time was something he had little of. He needed to be with the men, and it would be many hours before he could speak with Johnny. And even that was dependent on the speed of the German advance. Matthews returned and together they rolled the dead Inspector onto the blanket before carrying him out of the police station and up Church Lane, to the rear laneway and Doctor Haswell's car.

'If you don't mind, Clement, I will put him on the back seat. Rigor Mortis will start to set in soon and it will be impossible to straighten him out if he is in the boot.'

He found Phillip Haswell's pragmatism surprising, although he was glad of it. There was nothing Haswell could do for Russell now. And he had been correct not to call on the already overstretched ambulance personnel. He wished now that he had included the Doctor and not Stanley.

He closed the rear door of Haswell's car, his hand gently pushing the fold in the blanket that encompassed Russell's feet. Russell was not a tall man, but Clement would not have described the Inspector as especially short either. Yet wrapped in a police cell blanket on the rear seat of the Doctor's car, Russell had become small, even pathetic. Did one man's life amount to so little? The words of the order of service for the Burial of the Dead flashed into his mind. "We brought nothing into this world, and it is certain we can carry nothing out."

Phillip was speaking. 'I'll go now, if you don't mind, Clement. I would like to get him to the mortuary as soon as possible.'

'Of course. And thank you for all your assistance, Phillip.'

He stood back on the pavement and watched the car pull away. He and Constable Matthews returned to the station. From the duty desk he called the police station in Lewes. 'Could I speak with the Chief Inspector?' he asked.

He was put through to Chief Inspector Arthur Morris.

He explained what he and Constable Matthews had found in David Russell's office. 'Doctor Haswell is bringing the deceased to Lewes Hospital Mortuary as we speak. If you would come as soon as you can?'

He replaced the receiver back on the telephone. 'They said they would be here in about an hour, Constable.'

'I am grateful to you, Vicar. I know it will look bad for me. I'm a bit hard of hearing. It's to be expected at my age, I suppose, but I never heard anything. And I have no idea how the thief got into the safe. You need both sets of keys to do it.' He saw the Constable's eyes glance at the safe keys hanging on the hook on the wall opposite the desk.

'Perhaps we should find Stanley. If for no other reason than that he is Inspector Russell's next of kin.'

'Of course. Good idea, Vicar.' Matthews reached for his policeman's hat. 'Doctor Haswell put the time of death at about an hour ago. That would make it half past ten. About the same time Stanley came to see his father. Doesn't look good for Stanley either, does it?'

The list. Clement could think of nothing else as he and Constable Matthews walked towards Stanley's cottage. Was that why Inspector Russell had been murdered? Perhaps Russell had disturbed someone opening the safe? That implicated the man walking beside him, and Clement could not imagine that. Besides, no one knew about the list except himself and Inspector Russell. He pondered whether Russell had told anyone about it. Or even opened it and the murderer had just killed Inspector Russell in cold blood once the safe had been opened. He quickened his pace. He needed to get to the Operational Base without further delay. But the Lewes Police Chief Inspector would be suspicious if he went missing as well as Stanley, especially now he could not prove his involvement with the Auxiliary Units without the list. He understood now why Gubbins had been so insistent. But he also wondered if any of it now mattered. The Germans were invading and he was looking for Stanley. He was annoyed with Stanley. And he was annoyed with himself for including the silly boy in the first place.

He opened the gate and strode towards the front door of Stanley's cottage.

Constable Matthews knocked.

No answer.

Without waiting, Clement marched around the cottage to the rear, his temper rising. The back door was ajar. 'Stanley?' he shouted, entering the small scullery. Bending, he made his way into the house. Stanley was standing in the living room by the fireplace, a suitcase at his feet and his Fairbairn Sykes knife in his hand. Despite Stanley's tight grip on the blade, he could see the red fluid oozing between the chubby fingers.

'Stanley?'

'Reverend?'

'What has happened?' he asked, his eyes fixed on the blood-stained knife.

'I'm sorry, Reverend. I cannot be involved anymore. You'd better take my kit. It's upstairs.'

There was another knock on the door.

'Oh! She's come to the front,' Stanley said and ran to the door.

Constable Matthews stood in the doorway. Clement watched the policeman's expression change from one of greeting to wide-eyed horror as he took in the knife, covered in blood, still grasped in Stanley's hand.

'I'll be taking that, Sir!' Matthews said.

Chapter Twelve

Clement and Constable Matthews walked on either side of Stanley back to the police station. Stanley had not been willing to come with them, but not because he was demonstrating signs of guilt. In fact, Clement didn't understand Stanley's behaviour. All Stanley had done after Constable Matthews had taken the knife from his blood-stained grip was wipe the blood from his hand on his trousers, as though he had just jointed a roast. And Stanley's only comment had been that he needed to be at his house. None of it made any sense to Clement.

He sat in the waiting area while Constable Matthews went about the business of taking Stanley into custody. Fifteen minutes later he stood in front of the cell door and peered through the tiny hatch. Stanley was sitting on the bunk bed, his tie, shoelaces and belt removed. Clement thought the man looked a tragic figure. Physically large, with pale skin, light blue eyes and red hair, Stanley had been the butt of many porcine jests during his youth. He watched as Stanley stood and then paced the confined space, his loose shoes scuffing over the brick floor. But Stanley's agitation did not appear to have much to do with his current situation. He seemed distracted, almost joyous. There was a grin on his face like a child at Christmas. Clement turned and walked back out into the corridor to the second office, where Chief Inspector Morris from Lewes Police sat reading the report.

'Excuse me, Chief Inspector, could I speak with Stanley Russell?' he asked.

Chief Inspector Morris lifted his gaze from the papers and looked at him. 'Ten minutes, Reverend Wisdom.'

'Thank you.'

Morris stood and together they walked to the duty desk to retrieve the cell keys. This man seemed to Clement to be the antithesis of Inspector Russell. There was no bombast about Morris. In fact, a quiet, almost sedate manner was the first impression. Intentional or not, it was reassuring. But it concerned him that Morris may think this an open and shut case. Although Stanley had, for now, only been detained, and not yet formally arrested for the murder of his father, Stanley was obviously the main, and probably the only suspect. And being caught with the blood-smeared knife in his grasp was bound to lead to his conviction.

'Listen to me, Stanley,' said Clement, sitting on the cell bed. 'We only have a few minutes. Who did you think was at your door? Who were you waiting for?' He remembered the suitcase. 'Where were you going?'

Stanley tapped his nose with his index finger 'I'm sorry, Reverend. I cannot be in the group anymore.'

He was stunned. 'Do you know how serious this is, Stanley?'

'I have to go, Reverend. How long is this going to take? I have to get back to the house.'

He stared at Stanley. The man appeared to have no idea of the seriousness of his situation.

Stanley continued to pace the small cell floor, his face reddening, his agitation increasing. 'I wish they would hurry.'

'Stanley, you do know you have been detained, pending investigation, for the murder of your father?'

Stanley stopped his pacing and stared at him. He clearly had no idea about any of it.

'Your father was found murdered this morning. Found here. In his office. By me. His throat was cut. Guerrilla-style, Stanley. Done by someone who knew what they were doing. Doctor Haswell says it happened about the time you came to see your father. You were overheard arguing.'

Stanley sat down on the bed and leaned his head on the brick wall behind him. 'We are getting married. We are leaving Fearnley Maughton, Vicar. She just left to collect her things. But I need to go soon or she'll be back at the cottage.'

'Why were you holding the knife, Stanley?' he pressed.

'I thought while she was away, I should return my kit to you. But I couldn't find the knife.' Stanley leaned forward so that his nose was almost touching Clement's. 'When I did, it was covered in blood. I thought she must have found it and been playing with it. She could be hurt. That's it. She's hurt. That's why she is taking so long. I need to find her.'

'Where did you find it, Stanley?'

'In the scullery drawers, with the other knives.'

'Do you always have the back door unlocked, Stanley?' he asked.

'Yes,' Stanley said shrugging. 'I got nothing worth stealing.'

Clement's mind was reeling. It would be easy to enter the house unobserved and drop the knife into the drawer. He sat back on the bunk bed, his mind processing the facts as he knew them. He glanced at Stanley. He did not want to believe that Stanley Russell had killed his father. But if not Stanley, then who? And what was the girl's part in it all? He swallowed. Had she just taken fright at the idea of eloping with Stanley, and run away, or had she committed murder? Either way, what the girl had done was contemptible. But why would Elsie Wainwright kill David Russell?

'Stanley, there is something I must tell you,' he said and told Stanley about Elsie's empty room.

'Of course the room is empty, Vicar,' Stanley said. 'She went to pack her things.'

'But she didn't return to the cottage, Stanley. That was the arrangement, wasn't it?'

'She's hurt, I tell you. We're going to be married. She loves me.'

In that moment, Clement despised Elsie Wainwright.

'I will only ask once, Stanley, because I want to hear it from you,' he said. 'Did you kill your father?'

'No, Reverend! How did he die?' Stanley asked.

He told Stanley what he knew.

'Well, if I am going to swing for it, then I wish I had. But I wouldn't have killed him like that.'

He stared at Stanley. 'Why do you say that?'

'Now that I know how to kill, Vicar, if I had killed him, I would have bashed the bastard's head in. Not cut his throat. He wouldn't have suffered for more than a second. Not enough for what he did to me and my mother.'

He stared at Stanley, the image of the legs spread wide and the ferocious swing of the blade bursting from his memory. Physical and mental torment. Both mother and son. Hatred. Years of it. Hatred didn't make precision cuts, no matter how gory the end result. When a man killed with anger, the attack was... how did Major Bannon describe it? Frenzied. There would have been blood all over the room. Blood spatter; the photographs he had seen at Coleshill of dead men killed by gun and dagger flashed into his mind. The only variation to that scenario was the premeditated killing; the kind where the assassin has planned and prepared for the deed long in advance. That kind of calculated killing was never frenzied. But was Stanley capable of that? Clement frowned. Regardless of whether the attack was spontaneous or premeditated, there was no blood on the walls in Russell's office. The memory of the cascading maroon scarf filled his mind. Such a violent injury would have sent blood spurting forward. In his mind's eye he could see the grotesque windpipe surrounded by raw flesh. Such an attack not only cut the windpipe but also the main arteries of the neck. Why was the blood confined to Russell's neck and not all over the office? He pondered the girl. Could Stanley be protecting Elsie? He stared at Stanley. Even if he asked, he knew Stanley would not say. Stanley was in love and he would swing for the girl if he believed she had done it. He swallowed. 'I believe you,' he said. 'But I have to go, Stanley. I'll be back as soon as I can. I'll pray for you.' He stood and went to the cell door.

'I didn't do it, Vicar. And I know Elsie will be here for me,' Stanley said. But already he could hear the doubt creeping into Stanley's voice.

'Chief Inspector?' Clement called.

As he stood in the doorway, he turned to look back at Stanley. He nodded and smiled, hoping it would give Stanley encouragement. He wanted to share his thoughts with the Chief Inspector, but he had so little time. Everything now was dependent upon the speed of the German advance.

He stood in the corridor, the Chief Inspector beside him. From where he was standing he could see the police station clock on the wall, and he was already late. The men would be assembled now.

'Thank you. I must attend to something right now but could I speak with you further about Stanley?' he asked.

'Could I trouble you to show me where exactly you found the body, Reverend?'

He glanced again at the clock on the wall. The Chief Inspector would be suspicious if he failed to assist. Besides, his men were independent enough to handle whatever may arise without him.

'Of course,' he said.

They walked into Russell's office and he told Morris what he had seen and done. Morris said little as he retold his account of events. But he felt certain the man would check it all against Constable Matthew's statement.

'Is Constable Matthews alright?' he asked at length.

'Why do you ask, Reverend?'

'This is a small village. We all know each other. Constable Matthews has had quite a shock. And he is elderly and a bit deaf.'

'So I understand. I have sent him home. He is too close to this investigation. Constable Newson – one of my men from Lewes – and I will remain in Fearnley Maughton for the duration.'

Clement watched Morris. The speech had been delivered without once making eye contact. But it was neither ill-mannered nor dismissive. The man was concentrating on something. He followed the stern gaze to a set of keys hanging on the wall opposite the duty desk.

'Do you know what those keys open?' Morris asked.

Clement nodded. 'I suppose anyone who has asked Inspector Russell to keep anything in the safe in his office would have seen those keys. But to open the safe, two keys are required. At least, that is what Constable Matthews told me.'

Morris tilted his head. 'Where is the second key kept?'

'I don't know. It is just what Constable Matthews told me.' He thought of the key he had seen in David Russell's pocket but he did not know what it opened, so he had not actually lied.

Morris nodded. 'Thank you.'

There was a pause.

'Why were you here this morning?' Morris asked.

'I came to ask the Inspector if he knew where Stanley was.'

'You needed Stanley because?'

'He is a member of the Home Guard of which I am group leader. I am organising exercises, in view of the recent increase in German bombardment.'

He turned to push open the glass partition doors. Morris remained staring at the keys on the wall. The Chief Inspector had not said much, but Clement could tell the eyes did more talking than the tongue.

Chapter Thirteen

It was now nearly one o'clock. Even though he was late, Clement needed to retrieve Stanley's pack. Striding to the end of the street, he entered Stanley's cottage from the rear. As he walked into the cottage he glanced around the scullery, looking for the cutlery drawer. The utensil drawers were under the bench right beside the back door. He stared at the drawer. As long as the door was unlocked, and it always was, anyone could have placed the blood-smeared knife there. They didn't even need to enter the house to do it. Upstairs, his attention was caught by the bed in Stanley's bedroom. It was roughly made, the blanket askew and creased. In his mind's eye he saw the neat bed at *The Crown*. His eye scanned the room. He saw the pack wedged between the bed and the wall. Its location angered him. Their packs were to be hidden away from any eyes other than their own. And Stanley had left his kit where anyone in the room could not only see it but have access to it. He felt the corners of his mouth tighten in disapproval. Reaching for it, he swung it over his shoulder and returning downstairs left by the rear door.

It was just after two o'clock when he approached the location of the Operational Base in Maughton Forest. Off to his left he heard a rustle in the bushes. He stopped, falling to the ground. He had no weapon immediately available to him other than his knife. Stanley's Sten gun was in the bag but it would take him too long to open the pack, assemble the weapon and load it. And the noise would give away his position. He lay, motionless, in the first of the autumn leaves. With his nose pressed into the decaying leaf matter, he moved his left leg, bending his knee, his left hand feeling for the blade. Without a sound, he grasped the blade in his hand and lifted his head, his eyes sweeping the woodland. Up ahead the early afternoon sun shone through the trees, the gentle light flickering on the foliage. His eyes scanned the forest ahead. His ears strained for any noise. Nothing. A falling leaf caught the dappled sunlight as it fluttered earthwards. His eye caught it immediately and he saw it bounce then fall. Screwing his eyes tight, he focused on the spot. He could just make out the trip wire stretched across the forest floor at about ankle height. It crossed the path and went off into the bushes on the right side of the track near a large boulder. Grasping the knife to his chest he rolled sideways off the path and into the bushes at the edge and waited. Nothing stirred. He stood, and hunching low, ran through the trees before falling again to the ground about ten feet away from the boulder. He could see the wire. It was wrapped around the base of a tree but he could not see any explosive. Staying in the low shrubs, he skirted the rock, approaching it from higher in the woodlands. Crouching beside the rock, his eye followed the wire. The trip wire was secured to an explosive device at the base of the tree on the high side, making it invisible from the forest path. He recognised it immediately. It had the signs of George's handiwork all over it.

Waiting, he listened, the Fairbairn Sykes blade still in his grasp.

'Clement!'

It was Peter's voice; quiet and sharp.

Peter Kempton stood, his Sten gun in his hands. The man had twigs and branches all over his clothes. Peter made a sweeping gesture. He heard the movement behind him. Reg Naylor stood. The man had been hiding in a copse higher up the slope. Clement smiled. The disguise had been perfect. He had crawled right by Peter yet had not seen him. And Reg, no doubt, had had him in his sights since he arrived in the woods. He only hoped the Germans were as distracted as he was.

They walked in silence, about ten feet apart, further along the hillside then higher to the trees and the Operational Base. Peter placed a hand on a tree stump and pulled it sideways. Beneath it was the small trap door opening to their underground Operational Base, and one by one they descended the stairs into the subterranean bunker.

He glanced around the Operational Base. Although he had never been in it before, it was identical in every way to the one at Coleshill.

'What news?' Peter asked. 'We assumed something had gone wrong.'

He told them about Stanley.

'I thought he would pop that bastard one day,' Clive said.

'I don't think he did it,' he said. 'I think he is covering for the girl.'

'That slip of a girl couldn't have done it. Besides, why would she?' Clive replied.

'I have been asking myself the same question,' said Clement.

'And the invasion?' Peter asked.

Clement shook his head. 'I know nothing more than you do. So we maintain a watch and patrol tonight. We could be here for a while, so we'd better settle in,' he said, his mind still on Stanley. But right now there was little he could do. The group had been activated. Killing the invading enemy came first and Stanley would have to wait. But the effect of Stanley's absence was visible on the men's faces. 'Life expectancy; two weeks,' Clement muttered, wondering if Stanley's problems were now academic. He glanced at the faces of his men. George and Clive, who knew Stanley best, were clearly concerned but he could see that others were going about their routines as if Stanley was already ancient history.

'It no longer matters to us,' Reg added, voicing what he believed some were thinking. The man stood and removed his camouflaged suit. Grasping his Sten gun, Reg sat at a distance from the others, the weapon on his knees, rubbing an oiled cloth over the barrel.

'What's to report here,' he asked.

'Nothing, other than an unwary vicar,' Ned answered.

He nodded. He was not proud of his inattention, even if he had good cause. If the Germans had landed, his absentmindedness would have cost all their lives.

'With one man down I'll rework the watch,' Peter said.

The men dispersed and he watched them go about the routine tasks of life in the Operational Base. But there was little conversation. Stanley aside, he had another problem; the whereabouts of the list. So many questions flooded his mind. And he couldn't share any of them, not even with his second-in-command.

He sat at the table, the survey and ordnance maps of the area laid out before him. Poring over the maps, he plotted the evening's patrol routes. Stanley. Had Clive been correct about Stanley? Was the motive anger? If so, Stanley had the most to gain from his father's death. And Stanley had no alibi other than Elsie who, it appeared, had disappeared. Had Stanley thought that now he knew how to kill, and had protection because of his membership of an elite group, he could get away with murder? Yet, if Stanley had opened the safe, it would be for the money, not the list; a list the man didn't know existed. He swallowed, thinking of the five-pound notes he had seen in the safe. Why would Stanley leave a stack of five-pound notes if he had come for his inheritance? He felt himself shaking his head. Stanley did not kill his father. He believed it. But who other than himself and Russell knew about the existence of the list? Not his men and certainly not the elusive Elsie. He began to wonder whether Elsie was entirely innocent and had also met with foul play. Only he, Russell, Gubbins and

Johnny knew about the list. But only Russell did not know whose names were on it. And he was dead. A squeezing knot was forming in his stomach.

He focused on the maps and devised the route. 'We should get some rest. Tonight we need to be on high alert. George, you and Reg take the first watch. We'll change again in two hours. At midnight we will patrol the area east and south of Firle Beacon. And we'll check Firle Place on our way back.' The Operational Base was a small space for seven men. Tempers would be quickly raised. His team spread out, each tending to his own area of expertise. The long, narrow, arched tunnel was sectioned into a living area with a table and chairs and several bunk beds. Near the entry steps, sectioned off and behind the blast door, were the latrine on one side and the stove on the other. The flue rose from the stove, through the bunker and into a hollowed-out tree trunk above ground to disperse the smoke and cooking fumes. Beyond the living space was the supply and weapons store, and at the far end was the emergency escape door. Lamps hung from wooden beams at intervals along the narrow tunnel. He glanced at his men from time to time. They were occupied but the tension was palpable. He imagined that with each passing night, the routine would become more familiar.

At the end of the evening, he laid his head back onto the hard pillow on his bunk. Closing his eyes, he recited the Lord's Prayer and asked God for guidance and strength. But as the afternoon had become evening there had been no sightings of any enemy activity within the forest. In fact, each returning watch had reported that there had been no one sighted in the forest at all. It was as if all of England knew the Germans were on the foreshores and had stayed at home, waiting. Waiting. Yet he had not heard any church bells. He hoped Reverend Battersby had arrived in the village. With Mary away, he prayed the old man could manage to ring the bells and see to the villagers. He took a long deep breath. He wanted to be there. To shepherd and to advise. But Battersby, who had been well received, would do a good job. Besides, Clement believed he was doing more for them where he was, even if they didn't know about it.

Tension had increased during the evening. As the night descended and the patrol time approached, the men's nerves were only just under control. It was to be expected. None of them were guerrilla fighters. They were bakers and clergymen and solicitors; ordinary people waiting to do extraordinary things. He wanted and needed to stay focused as much for himself as the team. He swung his legs over the bunk, went to the table and stared again at the maps, going over every detail. What he found most frustrating was that he didn't even know where the invasion was taking place. He glanced at the men. Reg was oiling his Sten. George was checking wires and incendiary devices. Clive was sorting explosives. Ned and Peter were on watch. He checked his wristwatch. Peter and Ned would return in twenty minutes and it would be his turn to watch with George. He went to check his pack. But despite everything, Stanley was never far from his thoughts. Somehow Clement had to speak with Chief Inspector Morris about Elsie Wainwright's involvement.

For one horrible moment during his mental ramblings, he had questioned Johnny's allegiances. But Johnny already knew the names, and that alone exonerated him. Clement was a vicar, not a policeman, although, as the hours passed, again he began to feel less like one. At midnight they lifted their packs, and with Sten guns in hand left the Operational Base and headed south.

Chapter Fourteen

Tuesday 17th September 1940

Dawn. It had been a long night. And they had seen no one. It was always possible they had skirted advancing troops but Clement didn't believe so. Invasions required armoured vehicles and above all, tanks. And tanks are noisy. They can be heard and felt miles away. And even with the binoculars, he had not sighted any shipping from Firle Beacon that would indicate an amphibious invasion.

He watched his men remove their packs and stow their weapons before collapsing on the bunks. They had walked for over six hours and covered more than the forecasted eight miles. Full moons are a night patrol's worst enemy. He thought of his theory about full moons and bombing. He had been right about that. But for them, the strong moonlight had meant staying away from open fields and ridge tops where their silhouetted forms made them like ducks at a seaside shooting gallery. Being forced to stay in the valleys and criss-cross fields behind hedges and clusters of trees had turned eight miles into twelve. But despite everyone's nerves being on edge, they had not sighted the enemy.

'What now, Clement?'

It was Reg's voice.

Everyone was looking at him. Reg had voiced what they were all thinking. Just because they hadn't seen the enemy didn't mean the Germans hadn't landed. 'I need to contact Commander Winthorpe,' he told them. 'I need to report in and I want to find out where the invasion is taking place. He also should know about Stanley. I will return to the village and telephone the Commander. I'll be as quick as I can. If I am delayed I will let you know by a reverse dead letter drop. George, make sure you visit the bus shelter during the day. Get some rest. All of you. And well done last night.' He turned to go. 'Remain vigilant. In my absence Peter is in charge.'

'Clement. Perhaps you should have a weapon on you,' Peter said.

He shook his head. 'If I was caught either coming or going from here, the Germans would come looking for you. Stanley is in enough trouble, I don't need to worry about all of you too.'

He said his farewells and walked back through the woodland. Sometimes in the summer, if the weather was fine, instead of playing chess, he and Peter would walk the forest with Boadicea discussing theology. Then, the woodland paths were happy places, an escape from the routine pressures of life. Now he saw them as places of concealed death.

He skirted the village and entered Church Lane through the cemetery. Opening his door he walked along the hallway towards the kitchen. It was still early, not yet eight o'clock and possibly too early for Johnny to be in his office at The Admiralty. Even though Mary was not there, her fragrance lingered and he breathed it in. Filling the kettle, he placed it on the stove then went to his study. Reverend Battersby had left some correspondence on his desk. He sat and dealt with Church matters until he heard the clock in the hall chime nine. Walking into the hall he lifted the telephone receiver and dialled the number.

'Nothing to report in our sector. Any news?' he said.

'Nothing as yet,' Johnny answered.

He could hear the strain in Johnny's voice.

'We have a problem that you should know about.'

There was silence at the end of the line. He wasn't even sure that the line was still connected. 'Johnny?'

'Yes, I'm here. Not on the phone. Come. Same day, same place.'

The phone rang off.

He replaced the receiver. He had not expected so short a conversation. But he told himself it was because Johnny was on edge. Waiting always did that. He returned to his study and closed the door. In the stillness he heard the droning. As it increased, he stood and went to draw the curtains. The planes were early today. Even though it was daylight he decided to check the house. He opened the door to the hallway, and walking along it went into every room drawing the black-out curtains as a precaution. But there was something different about the noise. He stood in the middle of the hallway, listening. The sound was higher pitched, more like fighters. And they were low. Dorniers, possibly. Within seconds the noise was fierce. It seemed as though the aeroplane was above the house. Then came the unmistakable falling squeal. He turned and ran into the scullery and sat on the floor in the corner, his head between his arms. He stared at the locked scullery door, the Anderson Shelter only yards away. But there was no time to reach it. The detonation was so loud he called out, an involuntary shriek. The noise was horrific. The whole house shook. Several windows shattered, the sound of the breaking glass sudden and intense. His mind flashed to the scullery at the vicarage in Mayfair. A second later, another explosion. Smaller, or perhaps an aftershock? Standing, he ran to the front door and opened it, his eyes searching for the plane. Flames were rising from the roofs of the buildings and shops in the High Street. In his mind's eye he could see the couple in Trebeck street. It seemed months ago but in reality it was not even two weeks. He ran outside into the lane. The noise was different now. Short bursts of exploding cracks shattered the morning. Hearing the high-pitched squeal he looked up. A German Stuka was descending out of the sky. He wasn't sure if it was crashing into the village or strafing it. He could hear people screaming. Running down Church Lane, he leaned against the red brick wall of the police station and looked up. The plane pulled high, circled, and once again came in low. It was so loud. But from the formation, its presence in the village was not just a stray encounter designed to intimidate then fly away, it was intentionally mowing down anyone in the streets. He watched, horrified, as the plane once more strafed the High Street. The bullets cracked the air in bursts of two to three seconds before the plane rose into the sky. Turning, the aircraft lined up for a third run. He watched the single fighter return, the terrifying crack of rapid spraying bullets mingled with screaming. The plane thundered over the village. It seemed to be just above the rooftops then pulled high again, this time disappearing into the sky.

He ran down the lane and into the High Street. Some of the buildings and shops around the village green were partially destroyed, and fire was already taking hold. Peter Kempton's office was nothing more than rubble. The scene was something unimaginable. Windows and shop fronts had been blown out onto the streets, and flames now leapt high into the sky. People were lying on the footpaths and in the roadway, bleeding and dying. Others were staggering around in aimless circles, their clothes ripped into shreds. His eye fell on a pram, standing alone in the middle of the street, a woman prostrate beside it. His chest felt hollow. Looking up he saw *The Crown*. It appeared to be undamaged. He remembered it was the emergency assembly point. And thanks to Mary there were medical supplies there. 'Go to *The Crown*,' he bellowed.

He ran towards the woman lying in the street. He recognised the young mother immediately. Mrs Black had been shot through the chest and had died instantly. His eye turned to the baby. He placed his hand on the infant and felt its tiny breaths. He looked up. Two older women were comforting each other on the footpath.

'Can you take care of this child?'

'Dear God! Is Mrs Black dead?' one asked.

'Please take the child to *The Crown*, Mrs Beath, I must find Doctor Haswell.'

He ran back up the hill. The buildings at the top end of the High Street appeared not to have been so badly damaged. Without knocking, he opened the door and ran in. He prayed that Phillip Haswell was not out on his rounds in the country or dead in his own house. 'Phillip?' he shouted.

The front hallway was filled with dust. Covering his mouth with his hand, he looked into the front room which was the surgery. It seemed to be undamaged except for debris and dust from shattered brickwork falling onto the equipment and furnishings. He walked further into the house. 'Phillip?' he shouted again. He started to consider what he would do if he found Phillip Haswell dead. Daylight filtered through the dust haze. There was nothing left of Phillip's kitchen or scullery. Clement stared outside. Phillip Haswell was standing in his garden, or what was left of it. His Anderson shelter had taken a direct hit and had been completely destroyed. A crater ten feet deep was where the shelter had once stood. He stared again at his friend and church warden of several years.

'Phillip? Are you unharmed?'

The man was coughing and blinking dust and dirt from his eyes. 'I was in the lavatory, Clement,' he said, staring at the flattened brick and wooden structure a few feet away. 'I decided while I was outside to cut a few vegetables for my dinner. If I hadn't been on my haunches pulling up carrots at the end of my garden,' Phillip's voice trailed off. 'A few seconds earlier,' Phillip stopped again.

'I'm pleased you are unhurt, Phillip. But many of the villagers have been hit. There are several already dead. If you could come? Now?'

'Of course. I'll just get my bag.'

He saw the stunned expression on Phillip's face.

'At least the surgery will clean up. Is Elsie in attendance?' Phillip asked, as he collected some bandages from a cupboard with no doors. 'I hope these bandages will not put more infection into the wounds than they are supposed to prevent. Needs must, I suppose Clement. At least they will stem the flow of blood until we can get the wounded to hospital.'

'You didn't know Elsie has left Fearnley Maughton?'

Phillip stopped filling his medical bag and stared at him. 'What? Why?'

'I was hoping you could tell me,' he said.

'Young people today. They have no sense of duty. Can't be helped. We must do what we can, Clement. Thank the Lord for Mary's foresight and planning. Where are most of the wounded?'

'*The Crown*,' he said. 'It appears undamaged.

'Good man. Would you mind calling Lewes Ambulance station? And Clement,' Haswell paused. 'I think the villagers will need you but before you do, can you open the church? We will need somewhere to put the bodies. It is best the dead are not with the living for too long. Bad for morale.'

'Of course.'

He watched Phillip run down the street towards the destruction.

Clement ran back up Church Lane towards the vicarage. Why had the plane bombed Fearnley Maughton? There were no industries, no railheads or munitions factories. Had it just been a random release of leftover bombs? But the strafing runs had been intentional. That was sheer wickedness. Without stopping he opened his front door. Mary. Relief that she was not in the village was his immediate reaction, although her calm efficiency would be missed and not just by him. He pushed it from his mind and grasped the telephone to call Lewes Ambulance. Running into his study, he took the keys from the drawer and went to open the church. One of the long, stained-glass windows had been blasted inwards. He paused for a moment to reflect on the damage. The windows had been in place since the Reformation. 'Such vandalism,' he muttered. He drew back the blackout curtains to allow as much light into the building as possible. Closing the door, he ran back towards the village. He was now pleased that Major Bannon had trained them so hard. He had not done so much physical exercise in years. As he rounded the corner from Church Lane into the High Street he passed the police station. Stanley. He should check on Stanley and tell him what had happened. He ran into the building. Glass from the shattered front windows lay like snow over the floor. He looked up. There was no one behind the duty desk. He went straight to the damaged partition door and pushed it open. The body of a man in a Constable's uniform was lying face down on the floor in the corridor.

'Constable Newson,' he called. He bent down, grasped the man's shoulder and rolled him over.

He reeled back. The man was dead. But not from blast damage. A bullet hole the size of a sixpence glared back at him from the bloodless visage. It had entered the man's head through the left temple. But there was no exit wound. He swallowed hard. The man's brains would be nothing but slush, the bullet still within the skull. Most likely subsonic. Special. He stood and ran towards the cells where he knew Stanley was imprisoned. The cell door was open.

He stared at the vacant cell for what seemed like a full minute. His mind was reeling. He turned. 'Chief Inspector Morris?' he called. He ran from the cells and opened all the doors in the corridor. No one. One of the doors he opened led into a room with shelves around every wall. Various labelled items sat on the shelves. He realised he was staring at the evidence cupboard. His eye scanned the shelves. He could not see the Fairbairn Sykes knife. He licked his dry lips. There was no time for finding the commando knife. 'Chief Inspector Morris?' he called again. No one other than himself and the dead Constable were in the police station. He turned and left. Neither Stanley nor the dead Lewes Constable was now his priority. He would deal with it later. 'Let the dead look after the dead,' he quoted as he ran towards the village green.

Devastation is what he saw. He could hear the siren of the local fire brigade. ARP wardens from Lewes were already in attendance and appeared to be directing the injured into *The Crown*. Along the street in both directions he saw people lying on the ground. Fearnley Maughton, his pretty village, was almost unrecognisable. He ran towards the public house.

The main bar had been transformed into an infirmary. Tables had been placed side by side and upon each lay an injured person. Phillip Haswell was running between the tables, enlisting the help of anyone who could wrap a bandage or pack a wound. The barmaid was fetching hot water and emptying used buckets filled with blood-stained cloths, as blood dripped from the edges of the tables to the floor. Behind the bar, Ilene Greenwood, the postmistress, was shredding sheets from the linen store into long strips.

Haswell looked up as Clement entered.

'They are on their way,' he said, staring at the doctor's blood-stained clothes and hands.

Haswell nodded. 'Keep the hot water coming,' he shouted to the barmaid. 'Wet all the surfaces, we have to keep the dust levels down. And could someone get the ARP to put a sheet or blanket over that open window, please!'

He backed away. Haswell, although clearly finding the makeshift surgery stressful, was managing well enough. And the village women had sprung into action. With all the deaths in the village, Clement was going to need assistance organising the funerals. He should call Battersby. But for now his role was to pray with the dying and take the deceased to the church. His mind went to the team still dug in at the Operational Base. He had left Peter in charge. And with the Germans not yet on their shores, they would be alright. His place was here in the village with his flock, but he made a mental note that if things returned to something close to normal he would telephone Mary and ask her to return.

The telephonist at Lewes Ambulance had said they would send all three of their ambulances. Clement found the ARP warden and told the man to go to the main road and direct the vehicles, when they arrived, to the village green. Then he brought a stretcher outside and laid it on the ground beside the body of Emma Black. Looking around for able men to help him carry the deceased, he saw John Knowles standing, staring open-mouthed at the scene.

'John!' he called.

The man seemed dazed.

He called again.

'She's dead,' John Knowles muttered. 'She came looking for me.'

He realised with horror what the man was saying. Looking up, he could see the body of Margaret Knowles lying face down on the footpath outside what was left of Peter Kempton's office. He felt utterly ashamed. He had failed John Knowles by forgetting him, even though only for a short time. John Knowles had sought comfort from the church but found it in *The Crown*. And the man's wife had died because of his forgetfulness.

'The child?' he asked.

'At home with a neighbour,' John Knowles responded.

'Can you help me carry stretchers, John?' he asked.

All around him he saw carnage. His eye fell on a line of bodies, evacuees from London. The ARP Warden wanted them kept separate for identification purposes. He bent to lift the stretcher with John Knowles, his gaze on the lengthening queue waiting for treatment. Gladys, the girl from Stanley's shop, was sitting by the door into *The Crown*, bandaging the less injured and checking names against Mary's roll. Perhaps it had been Mary's drill for invasion day, for those who could went quickly to their allotted roles, and between himself and Phillip Haswell there was some order to the chaos.

For several hours he alternated between carrying the dead to *All Saints* and praying with the dying and injured. Battersby had arrived in the village, although Clement wasn't sure when, and had gone straight to his task of comforting the wounded.

By late afternoon all the injured had been taken to Lewes Hospital and a silence had descended over the village. Fearnley Maughton was shattered. Thin plumes of smoke rose about the destroyed rubble. Buildings could be repaired but nothing would eradicate the memory. In his mind's eye he could see their faces. People he had known for years. Gunshot wounds. He closed his eyes remembering the jagged and bloody, raw and gaping wounds of brutality. The burns victims had impacted his mind most; the hideous charred blackness of burnt flesh. For those who survived, theirs would be the long and silent suffering of enduring pain and disfigurement.

He and Reverend Battersby sat in the dining room at *The Crown*. He could see Battersby's exhaustion. Clement learned that the man had come from Lewes in one of the ambulances, and he was grateful for the practical and spiritual assistance.

'There is a bed for you at the vicarage,' he said. 'I cannot thank you enough for all your help. With Mary away, I could not have done it without you.'

'It is a sad day for the village and for our nation,' Battersby said, sipping some tea. The old cleric sighed. 'Perhaps it is a sad day for the world. Thank you for your offer of a bed but one of the ARP wardens is giving me a lift back to Lewes. Should I come tomorrow?'

He nodded. 'I will telephone my wife and ask her to return. As you know I have some Home Guard business which cannot be ignored, and I may have to be away for a few days. I'm sorry to put so much on your shoulders, Battersby.'

'I know you have other duties. You do what you need to, Clement.'

He walked outside with Reverend Battersby and watched as the car left the village.

Chapter Fifteen

It was just on sunset when Clement scribbled a note for the team telling them that he would not be back before Thursday night at the earliest. It was a longer time than he, and no doubt the team, had anticipated but he knew Peter would follow the routines they had learned while at Coleshill. Placing the note into the dead letter drop collection point, he then returned to the vicarage. For over ten hours he had ferried the dead, prayed with the dying and the living, and done whatever he could to assist. But he knew that, as their vicar, his greatest use to them was in the future. Dealing with trauma, both physical and mental, always led to anger and seeking someone to blame. And the first one they held responsible was God. This he knew from his time at St Thomas' Hospital. But that depended on them having the luxury of time to apportion blame. If the Germans were invading in the near future, Clement didn't want to think of what horrors lay in store for them. He, presumably, would be dead.

As he closed the door to the vicarage he realized he had been awake for thirty-six hours. He felt physically drained and emotionally numb. Nineteen bodies lay on the stone floor in his church, six of them evacuees. He felt the tragic irony; they had come to Fearnley Maughton to escape dying in London. Closing his study door, he heard the soothing click of the lock, and falling into his red leather chair he kicked his shoes from his feet. He hadn't had a drink of any kind for hours and now he really wanted a cup of tea.

During the time he had spent with John Knowles, moving the deceased, he had ascertained that John, despite his cryptic comment to Stanley in *The Crown* about his "special Army friends", really didn't know anything about the Auxiliary Units. He closed his eyes, the image of Margaret Knowles lying dead on the street etched in his mind. John had insisted on carrying her himself. His thoughts went to the infant. The child would need John now. Clement hoped that his words at the public house about judging the child would find resonance with John. During their repeated trips into the church he had offered to baptize the infant. Although if the Germans occupied England he wasn't sure what he would be baptising the child into. Would the Church of England survive? He pulled himself up from the chair and trudged along the corridor to the kitchen. He was too exhausted to philosophise tonight. He filled the kettle and placed it on the stove. Lifting the tea towel from the cups and saucers on the tray, he put a heaped scoop of tea in the pot. It was extravagant, but this night he needed it. So many faces he knew. Good men and women of the village, whose lives had been cruelly cut short. And children. Too many children. One just an infant. He poured the milk into a jug. What did small children know of the Nazis? When the Germans did invade and drove into Fearnley Maughton, he would seek revenge for the little children. He closed his eyes. He was tired. Was he right to think such thoughts? He remembered Gubbins' words about killing. But killing the enemy because they were the enemy was one thing. Killing for revenge? That was not right. *Vengeance is mine*, said the Lord. And he was a man of God. 'No more philosophy,' he muttered as the kettle whistled.

He almost heard it before it happened. Why did the telephone ring or the front door bell sound just as one was about to sip the hot, soothing liquid? It was one of life's eternal mysteries. But tonight, more than any night, he could not ignore it.

He put the tray on the kitchen table and found another cup and saucer. 'Coming!' he shouted.

Turning out the hallway light, he went to open the front door. There stood Chief Inspector Morris.

'Reverend Wisdom. Could I have a word?'

'Of course,' Clement said. He hadn't thought of the dead Constable or Stanley in hours.

Chief Inspector Arthur Morris was, he estimated, approximately fifty years old. He had thin, neatly combed, greying hair and an unhurried manner.

'Please,' Clement said, gesturing towards one of the winged armchairs in his study. 'I'm sorry the room is so cold. My wife is away at present, seeing to her elderly sister. But, at least, I can offer you a cup of tea.'

'Thank you.' The policeman sat down. 'Reverend Wisdom, could I ask you a direct question? Are you involved in anything other than clerical duties?'

His mind raced as he poured the tea. He could not answer directly. Handing the cup to the Chief Inspector, he poured his own tea and sat in the other winged armchair. 'I am group leader of the Home Guard here in Fearnley Maughton.'

'Anything else?' Morris paused. 'Is Stanley Russell also involved?'

'He was in the Home Guard.'

'Was, Reverend Wisdom?'

The silence in the room was as cold as the temperature. 'I'm sorry, but I cannot discuss it.'

Morris nodded. 'Constable Newson was killed with a nine-millimetre bullet at close range. Would you like to tell me what you know about it?'

Clement had nothing to hide, but he wondered how the Chief Inspector knew he had been there.

'I did go into the police station,' he began, and he told Morris what he had seen. The man listened as Clement told him about the dead Constable and that Stanley was not in his cell.

'And you left the police station exactly as you found it?'

He nodded.

'Did you retrieve the Fairbairn Sykes knife from the evidence cupboard?'

There was another silence.

If his activities had been so easily spotted by the outsider from Lewes, he wondered if Gubbins should dissolve the group and elect a new leader. 'No,' he replied.

Another minute passed without comment. He watched the Chief Inspector sip his tea.

'My father was a vicar,' Morris said.

'Really?'

'Could you have gone to the police station during the raid and arranged for Stanley Russell's escape?'

It was a direct question and one that needed a direct answer.

'Despite what I, or anyone else for that matter, may be called upon to do to defend our nation, Chief Inspector, our country's enemy is Germany, not English police Constables.'

Clement bit his tongue as he thought about what he had been asked to do to Inspector Russell. For one second he pondered Morris' future. But Chief Inspector Morris was in Fearnley Maughton, not Lewes. Perhaps the investigation into Russell's death had prevented Morris from suffering the same fate.

Morris sipped his tea, but Clement noted that his expression had not changed. 'I grew up on the Wellington Estates in Stratfield Saye, in Hampshire,' Morris said. 'I was named after Arthur Wellesley, a man of extraordinary insight. And a nose, a large one as it happens, for predicting future needs. Reverend Wisdom, I do not want to know what you and Stanley Russell were or are involved in. But Stanley Russell is in very serious trouble. Especially if the man had access to special and unusual weapons. If you have any idea where he could be, I must insist you inform me without delay. If Stanley Russell is, or for that matter if you are, depending on classified wartime activities to pervert the course of justice, I would have to arrest you both pending an investigation. Or until ordered otherwise.'

Morris' intense brown eyes were staring at him. They were not hostile but they were authoritative.

'Whilst I cannot discuss any other role I may or may not have, I must tell you that I do not believe Stanley Russell killed his father.'

'Why?'

Clement told Morris about Stanley's childhood. 'Such anger once unleashed, Chief Inspector, would be violent. Emotion, not reason, takes control and hatred would make for a frenzied attack.' David Russell's office flashed into his mind. 'But I will tell you something I thought was odd.'

He saw Morris tilt his head, the eyebrow slightly raised.

'I know this will sound strange, especially from a man of the cloth, but there was just not enough blood. I served in the Great War, Chief Inspector, and I have seen what bayonet wounds do to necks.'

Morris nodded. 'I think you are right.'

Clement knew that regardless of his opinion, everything pointed to Stanley's guilt. He felt sorry for the gullible lad, especially when it came to Elsie Wainwright. And he felt responsible for getting Stanley involved in the first place. He pondered the girl. 'Perhaps you should know that Elsie Wainwright, our recently arrived District Nurse, has also disappeared from the village. We could have done with her nursing skills today. She may be completely innocent. She may even be dead herself, either from German dive bombers or some other foul play. But in light of what I told you about the relationship between Stanley and Elsie, it would appear that she and Stanley have vanished together as Stanley had originally intended to do. It could also explain the empty room at *The Crown* and the open safe.'

He watched the Chief Inspector processing this information.

'Why would that be?' Morris asked.

'Constable Matthews heard Stanley and his father arguing about money. Inspector Russell did keep money in the safe. I saw some. But if Stanley wanted his inheritance, why did he leave several five-pound notes in the safe? It must have been a tidy sum.'

'Did you see anything else in the safe, Reverend?'

He shook his head. 'There were some papers, but I do not know what they were.'

Morris sipped his tea but said nothing.

Clement wondered about the Chief Inspector's silences. They were palpable. 'I saw that the safe was open. But, I swear before Almighty God, that I did not take anything from it.'

Morris nodded.

'I'm sorry I didn't mention Elsie's disappearance sooner. But with all that happened today, I forgot about it. What will you do now, Chief Inspector?'

'Arthur, Reverend. We will be seeing quite a bit of each other over the next few weeks, I have no doubt.'

'You think Stanley did it, with the assistance of the girl?'

'It certainly looks that way. Well, it has been a long day. Thank you for the tea.'

'Thank you, Arthur. And my name is Clement.'

'Thank you, Clement.' Arthur Morris moved towards the study door. 'I will be staying in Fearnley Maughton for a few days, at *The Crown*. If Stanley should contact you or you have any other information, no matter how insignificant you may think it, please tell me as soon as possible.' He paused. 'If Stanley Russell is innocent, Clement, then we have a very cunning murderer who could still be here in Fearnley Maughton.'

Clement stared at Morris.

Morris must have seen his expression of alarm. 'If Stanley Russell did have an accomplice who shot Constable Newson, that person, whether male or female, would have to have access to a weapon which uses a nine-millimetre bullet.'

His mind raced to Stanley's pack. He had not checked to see if the Sten gun was actually in the kit bag.

'Furthermore, if Stanley Russell had such a weapon and if Elsie and he were planning an elopement, it is probable that the girl was waiting for just such an opportunity to stage a rescue. But did that rescue include premeditated murder? Either way, given what was happening outside today, no one would have paid much heed to two people running through the streets. Well, good night, Clement.'

Clement switched off the hall light and opened his front door. The strong moonlight flooded into the front hall, the pale grey-blue glow lighting up his front garden and the gate to Church Lane.

They shook hands. There was an honesty about Morris that Clement very much liked. He was pleased for Stanley that Morris was the officer investigating this business. If Stanley was innocent, there was a greater chance of proving it with a man like Morris on the case. He stepped back to close the door, but Morris held his gaze.

'It may not surprise you, Clement, that while Fearnley Maughton was being bombed today, I was in Lewes at the hospital. I attended the post-mortem of Inspector Russell. He was shot with a gun using a nine-millimetre bullet.'

Chapter Sixteen

Wednesday 18th September 1940

Despite his exhaustion, Clement had found sleep difficult. He rose and opened the curtains, wondering about his men and whether the Germans had landed during the night. Blue sky greeted him; the early morning sun was highlighting the changing leaves of the trees in the churchyard. He checked his watch. It was not quite seven o'clock but despite his anxiety about the invasion, he couldn't get Chief Inspector Morris out of his mind. Nor what the man had told him. All the evidence pointed to Stanley's guilt. And to Elsie as his accomplice. Yet he was convinced that Stanley had not murdered his father. Clement had decided, however, that whoever had killed David Russell wanted Stanley to take the blame. Such wickedness astounded him. But what of Constable Newson? That was not a shot fired at random. Neither was it a bullet commonly found. Could the girl have shot him in such a cold-blooded way? But if not Elsie, then who? What worried and appalled Clement most was that it now seemed probable that he knew the murderer. He visualized the hole in the Constable's head. Subsonic bullets. Special. He pondered his team. But he knew these men. He had hand-picked them and trusted them with his life. Although, Reg Naylor had been a revelation with his skill and aptitude for sniping. Young George had set up the trip wires, and Clive the explosives. Even Peter, who had an aptitude for disguise and stealth, could have returned to the village at any time. All of them had the skill to move in and out of the village without being seen. He stared through his window, feeling wretched.

How could he doubt his team? Good and decent men who had put duty ahead of personal safety. And why would any of them kill the Inspector? There was no motive. They knew nothing about the list or David Russell's involvement.

He would have to wait until tomorrow when he could see Johnny. Although, he did not know what Johnny could do. Clement felt that just sharing his thoughts would be helpful. He should tender his resignation if such action was permitted. But above all, he wanted to hear Mary's voice.

He dialled Gwen's number, forgetting the earliness of the hour.

'Hello?' a man's voice said.

He rang off. Still holding the receiver in his right hand he depressed the dial tone buttons and redialled the number. He had phoned that number so many times he knew it by heart.

The lines were crossed. That was it. He rang again.

'Hello?'

'Mary?'

'Is that you, Clement? Hello?'

'Mary, it's Clement,' he shouted. 'I'm sorry to call so early. I hope I haven't woken Gwen.'

'Clement? The line is so bad at this end.'

He stepped down from the bus and looked along the Lewes High Street. Everything looked normal to him. Why had the Stuka strafed Fearnley Maughton and not Lewes? He looked up at Lewes Castle. Perhaps the proximity of the high Keep to the roadways had prevented the plane from flying low over Lewes. 'Random wickedness,' he muttered. He walked towards the town centre and purchased a newspaper. But there was no mention of invasion and no pictures of high-ranking German officers standing on the steps of the Houses of Parliament. He swallowed, feeling the relief. He walked on, down the hill towards the railway station, the newspaper under his arm. As he passed Lewes Police Station he thought of Stanley. He knew that Chief Inspector Morris, although still in Fearnley Maughton, had posted a nationwide alert for Stanley and Elsie.

He shook his head. Ordinary people; a butcher and a nurse. Did war make ordinary people do extraordinary things? Of course it did, but he had never questioned that the extraordinary things were not heroic.

He stood on the platform as the train pulled into the station. The slender ankles stepped from the train and Clement embraced his wife.

'Clement, it is so good to see you. How is the village? What a terrible thing. I can hardly believe it. And young Mrs Black dead.'

'I'm so pleased you are back. It has been hectic since the bombing, and it is taking its toll on poor old Battersby. There are twenty-two funerals to arrange. Three of the burns victims died in Lewes Hospital. I still can't believe it. And this business with Stanley. I think you could well have been right about the girl. She has led Stanley astray, I'm sure.'

They walked together to the bus shelter and waited. He remembered the day they had met Elsie Wainwright. 'You were correct about her, Mary.'

They were sitting in the kitchen having lunch when the front door bell rang.

'I'll go,' she said. 'You both look exhausted.'

Clement saw the appreciative smile on Battersby's face. He, too, was grateful. It had been a busy morning. Before going to Lewes to meet Mary, he and Reverend Battersby had spent the morning visiting the injured. And this afternoon, Battersby was taking the first of the funerals. Clement felt guilty that he wouldn't be there. But in a way, his presence in the village yesterday had been by divine intervention. If the Germans had invaded their sector, he wouldn't have been in the village at all. Although he hadn't mentioned it to Battersby, he had wanted to check on Geraldine Naylor first. She had been indoors at the time of the strafing, but as the house was half a mile from the village, there had been no damage. Other than Mary, Geraldine was the only other spouse of his team still in Fearnley Maughton. Clive's wife had gone to stay with distant relatives in Wales, and George was single. Peter and Ned were both widowers. And Stanley. He couldn't think about Stanley.

He heard the familiar voice and went to the front door. 'Chief Inspector Morris, you've met my wife, Mary. What can I do for you?'

'How do you do?' Morris said, raising his hat.

Mary smiled. 'I'll get the tea, Clement.'

'That won't be necessary, Mrs Wisdom,' Morris said. 'I was wondering if your husband would come with me to the police station. Not to detain him, I assure you, but as he was the first to find the late Inspector Russell, I was wondering if he would go over one more time what he remembers?'

'Of course,' Clement said, and reached for his coat and hat.

He smiled at Mary as she closed the door behind him.

'How long have you been in Fearnley Maughton, Clement?'

'Twenty years. Mary and I moved here just after we were married.'

'I won't keep you long. I know you must be in great demand after yesterday's events.'

'I've been out all morning. It will take the villagers some time to get over this. It was terrible. But I suppose we have been lucky until now to have escaped. Unlike so many other places. Hastings, for example, has been hit almost repeatedly by random bombings. They say the

Germans drop any leftover bombs as they leave England. I think we just happened to be in its way yesterday.'

'I have heard that too,' Morris added.

They rounded the corner onto the High Street.

'I don't know that I can add anything to what I have already told you,' he said.

'You may well be right, Clement. But sometimes just being in the same place will jog the memory.'

Chief Inspector Morris opened the door to the police station and they walked in.

'Good morning, Sir, Reverend,' Constable Matthews said as they entered.

'I thought you took Matthews off-duty for the investigation.'

'I did. But in view of Constable Newson's death, I need him. And he can handle other things.'

Morris pushed open the partition door and they walked towards David Russell's office. The room was cold, the office furniture still as it was the day Clement had found Russell's body.

'You say you found Russell on the floor?' Morris asked.

'Yes. In fact, I could not see him from the doorway. I entered the room and found him lying on the floor beside the desk and a little behind it. His foot was the only part of him visible from the doorway.'

'The window was open, I understand.'

'Yes. I remember the curtains moving in the breeze.'

'Did you see anyone outside?'

'No. But Russell's car was in the rear lane. You can see it from the window,' he said, pointing through the taped glass panes.

'And the safe was open?'

'Yes,' he said, hoping that the Chief Inspector would not pursue the question of the safe and its contents.

'Just for now, let's make the assumption that the murderer was not Stanley Russell.'

He felt a wave of relief. But before he could say anything, Morris continued.

'Nor Constable Matthews. Then the murderer came in through the window.'

'But surely Inspector Russell would see someone entering his office through the window. Unless he was already on the floor?'

Morris shook his head. 'No. I believe Russell was seated in his chair.'

'Which means he knew the person?' Clement said, thinking again of Stanley.

'Perhaps. Would you like to see the Coroner's Report?'

Clement had never been involved in a police investigation, much less a murder enquiry. He wondered why Morris was including him, but he reached forward and took the proffered file.

'The relevant part is marked,' Morris said.

'There are three wounds to the head,' Clement read aloud. That surprised him. He looked up at Morris then continued. 'The first injury is a contusion to the back of the head, caused by a blunt instrument but not occasioning death. The second and fatal injury was caused by a gunshot wound to the neck fired at point-blank range. The third wound is a deep incision to the throat which severed the tracheae and carotid arteries. The third injury was sustained after death.' He looked at Morris. 'Why would anyone hit him over the head then kill him twice?'

'Good question.' Morris said, walking around the room.

He watched as Morris' eyes scrutinized every surface. 'Clement, would you mind sitting in Inspector Russell's chair?'

Clement sat in the chair behind the desk, as he had remembered Russell doing the day he had come with the list.

'Someone comes in through the window and hits the Inspector over the head,' Morris began.

'Perhaps Russell has his head down. Perhaps the safe is already open when he is hit.'

'It is possible, but he falls or rather slumps in the chair. If he were leaning forward, as he would if he was head down in the safe, he would fall forward off the chair, hitting his forehead on the floor or the edge of the safe. No. I think he knew the person who came through the window. And given that the window was open, he may have even been expecting them. And I think he was seated in his chair when he was hit. Now, Clement, take a look at the edge of the chair. Do you see dark staining on the armrest? Where the armrest joins the seat?'

He swivelled around to see the armrest. Caught between the tight folds of the leather upholstery was a thin, blackish smear. 'Is it dried blood? It isn't very much, is it?'

'I agree. But it is my opinion that either the wound to the back of Russell's head was not intended to kill, or the attacker was not strong enough for the blow to cause death.'

'A woman?' he asked. He could only think of one.

Morris lifted his eyebrows in response. Russell's body is slumped in the chair. The murderer turns the chair to face the side wall, and then Russell is pulled onto the floor where he is shot. The blood in the leather is from the wound on Inspector Russell's head as he is pulled to the floor.'

'Then, to disguise the shot, his throat is cut.'

'So it would seem.'

'But?'

'Yes. There is cause to question.'

'Surely even Constable Matthews would have heard a shot,' he said.

'Perhaps.'

Clement watched Morris, who had stopped talking and was staring at the floor. He could see the deep furrow in the man's brow.

He waited.

'Would you lie on the floor exactly in the position you found Inspector Russell?' Morris asked.

Clement lay down, half-twisting his body to replicate the prostrate Russell. Morris came and stood beside him, extending his arm with his fingers pointed, like a pistol, and knelt down beside his head. Clement could feel Morris' index finger on his neck.

'The throat wound covered the entry and exit points of the shot. Which means that the murderer was kneeling or lying beside Russell's body on the floor.'

Clement sat up. 'But if the murderer shot Russell and it killed him, why would he or she even bother to cover it by cutting the man's throat?'

'If I was to fire a pistol at such close range there would be powder and burn marks on the skin,' Morris went on. 'The knife wound would cover the burn marks and the entry and exit wounds.'

'Forgive me for questioning your judgement, Arthur, but it does not make sense.'

'It would if the killer wanted the murder to resemble a knife attack. Lie back down again, Clement, if you would?'

Morris stood, and stepping over him, looked on the other side of his neck. 'As no bullet was found on post-mortem, the bullet must have exited the neck and travelled...' Morris stopped speaking.

Clement turned his head and stared to where Morris' finger was drawing an imaginary line from Clement's neck outwards. 'I can see something,' he said. He pointed to the wall.

Morris lifted a curtain and they stared at a neat round hole in the skirting board.

Neither of them spoke.

None of it made any sense to Clement. He glanced at Morris. Morris' brow remained knitted. 'Would you mind not mentioning this to anyone?' Morris said. 'I want to play this as if we think Stanley is guilty.'

'You think he is innocent?'

'I didn't say that. I have an open mind on it for now. But I think it is more complex than it appears.' Morris went to the door and called to Constable Matthews.

'Constable, when Inspector Russell was in his office was it his habit to have his office door open or closed?' Morris asked.

'It was usually ajar, Sir. The Inspector didn't welcome unexpected interruptions. But he always wanted to hear what was going on outside, if you know what I mean, Sir.'

'And he could see if anyone was standing at his doorway?'

'That would be difficult, Sir. But he had good hearing,' Matthews said, pointing to his policeman's boots. 'And he kept a close eye on the supply cupboard. What with the rationing, Sir.'

Morris paused. 'When Stanley Russell was in his father's office, where were you, Constable?'

'At the front desk, Sir.'

'But you heard them arguing?' Morris asked.

'I'm surprised the whole village didn't, Sir.'

'Did you leave your desk at any time after Stanley Russell left his father's office?'

Matthews paused. 'I did visit the supply cupboard. I have the requisition form, if you would like to see it, Sir?'

'That won't be necessary. The cupboard is just outside this door, isn't it, Constable?'

'Yes, Sir.'

'Did you see Inspector Russell?'

'No, Sir. But I did feel the breeze. I knew the window must have been open.'

'Was that unusual?'

'Most unusual, Sir. Inspector Russell was not the outdoor type.'

'Could you stand in the corridor, Constable, just outside the supply cupboard door? Reverend Wisdom will say something and I would like you to tell me what he says. Can you do that? And leave the door to this office as it would have been that morning.'

'Of course, Sir.'

Matthews left the office, placing the door in its customary position.

'Clement, would you cough, just the once?' Morris whispered.

Clement nodded, then emitted a short, forced cough.

'Well, Constable?' Morris shouted.

The Constable pushed open the door and stood in the doorway. 'I'm sorry, Sir. I was listening hard. But I didn't hear the Reverend say anything. Actually I thought I heard him cough.' Matthews paused, the man's face a study in concentration.

'What is it, Constable?' Morris asked.

'I heard him cough, Sir. Inspector Russell, that is. He had a loud cough and a very loud sneeze. But this was...'

'Go on,' Morris said.

Matthews shook his head. 'Different, Sir. Shorter. And hard. Just the cough. Nothing else. Then the door closed.'

'The door closed?' Morris asked.

'Yes, Sir.'

'Thank you, Constable. You may return to your desk now.'

Clement watched the bemused Matthews walk back along the corridor to the duty desk. He turned to face Morris.

'A silenced weapon?' he asked.

146

'It would be my guess.'

Chapter Seventeen

Thursday 19th September 1940

Clement left the vicarage dressed in his Home Guard uniform. He wanted to see the men before going to London; to hear about any sightings and to let Reg know he had seen Geraldine. George, who had collected his note from the dead letter drop the previous day, would have informed them about the devastation in the village. He pondered their reaction to the raid. But what he considered equally as pressing was the contents of Stanley's pack. He checked his watch. It would be another two hours until dawn. Four o'clock. The coldest hour of the night. The ground was damp. He had heard the rain during the hours he had lain awake. Clouds now scudded across the moon, the strong light coming and going in uneven flashes. At least for now there was no rain. But with the clearer skies came a cool night. He pulled the collar up on his jacket. Standing at the front gate of his home, he looked up and down Church Lane. Nothing stirred. Not that he expected there to be anyone around at that hour. But it was remarkable how the intermittent moonlight made everything look sinister. It heightened the nerves. And it was so colourless: black, grey, pallid blue, stark white. It reminded him of the black and white Pathé newsreels at the picture theatres. Hurrying away, he strode towards the church. His men had only been at the Operational Base for forty hours but it seemed like a week. Half a lifetime. He opened his church, the door creaking closed behind him. He went straight to the church office. In daylight everything was familiar and unthreatening. But at night, particularly in the pre-dawn hours, everything seemed silent and alien. Shadows concealed imagined beings, and what sounds could be heard were intensified, juxtaposed with crisp silence. Unlocking the filing cabinet drawer, he took out his knife and strapped it to his inner left calf. It was becoming second nature, but he did not consider this an accomplishment. He pulled his trouser leg down over the weapon, and glanced at the neat piles of paperwork Reverend Battersby had left on the table in the vestry. He thought of Mary, who was still asleep in their bed. But with her return another anxiety had arisen. If Stanley was innocent, as he believed, then a murderer was on the loose in Fearnley Maughton. The neat hole in the skirting board flashed into his mind. He understood why the murderer would not want to leave the bullet, but whoever this killer was, the person was cool-headed enough to remove it. They also had the time to do it. Those two facts ricocheted around Clement's brain. Calm, rational thinking was dictating the murderer's actions. He shivered, but not from the cold. Was the murderer following a plan, a well-constructed and thought-out strategy? He knew now that they were dealing with neither an impassioned murderer nor an assassin. Clement had been taught at Coleshill that for the assassin it was about the kill. Personal issues played no part, because the assassin did not know the assassinated. But the murder of David Russell confused the personal with the impersonal. Was that the murderer's intent? But what was the motive? Whichever way he thought about it, he felt confused. He thought of Elsie Wainwright. But there was little he could do there. Finding Stanley and Elsie was in the hands of the police now. But while he had his reservations about the girl, he was almost sure that Stanley had been framed. He worried that he may know the killer. But if he did, why had the murderer waited until now? What had precipitated the murder of David Russell? He thought of John Knowles' threat the day the child was born. But he couldn't imagine John Knowles calmly killing David Russell. John's threat had been made in the heat of the moment. And as he already knew, the killings of David Russell and Constable Newson had not been frenzied. Besides, John Knowles' threat had not extended to killing Constable Newson or assisting Stanley in his escape.

He looked up as a flash of moonlight lit up the churchyard. Reaching for his keys, he closed the door to the church and hurried into the darkness, crossing the fields, heading for the woodland. The dawn light was tinging the sky as he approached the forest. He was about fifty yards from the Operational Base when he heard them. Birdsong filled the woodland, and Clement dropped to the leafy floor. He paused, then responded with the raucous warble of the Jay. Within seconds Ned and Clive were around him.

As he crawled through the narrow opening to the Operational Base, he saw Reg in the low light of a lamp. He was sitting with his Sten gun over his knees, the oil rag in his hand. Reg looked up as Clement sat at the table.

'What is happening, Clement?' Peter asked, as the men gathered around the table.

'You heard the Stuka?'

'George went into the village in the night and collected your note. He told us about the destruction.

'Twenty-two dead,' Clement said. He saw their wide-eyed horror and told them what had happened. 'It could have been more, had we not had our invasion day plans. But twenty-two is too many for our small village. I checked on Geraldine this morning, Reg. She knows you are doing your bit and while she is worried, she is unharmed and the house is undamaged. I also saw one of your Land Army girls, Ned. She told me that they were not hit. But the village has been damaged quite badly. I am sorry to tell you, Peter, that your office took a direct hit.' He remembered Doctor Haswell's garden. 'So did Phillip Haswell's Anderson Shelter.'

'So George said,' Peter answered. 'Is it completely flattened?'

'A direct hit. Peter, if you had been there you would have been killed.'

'I suppose I should be grateful for that,' Peter replied.

Clement could only imagine what it would be like to lose, at a single blow, one's life's work. But his friend was alive, at least for now. 'Anything to report here?' he asked.

'Only one incident, which occurred during my watch,' Peter said. 'I tracked a young man in the forest between two and four this morning. He must have slept there overnight but he left just before four o'clock. He was heading south. He didn't meet anyone and he did not stay long. He appeared to be foraging for forest food.'

'What did he look like?' he asked.

'He wasn't wearing a German uniform,' Reg said. 'Apparently.'

Clement glanced at Reg, who continued to polish his weapon.

'Who was on watch with you, Peter?' he asked.

He saw Peter shoot a glance at Reg.

'I didn't recognise him, Clement,' Peter added. 'About thirty, rather unkempt. Dark hair and whiskers. He was wearing a coat, but it was old and quite worn. Put it this way, he was dressed like he should be if he is that hard up for food he needs to forage in woodlands in the early hours of the morning,' Peter said.

'He could be a deserter,' Reg said.

'Did you see this man, Reg?' he asked.

Reg shook his head. 'The coat. Peter said it had epaulettes. And there is some sort of underground naval installation near Cuckmere Haven.'

Clement felt the frown crease his forehead. Johnny had not mentioned any Royal Navy bases within or near their sector. Besides, Cuckmere Haven was specifically off-limits. He turned his attention from Reg to Peter.

'Reg did a solo patrol to the coast during our watch this morning,' Peter told him.

Clement was astonished. 'That was never what we are about, Reg. We patrol in groups of no less than two. You could have got yourself and others here killed.'

'In this moonlight a patrol is too obvious. We learned that the night before. Sitting ducks! Besides, Peter and I became separated. And I work better alone,' Reg added.

Clement looked around the faces. He could see disapproval in the eyes of Clive and George. From the way the two men had seated themselves, he guessed there had been heated words. Living in the confined Operational Base was taking its toll, and they had been there less than two days.

'So where is this invasion, Clement? Because it is not here, nor, apparently, is it at Cuckmere Haven,' Peter said.

'I'm seeing Commander Winthorpe this morning at ten. I have been helping the Chief Inspector from Lewes.' He leaned back in the chair. 'It doesn't look good for Stanley. The police have issued a warrant for his immediate arrest and sent a description of him and the girl up and down the country.'

'How do you issue an arrest warrant for someone already in custody?' Clive asked.

'I'm sorry, of course, you do not know. Stanley has escaped. And someone else has been shot; a Constable from Lewes who was at the police station at the time. It happened during the raid. Did any of you come into the village during the attack?'

'None of us left the base during daylight hours. And during last night we patrolled to the south and east,' Peter said. 'Anyway, from what you have told us, it is just as well none of us was there, especially me.'

'Of course. I'm sorry,' he said.

'You think we freed Stanley?' George asked.

He stared at the boy. Or was George now a man? Something was different. For the first time since he had known George, the boy looked alive. The young face had transformed into the countenance of a warrior, and the pale visage of cardiac arrhythmia was nowhere to be seen.'

Clement swallowed. His mind bubbled with possibilities.

'So, once you are back from London are you here to stay?' Reg asked.

He heard the barb. 'I'm sorry. It was my decision to include Stanley and I feel responsible. I also believe he is not guilty.'

'You may want to revise that, Clement,' Reg added, throwing Stanley's pack onto the floor. It landed with a thud in front of him.

He looked at Reg. 'You mean the Sten isn't there?'

'That's exactly what I mean,' Reg said.

'And a magazine of ammunition is missing, Clement,' Peter added.

He leaned back in his chair. He felt tired. His legs ached, and his head. He wanted to believe Stanley innocent. And the girl.

'People have been hung for less,' Reg said, breaking the silence.

'If Stanley is guilty, I for one would not blame him,' Clive added. 'That father of his was a sadistic bastard. If anyone deserved to die it was David Russell. Pity there has to be an investigation. If he had been killed during the raid, no one would be any the wiser.'

'This Chief Inspector from Lewes, is he likely to cause us trouble?' Reg asked.

Clement shook his head.

'You haven't told him anything, I hope, Clement,' Peter said. 'We are trusting you not to give us away.'

'Of course your identity is safe. I would never tell anyone,' he said, which he knew to be correct. But with the list gone, he could not speak for others.

'What do you want us to do?' Peter asked.

He thought for a moment. He glanced at the faces staring at him, waiting for him to make a decision. Even though the alert had been issued, he believed the greater danger was from Arthur Morris, especially as, according to Johnny and *The Argus*, no invasion had yet taken place. The Chief Inspector would be asking questions, and if the town solicitor, the baker, the postman, a local farmer and a landowner could not be found he would have to invent an excuse. 'Other than the vagrant, you saw no enemy activity of any kind last night?'

'None! And not a ship in sight,' Reg answered.

'Perhaps you should go home. Peter, would you compile the report and George, will you drop it as usual? Make sure to include a description of the vagrant. Then go home. But please be careful. With Lewes Police in the village, it could be wise to conceal your packs. All of you would be suspects if Chief Inspector Morris discovers you have weapons which use nine-millimetre bullets, and Fairbairn Sykes knives. I should only be in London today. We'll meet at Peter's place tomorrow night at eight, if that is alright with you, Peter. '

Clement left the Operational Base and walked back through the woodland towards the village. He wondered about his team. The level of tension in the underground base was unnerving and he was glad to be away from the men. Had they become divided because of Reg's actions? It had been risky to patrol alone. And, Clement considered, unnecessary. More than unnecessary, it was specifically against General Headquarters' orders. Reg should have been disciplined for his breach of procedure. But his actions had also confirmed that no enemy amphibious invasion had occurred in their sector. Regardless, dissention was always corrosive. And spawned the bane of any team; mistrust. Standing them down, he hoped, would give them breathing space.

It was light now. He checked his watch. Ten minutes past six. Mary would be awake within the hour. He wanted to return home via the church, firstly to return his knife but also to grab a book in case Mary was already awake. He was tired but he could sleep on the train.

He broke into a slow run. As his feet fell into a rhythmic pounding, he contemplated the person who had the list. If the list had been taken by a local, what would they do with the information? Perhaps it was thrown away as meaningless. Perhaps the theft had always been about money. He shook his head. Ordinary people did not know how to break into safes. Neither did they remove bullets from skirting boards. Besides, if it had been about money why would the thieves leave some? His thoughts returned to the list. It contained only names. There was no indication of their mission. What was he missing? He quickened his pace, his eye on the brown mulching leaves beneath his feet. If the murderer had intended to get the list, then they had to have known its location and its content. He slowed and stopped. The morning birdsong had quietened. He had previously pondered whether the murder of David Russell had been personal or a means to get the list, but perhaps that was not the right question. Who would want the list? The Germans. Of course, that stood to reason, but there would have to be someone willing to do it. A collaborator. He thought of the vagrant. An outsider would have been seen. Especially one shabbily dressed. Besides, everyone in the village had lived there for years. Except one. Elsie.

Clement was back on the platform at Lewes station at nine o'clock. Mary had been more than usually quiet during breakfast, and he wondered if she had awoken in the night and found him missing from their bed. She hadn't said anything. He wanted so much to tell her not to be worried about him. And he would have valued her assessment of all that had happened. But it was impossible. Secrets. Whether during a war or between husband and wife, secrets divided.

Two hours later the train slowed and entered the familiar railway terminus. A Dornier bomber had crashed onto Victoria Station the previous Sunday during heavy bombing. Twisted wreckage still lay in piles around the old building, but whilst the damage had rendered the railway station inoperable for a few days, people now hurried about as though nothing unusual had happened. He stared at the faces. What he saw made him smile. It also made him oddly proud. It was as if the mighty city and its people were thumbing their collective noses at Hitler and his Luftwaffe.

He turned, his eye scanning the waiting crowd in the street, searching for the Naval Commander's uniform. But Johnny was nowhere to be seen. Clement felt his heart sink. He didn't like being a disappointment to anyone, especially Johnny who had shown such faith in him. Looking along the street, he saw the car. It was parked outside the public house on the corner where he had seen it last time. He waited. A few seconds later he saw the car leave the curb and join the main stream of traffic. Turning, the vehicle pulled up beside him and the driver got out. Clement recognised the man who opened the door for him, but there was no conversation. He wondered if it was a frosty portent of things to come.

Johnny met him in the entrance foyer of Number Seven, Whitehall Place. They shook hands but he thought it was not the eager greeting he had previously been shown. He followed Johnny up the familiar staircase.

He smiled at the secretary.

She smiled back.

The door opened and he entered Gubbins' office. The window behind Gubbins' desk had been taped with criss-cross panels, making the window look like something from Hampton Court. Intrigue, war, strategies, murder; nothing much had changed in four hundred years.

'Winthorpe tells me, Wisdom, that you are having problems?' Gubbins said. 'I could do with some good news, Reverend.'

He thought Gubbins looked exhausted. Everything and everyone had altered in some way.

'I'm not sure I can provide that, Colonel,' he replied.

Gubbins remained silent while he told them about the strafing, the murder of David Russell and Constable Newson, and the subsequent disappearance of Stanley, Elsie and the list.

Gubbins' face clouded. The man remained silent for a few minutes. He heard the clacking of the secretary's typewriter in the outer office.

'The vagrant is interesting. John, will you have some of your other people look into that one?'

'And Elsie Wainwright?' Clement asked.

'You say she answered an advertisement placed in *The Times*?'

He nodded. 'She said her parents were from Eastbourne, although now deceased. I don't know anything else about her. She did say she had come from London.' He paused. 'She had very little luggage.'

He looked up at Gubbins who was scribbling notes in a file.

'Many people don't have much to show for their lives now, Clement,' Gubbins said. 'But perhaps you are right to be suspicious.' Gubbins pressed a button on a wooden box to the right of his desk. A woman's voice responded. 'Miss Bradwynn, would you look into an Elizabeth Wainwright? John will give you the details. We need to find your runaways, Clement.'

'And the invasion, Colonel?' he asked.

'It appears that the war in the air is not abating. But there have been no sightings of any landing craft on our shores that would indicate an amphibious invasion. Hitler may well have planned his invasion to follow their control of the air. Fortunately, as yet, they have failed to achieve this.' Gubbins stood and walked to his window. The man was staring at a barrage balloon framed in the centre of his cross-hatched window.

What now? Clement thought, staring at the Colonel's back.

'Where are your men at present, Clement?'

'As we have not found any sign of the German invasion, I have stood them down, Colonel, pending your orders. What with the raid on the village, the murders and Stanley's disappearance, emotions are running high and the Operational Base is a confined space for volatile spirits.'

'I agree. Have your meeting with them tomorrow evening, but it could be a good idea if they were to have a refresher course at Coleshill. Arrange it for this weekend, would you, John?'

He saw Johnny's surprised glance at Gubbins, but Johnny did not question the Colonel's request. Or was it an order? Either way, it would be obeyed.

Clement was not a suspicious man, but it was evident even to him that Gubbins was having reservations about something. The man had said "they" not "you". Did the visit to Coleshill not include him? And why would Gubbins want them to go to Coleshill again so soon anyway?

Gubbins turned. 'Well, I won't keep you. Clement, stay in touch with this Chief Inspector Morris. The runaways must be found. For now we must assume that Stanley Russell has confided in Miss Wainwright. We cannot have them talking.'

Gubbins sat down and picked up some papers. The interview was over. Johnny went to the door and held it open. What Gubbins had said about Stanley worried Clement, and he wondered if he would ever see Stanley again. Whether hung for murder or killed in secret, he felt sure Stanley Russell was a dead man. But Stanley aside, why were his men returning to Coleshill? A shudder ran through him. Johnny's surprised reaction also worried him. He stood and left Gubbins' office more confused than when he had entered it.

Neither he nor Johnny spoke. Clement wondered whether he should mention that Reg had been at Cuckmere Haven. In view of all that had happened with his cell, and that Johnny had told them to stay away from the place, he decided it would be better left for another time. Besides, the speculation as to why his men were going to Coleshill was gnawing in his stomach. He had not questioned Gubbins' purpose, mostly because he did not wish to know the answer. 'How will Miss Bradwynn find out about Elsie Wainwright?'

'That's her job, Clement. As well as looking after Gubbins. And old Billy, as she is affectionately known to all, is good at it. By the time we have had lunch she will have something for us.'

'Really? More than just a secretary, then?'

'Most people at the Admiralty have more than one role, Clement. How long is it since you had some old-fashioned broth and really good fresh bread?'

'As tempting as that sounds, Johnny, what I really need is sleep.'

'Food first. Then after we have read what Billy Bradwynn has for us, I will drop you at the station. You can sleep on the train.'

'I should call my second-in-command and confirm the stand-down,' he said.

'Food first,' Johnny repeated, and leaving Number Seven, they walked towards Trafalgar Square and entered

St Martin-in-the-Fields Church in which a soup kitchen had been set up in the crypt.

An hour later they returned to Gubbins' office. Miss Bradwynn handed an envelope to Johnny. Gubbins wasn't there so they went up another floor, to the smallest office Clement had ever seen.

'This is my cupboard,' Johnny said, squeezing past the desk to sit in the chair. 'Only for the duration of the war, I am happy to say.'

Clement looked at the tiny round window set high in the wall. Even if Johnny could stand behind his desk it was impossible to see out. Not even a barrage balloon disturbed the whitish-grey sky, the only thing visible through the pane of glass.

Johnny gestured towards the phone on the desk. 'You can use this phone to call your second-in-command, Clement.'

'Is everything alright, Clement?' Peter asked.

'Yes. I'm a little tired, that's all, Peter. Not so young anymore, you know how it is. I should be home late tonight, but I will see you and the team tomorrow night at eight. And Gubbins has confirmed the stand-down.' But Gubbins' true motive for sending his men back to Coleshill worried him. Was it to hone their skills? Or was it to remove this troublesome team permanently? Secretly. Silently. Surely their training and knowledge would be needed, especially with the German invasion so imminent. They had, after all, signed The Official Secrets Act. Clement hoped he was just being paranoid. But his paranoia didn't extend to Stanley. He felt the weight of despair for the gullible lad; Stanley's actions had placed the organisation in real jeopardy. But surely the other members of his team were safe? He felt his stomach knot.

'Any news of Stanley?' Peter was asking.

'None.'

He rang off. He glanced at Johnny.

Johnny was smiling at him but he didn't, couldn't respond. He dreaded what lay ahead for his men. And he hated the deception he was obliged to perpetrate on a trusted friend.

Johnny opened the envelope and pulled out the papers. 'Elizabeth Patricia Wainwright, born fourth of December 1914 to John Abercrombie Wainwright and Audrey Louise Wainwright of Eastbourne. Attended Roedean School...' Johnny's eyebrows raised at the mention of the prestigious school, before continuing '...then undertook Nursing training at Guy's Hospital.' Johnny's eye scanned the page. 'She held a few positions in hospitals before taking her previous position as midwife at Charing Cross Hospital in 1939. Parents both deceased. Father was a doctor in Eastbourne. The mother was French. Also a nurse until she married, then home duties. No siblings. A marriage certificate for her parents has not been found, although Billy has made a note that in view of Mrs Wainwright's French nationality, Doctor and Mrs Wainwright could have been married on the continent.'

Johnny handed the paper to him.

'She said her parents were quite old when they had her,' Clement added.

'And here is a copy of *The Times*' advertisement,' Johnny said, handing him the newspaper cutting. 'All seems to be correct. I'm sorry to say, Clement, but it appears that your man is guilty and has run away with a hardworking, but rather well-educated English rose.'

Clement sat alone in the tea room at Victoria Station. He felt exhausted. But all he could see in his mind was Elsie Wainwright sitting on the counter in *The Crown*. She was undoubtedly beautiful, and possibly well-educated, but she hadn't exhibited it that day in the public house. He could hear her voice now. Gone was the genteel lilt he had heard in the bus shelter in Lewes. It had been replaced with the hard-edged sound of vulgarity. As far as he was concerned, she had the manners of a bar room harlot. English rose. He visualised the Reverend James Moore's wife, Helen. She was an English rose. Such women were above the likes of Elsie Wainwright. He suddenly felt sorry for the girl's deceased parents. He had seen it before, older parents who indulged the child they had so long waited to have. The police would find Stanley and Elsie, and when they did, they or Gubbins would deal with the pair. Guilt weighed on Clement for involving Stanley in the mission. He should have realised that despite his age, Stanley was still really a child: trusting, gullible in the hands of the wicked, and desperate for affection. Love and approval, which should have been forthcoming from his father, would have forged a different Stanley. On the train Clement closed his eyes. He couldn't think about Stanley anymore.

Chapter Eighteen

As he walked to the bus shelter in Lewes a horn sounded.

'Clement? Can I give you a lift?'

'Arthur? How very kind of you. I won't say no. It's been a long day.'

'Do I dare ask where you have been?'

He laughed. 'It's not that secret. Home Guard paperwork, actually.'

'Ah! Don't they say the devil is in the detail?'

Home. Mary. He opened the door. He could hear her in the kitchen singing her little ditties. He smiled and put down his satchel. At that moment the telephone rang.

'Hello?'

'Reverend Wisdom?'

'Speaking.'

'Please be in the graveyard in five minutes. You will be contacted.'

The line went dead.

'Hello?' he said again. He looked up. He could hear Mary still singing in the scullery. The caller had been insistent. He stared at the geometric pattern on the hall runner in the corridor, pondering whether he should go or not. He wanted to ignore the call but he knew he couldn't. He searched his memory for anything in the caller's voice that sounded familiar. They had said so few words. Could it have been Stanley? For that reason alone, he needed to go.

'Clement?' she called, appearing at the door to the kitchen.

He looked up and smiled, and reached for the hat that he had only moments before placed on the stand.

'Are you going out again?' Mary asked, her head tilting in the direction of the telephone.

'Wrong number,' he lied. He bit his tongue. He stared again at the hall runner. 'I just remembered I wanted a book from the church office. I thought I would get it before I get too settled.'

'Don't be too long. I'll be serving dinner in ten minutes. How was London?'

'I won't be long,' he called, avoiding her question, at least for now. Closing the door he trudged in the semi-darkness towards *All Saints*. It was a path he had trodden so many times that he almost never thought about it. He stopped and listened. Had he complied too willingly? His eyes scanned the path ahead. And behind. And sideways. In the decreasing light his ears were straining. He wasn't sure what lay in store for him. Perhaps he should have been carrying a pistol. He put his hands into the pockets of his coat, searching for anything he could use as a weapon. If accosted now, all he had were his hands. The unarmed combat lessons at Coleshill flashed into his mind. Coleshill. Did assassination await his men there because they knew too much about Gubbins' Auxiliary Units? How dreadful to be killed by your own and in such a way. Their bodies would never be found. A story would be concocted for the families. But he would know. Or would he? Perhaps the same fate awaited him. Now. He began to recite *The Lord's Prayer*.

As he approached the old cemetery at the side of the church, he could see a figure standing behind the grave of Sam Lyle, the old village grocer who had died in 1934. Clement knew it was Sam's grave. It was the only one with an elaborate headstone. He had liked Sam and enjoyed the man's odd sense of humour, but he considered the tall winged-angel to be in bad taste. A man he did not recognise stepped forward from behind the angel's wings.

The stranger was wearing a long black overcoat, a dark hat and a plaid scarf.

'Reverend Wisdom?'

'Yes,' he said, drawing in his breath in preparation.

'It is vital that your reports are transmitted every day. But we cannot transmit what we do not receive. Your failure to drop your report is a serious breach of the trust which has been placed in you.'

'I can assure you that the reports are attended to and dropped every day,' he said.

'Perhaps you have another escapee, Reverend. See to it immediately. It is never to happen again.'

The man turned and walked away.

Was he Gubbins' man? Or Johnny's? Clement didn't even know if the man was English. The Germans had spies who had been educated in England. Major Bannon had said that the enemy had so many spies in England that they should be suspicious of everyone. 'What is the world coming to?' he muttered. He stared at Sam Lyle's winged angel. Regardless, the plaid-wearing man knew about the dead letter drop. And if Stanley wasn't enough, now George was letting him down. All around him the world was going mad. Yet he had hoped that in his village, he could rely on his selected men.

He turned and walked back towards Church Lane. He rested his hand on the front gate before going in. As exhausted as he felt, this should not wait. He visualised Mary and his dinner. He screwed his eyes shut. He would sooner face Gubbins than an irate Mary if his dinner was spoiled. He decided that after dinner he would check with Peter Kempton if the report had been written.

Two hours later he collected his bicycle from the side of the house and cycled down Church Lane to the High Street. He was annoyed with George, especially as he was so tired. Cycling through the devastated village and out to

Peter's cottage in the dark was not his idea of enjoyment. As he passed the rear lane behind the police station, Clement caught sight of the Doctor pulling into his usual parking space. He had been so preoccupied with George and the missing report that he had not seen the car until the last moment. And with the vehicle headlights covered with the strange downward-deflecting shades all cars had been required to install, he was surprised he had seen it at all. That he might have been run over by Phillip Haswell, who would not have seen him, made him more determined to chastise George for his cavalier attitude. Clement had not seen much of Phillip lately and he was sorry for that, but between Stanley, the Auxiliary Unit and the dead and injured, they had both been kept busy. He reflected on Phillip Haswell and the amazing work he had done in *The Crown*. No doubt more than a few owed their lives to Phillip's skill. But Clement felt guilty for not yet spending time with the wounded.

He pedalled on. In the silence he heard the low drone. But it was high and distant. Ten minutes later Peter's cottage came into view, and swinging his leg over the bicycle Clement leaned it against the fence.

Peter lived in a two-storey cottage on the outskirts of the village. It was a pretty dwelling, although the shrubs and climbing roses were now overgrown. These were the things wives tended to take care of. He knocked at the door.

He heard Peter's step and the tinkle of Boadicea's collar on the other side of the door. He could hear the dog's agitation. The door opened. Peter was holding Boadicea's lead in his hand.

'Clement? I have already rescheduled the meeting for tomorrow night,' Peter said, standing in the doorway.

'I haven't come about that,' he said.

Peter stood back and gestured for his friend to enter. Clement closed the door behind him. 'Will you have some tea?'

'No thank you, Peter. Is there anyone else in the house at present?'

'No. But I don't imagine you have cycled here at this hour to check on my moral wellbeing.'

'Quite. Sorry. As I said, Gubbins has agreed to the stand down. His view is that the Germans are waiting to win aerial supremacy before invading. But he wants us to keep meeting and training.' He swallowed. He was not a good liar. 'The reason I have come, Peter, is to check that you handed in the report this morning?'

'Of course, Clement. Just as you asked. I gave them a description of the vagrant and that we had patrolled to the coast. I didn't say that it was a solo patrol. And I didn't mention what Reg told us about the activity at Cuckmere Haven. My guess is that they already know about it anyway, which is why we were asked to stay away. I also stated that they, whoever they are, should check on the vagrant who we believed could be a Royal Navy deserter. Is there a problem?'

He leaned back in the chair. 'I was contacted by whoever it is who collects the drops. Well, that may not be true. The voice on the phone told me to go to the cemetery to meet a man who chastised me for not submitting my report.'

'The report was done, Clement, and given to George as usual.'

'I never doubted it. But something is amiss. What happened in the village today?'

'Nothing much. Most people are still sombre and I have been all day at what was my office. Years of records have been destroyed. People's wills, personal records, accounts, all gone. What I could salvage is in my garage. I think I am getting too old for it all anyway. And now faceless men are

167

harassing you over some perceived delay in submitting a report that contains nothing of any real value. Have you spoken with George?'

He shook his head. 'I'll go now and see him. I just hope he is at home.' He stood and walked to the door.

Peter pulled the blackout curtain over the doorway.

Clement patted Boadicea. 'I'll see you tomorrow night, Peter.'

'Good night, Clement.'

He heard the door close. It was darker now and late. And he wasn't sure he would find George. George had a liking for the night life and the picture theatres in Brighton in particular. He couldn't blame the boy. There was little for the young to do in Fearnley Maughton.

He cycled back to the village and went straight to the Post Office, leaning his bicycle against the stonework of the old building. George rented a room above the Post Office from Ilene Greenwood. Clement prayed that George would be in. He was tired now and just wanted to be at home with Mary. He knocked at the door. It was several minutes before Ilene Greenwood appeared.

'Hasn't been in all evening, Reverend,' Ilene Greenwood told him.

'But you saw him today?'

'No, Reverend. Until recently George has been such a good boy. A real blessing to me here at the Post Office. But lately he has been away all day and all night. Breezes in, then breezes out. And he won't tell me where.'

'When you do see him, Mrs Greenwood, would you please ask him to come and see me?'

'Of course, Reverend. I hope he isn't in any sort of trouble.'

He lifted his hat in farewell. He had stood his team down, but that did not include trips to the seaside.

Chapter Nineteen

Friday 20th September 1940

Large grey clouds hung in the sky. Clement hadn't slept well and rain had fallen throughout the night. He hoped it had made the German bombers miss their targets. He waited until nine o'clock, then taking his bicycle he rode down Church Lane and into the High Street. Leaning the bicycle against the wall of the Post Office, he stuck his head around the door. Ilene Greenwood was on the switchboard. He raised an eyebrow at her and she shook her head. He sighed. But it was a deep and audible sigh. Frustration was exacerbating his tiredness and his stomach was knotting. Closing the door, he collected his bicycle but a seed had taken root in his mind and he needed to know. Swinging his leg over the bicycle, he cycled out of the village towards Peter's house.

Peter Kempton was standing in the doorway to his cottage when Clement arrived.

'What did George have to say for himself?' Peter asked.

He leaned his bicycle against the fence. 'Peter, will you come with me to the Operational Base?'

'Of course, Clement. You look concerned. You found George alright then?'

'That's just it, Peter. I haven't. Of course, he could have forgotten to drop the report and has perhaps gone off to Brighton or Eastbourne. You know how he likes the night life.'

'I do know. But that is unlike George. He takes his duties very seriously. Too seriously at times.'

'I can only think that if he is not enjoying himself on the coast he has returned for some reason to the Operational Base. Perhaps he left something there. Or he may have stepped into a trap. We should expect vagrants coming into the woods to trap and forage, what with the tightening of rationing. George could be injured. Would you mind coming with me, Peter?'

'Of course. I'll bring Boadicea, but wouldn't Doctor Haswell be better?'

'I'd sooner keep it in the family until we know where he is.'

Peter nodded and attached the lead to Boadicea's collar.

At the edge of the woodland, Peter released Boadicea from her leash. The Labrador ran off, her nose to the forest floor.

'We haven't laid any traps in the area, have we?' he asked.

'No. But when we have to take to the Operational Base again, it could be a good idea.'

They walked in silence but Clement kept his eye on the path, looking for any sign of recent activity.

Boadicea was barking some way ahead.

They stopped. An uneasy silence wrapped around them.

'Should I whistle for Boadicea to return?' Peter asked.

He nodded, his heart pounding. 'Don't want to walk into an enemy trap.'

Peter whistled, then called. 'Boadicea!'

They could hear the dog barking, its insistent yelping magnified in the damp woodland air.

Clement looked at his friend. 'I think Boadicea is at the Operational Base. You didn't leave any cooking refuse, did you?'

Peter whistled again. 'Of course not, Clement. All ship-shape and Bristol fashion.'

They waited.

Within minutes Boadicea reappeared beside them in the bushes. The dog was excited and ran off again.

Clement was aware that his heart rate had increased, and a sense of dread had gripped the back of his throat. In the forest stillness every sound around him seemed to have intensified. 'Do you have any weapons on you?' he whispered.

'No. Do we go on or go back?' Peter asked in a low voice.

He looked down at the ground and his eye fixed on a damp leaf stuck to Peter's shoe. He needed to make a decision. 'You circle around. Take the right side of the path. I'll take the left. If we see no one, we meet on the path below the Operational Base. If there is someone there, go straight back to your house and I'll meet you later.'

Crouching low, Clement ran into the trees and fell to the ground. He could see Peter higher up the hillside but within a minute he had lost sight of his friend in the undergrowth. Rising to his knees, his eye scanned the forest around him. The only movement was the leaves in the rustling wind. He listened hard. He could hear the scratching sounds of foraging birds. He thought they made similar sounds to stalking humans.

Although the Operational Base was half a mile inside the forest, it took Clement over an hour to criss-cross the forest and arrive at the path below the underground base.

Peter stepped out from behind a boulder and joined him on the path.

'Anything?' Clement whispered.

'Nothing.'

Together they walked up the hill towards the Operational Base. But neither had spoken further, their eyes and ears straining for any movement, their senses on high alert. Ten feet from the tree stump opening to the underground bunker, George lay on the ground amongst the fallen autumn leaves. The boy's intense blue eyes stared out from the ashen face and gazed up at the forest trees. His mouth was open. A hole, the diameter of a sixpence, sat between his eyes.

It was several seconds before either of them spoke.

Clement turned around. 'Dear God!'

'Germans?' Peter whispered.

He shook his head. 'I don't think so. If George was killed by the Germans, where are they? They would surely have entered the village by now.'

'You're saying it was someone local?'

He swallowed. 'I think the murderer is English.' He looked out across the slope, his eye scanning the trees and dense foliage. 'We must look for the bullet!'

'It would be difficult to find here, Clement. Especially after last night's rain. Why do you want it?'

'Constable Newson was killed with a bullet fired from a gun which uses nine-millimetre rounds.'

'Like a Sten gun? You are not thinking that Stanley killed George?'

He shook his head. 'No. But it could be the same weapon as the one that killed Constable Newson.'

'Is there something you are not mentioning, Clement?' Peter asked.

'It is possible David Russell was also killed with a nine-millimetre bullet.'

'I thought he had his throat cut?'

He nodded. 'Both.'

He heard Peter's long exhaled breath.

'Someone is sending us a message, Clement,' Peter said, and squatted. His friend reached forward, his hand outstretched to close George's eyes.

'Don't touch him, Peter. He may be lying on a grenade.'

'Dear God! What do we do? The bullet is probably in the ground under him. Besides, we cannot leave him here, so close to the Operational Base.'

He nodded.

'There is some rope in the store cupboard in the bunker. We could drag him further down the slope,' Peter suggested.

'We must assume that whoever killed George has left him here for a reason. The Operational Base may be booby-trapped. It is a risk only I can take. Stand well away, Peter.'

'Clement?'

'Life expectancy two weeks, Peter. It may be less for me. Tell Mary I loved her, if it blows.' He shook Peter's hand. Peter and Boadicea walked away, down the hillside.

Clement grasped the tree stump and pushed it sideways, exposing the tunnel, then jumped backwards and waited. Bending down, he stared into the narrow space. It was dark inside. It did not matter. He knew where to find rope. He placed one foot onto the top step of the descending stairs, then his other foot onto the next step. He looked down, his eye scanning the narrow, dark space. Several minutes went by before he placed his foot onto the floor of the Operational Base. By then his eyesight had grown accustomed to the diminished light. His eye traced the airspace in front of him. Then the ground. He couldn't see any wire. He stepped forward, placing one foot in front of the other. His skin felt hot and he could feel the perspiration building on his upper lip. He walked at a snail's pace past the stove and doorway to the latrine, into the living areas, past the bunks and into the rear of the base, almost the entire length until he stood beside the storage cupboard. He took several deep breaths, then placed his hand on the doorknob and squeezed the handle. The cabinet opened. He reached in and withdrew a length of rope.

He licked his upper lip. He could taste the salty sweat. Retracing his steps, he climbed back up the stairs and pulled himself through the trapdoor to the forest. Peter was staring at him from the pathway lower down the hillside. They both seemed to breathe a sigh of relief.

He held his hand up to stop Peter from returning. Unravelling the rope, he tied one end to George's feet and backed away down the hillside to the forest path.

Peter joined him, and together they pulled George's dead body down the slope away from its resting place.

Nothing.

Silence.

They waited, in case of a delayed detonation.

Nothing.

'I should go this time, Clement,' Peter said.

'No, Peter.'

He walked back up the hill, past George's still body. He had expected to find the bullet under George, but he had not expected what he saw. The canvas shoulder bag George used to carry the daily reports lay in the autumn leaves.

Clement squatted down and palmed away the leaves around the canvas pouch. He couldn't see any wires, Neither could he see the bullet. His eye checked around the edges of the pouch before he reached down for it.

He lifted the sack and opened it.

Empty.

Chapter Twenty

'Clement! Come in,' Arthur Morris said. 'Won't you sit down?'

As Inspector Russell's office was a crime scene, Morris had chosen to use the second office. Clement glanced around the small room as he took the indicated seat before Morris' desk. He had already noted the photograph in the waiting area. And his eye had caught the other changes. They would be considered minor, but they were indicative of the man now in charge. A large, framed picture of the King hung on the wall in the office of Morris' choosing, and a similarly-sized picture of the Prime Minister looked down on those waiting in the reception area. Fire buckets filled with sand had been placed around the public areas and rear hall and the front reception desk, which was Constable Matthews' domain. It was the epitome of order. He noted Morris' desk. Neat stacks of files sat around the timber desk. The whole place had taken on the guise of quiet efficiency.

'Arthur,' said Clement, 'Peter Kempton and I have just returned from walking in the forest. We have found a body.'

Morris leaned back in his chair, a frown forming on his brow. 'Do you know who it is?'

'George Evans, the young postman.'

'I am assuming, Clement, by your reaction, that you do not believe Mr Evans' death to be accidental?'

'No. He has been shot. Between the eyes.' He could feel his stomach beginning to churn. The sight of young George lying dead in the forest flashed into his mind.

'You can positively identify the deceased?'

He swallowed, suppressing a surge of acid. He nodded.

'How long ago did you find him?'

He checked his watch. 'Forty minutes.'

'Was the body cold to touch?'

Clement nodded.

'And rigid?'

He shook his head.

'Have you told anyone else about this?'

'No. I did try to find the bullet but in the thick leaf litter, I couldn't.'

'We should leave now, if you can. And your friend Mr Kempton?'

'Is waiting outside.'

'We'll go in my car.'

Twenty minutes later they were standing beside George.

Clement had seen plenty of corpses before, but in death the young man seemed a mere child. Too young to die. He sighed. That was not true. George had gallantly volunteered; his death had been inevitable. But not like this.

He and Peter watched as Arthur Morris walked around George. Without touching the lad, Morris scanned the body, his gaze following both legs and arms and settling on the hole in George's forehead. Morris turned around and gazed up the hillside. 'Is this where you found him?'

'Yes,' Clement said.

Morris turned to face him.

'You say you didn't find the bullet?' Morris asked.

'That's right.'

Another pause.

'Well, I don't believe you would find it here. Because I don't believe George Evans was killed here. And it could be that George Evans wasn't killed where you found him either. Would you like to tell me where that was?'

176

He glanced at Peter. 'Higher up the hillside,' he said, feeling like a small boy who had taken sweets from the counter.

'Thank you. And you moved him because?'

'I was afraid there may have been a grenade under him,' he said.

Pause.

'Clement, I said I didn't want to know what you were involved in, but I think the time has come for me to speak to your commanding officer.'

He nodded. 'Yes. I will telephone my immediate superior and ask if you can see him.'

'His name is?'

'Commander Winthorpe.'

'And I am assuming Mr Kempton also knows about this?'

Peter nodded.

'Thank you,' Morris said, and turned to walk up the hillside.

He watched Morris squat over the place where they had found George. The Chief Inspector's hand smoothed away some of the leaves, exposing the soft, moist soil. They waited, neither of them speaking. Clement saw Morris take a small tool, like a hand trowel, from his coat pocket and dig the ground. Within minutes Morris reached into his coat, retrieving his handkerchief. The Chief Inspector then stood, and he saw the white handkerchief go back into the coat pocket.

'Must have found the bullet,' Peter said.

Clement nodded, but his gaze was on Morris. Finding the bullet would help. Although if it was nine-millimetre calibre, this would not be good for Stanley. He saw Morris turn and look towards the tree stump over the entrance to the Operational Base. Morris walked towards it, paused, then turned away and walked back down the hill to rejoin them.

'You think he was killed elsewhere and brought here?' he asked as Morris joined them on the path.

'I don't anymore.'

Morris lifted his handkerchief from his coat pocket and opened it. Two bullets lay in the Chief Inspector's palm. 'Did you and Mr Kempton drive a car here this morning?'

'No,' Clement answered, his eyes staring at the two bullets.

'And you did not notice the recent tyre tracks where I parked the police car?' Morris said.

'No,' he said.

Peter shook his head.

'And there are several sets of footprints at the entrance to the woodland. Too many, perhaps?' Morris paused. 'It is my opinion that whoever killed George Evans didn't want his body found by just anyone.'

All the team members came and went from the forest using the track. But so did anyone else entering the woods. It had never occurred to Clement that the friable soil, once compacted, would hold footprints for some time, even after rain. He pondered the car tracks. He had not seen them. But then, as he often said, he was a vicar not a policeman. And what of the second bullet? Morris had not made further mention of it. The image of George's pallid face flashed into Clement's mind, the ugly purple hole staring out at him. Perhaps the killer had fired twice. But the shot was fired at point-blank range. How could the killer have managed that without George knowing of the killer's presence? He guessed Morris would have already considered this. But one thing now seemed obvious to him: the killer was playing games with them.

'But,' Morris began, interrupting his thoughts. 'Did the killer bring Mr Evans here, then shoot him? Or did he happen upon Mr Evans? Or did Mr Evans happen unexpectedly upon him? Or her? Or was it a rendezvous?'

He felt himself nodding. That would explain the close proximity. And if it was "her", why George had been so close to his killer.

'Moreover,' Morris continued, 'would it not seem logical to bury the body? A forest, surely, is the ideal place to bury a corpse, especially when there is little likelihood of being disturbed. Most murderers do not want their victim's body discovered. So I must ask myself, why does the murderer want Mr Evans to be found?'

They walked back along the track to the parked car in silence. Until he could speak with Johnny, there was nothing Clement could say to Morris. He stared at the footprints on the pathway. They were all large. Not the size or shape of a woman's shoe. Morris was also staring at the prints but remained silent. The Chief Inspector walked ahead of them while he and Peter returned to the car. They stood watching Morris squatting over the tyre tracks. Clement didn't own a car, so he didn't know if there was anything unusual about them. But he guessed from Chief Inspector Morris' preoccupation with the marks that something had caught the man's ever-vigilant eye.

'I will arrange for the police from Lewes to remove Mr Evan's body,' Morris said, standing.

They drove away from the forest and pulled onto the road heading for Fearnley Maughton.

'Do you think it was a car or a van?' Clement asked, thinking of Clive.

Morris shot him a glance. 'I believe it would be a car.'

'Can you be so decided?'

Morris nodded. 'The killer wanted George Evans found, Clement. However, he or she does not want to be caught.' Morris paused. 'A van with a name emblazoned on the side is far too memorable. Even if that van had been stolen. I have been a detective for over twenty years, and in almost every case of murder with which I have ever been associated, there is always a witness. Someone will have seen something. Unfortunately, that something is so routine that no one questions it.'

They pulled into the police parking area and went inside.

While Morris arranged for Lewes Police to collect George's body, Clement telephoned Johnny from the Chief Inspector's office.

'Something else has happened,' he said. He looked at Peter. He could only imagine what Johnny was thinking.

There was silence for a few seconds.

'You may remember I mentioned a man from Lewes. He would like to speak with you.'

'Usual place, Clement. Tomorrow. Bring your new friend. As for all your other friends, they are expected at the holiday camp this weekend.'

Johnny rang off.

He replaced the receiver. He had never felt so wretched in his life. Everything was falling down around him. And to make matters worse, he believed that Johnny was regretting getting him involved in the first place. He looked at his friend of many years. Did death await Peter and the others of his team at Coleshill? His head was pounding and he could feel the acid surge in his stomach.

Morris came in and sat in the chair behind the desk.

'I suppose you have no news of Stanley or the girl, Arthur?'

Morris shook his head.

Two of his men lost. He worried about Stanley who, even though living, was as good as dead unless he or Morris could prove Stanley's innocence. And George. George's death was a wicked and cruel act. It would have a very bad effect on the others, especially Reg. The man was already a loner, and Clement was worried about Reg's mental state. If Coleshill was really for a refresher, he was glad of it. But if Coleshill was for another purpose... He screwed his eyes shut. He couldn't think about it. Morris was asking Peter his recollections of finding George. Clement stood up and stared out the window. Close by the window was David Russell's black car. On the other side of the laneway Phillip Haswell was getting into his. He waved to his church warden, trying to catch Phillip's attention. He wanted to ask about the injured. But Phillip had not seen him. Clement turned around and watched as Peter read over the statement he had given to Morris. The odd thing about a view from a window is that there is, potentially, one hundred and eighty-degree visibility. But it is not the same from the outside. Seeing in is like looking down a tunnel: restricted and dark. He stared at Morris.

'Clement?' Morris asked.

'David Russell had to have been expecting the person who murdered him,' he said.

'Go on,' Morris said.

He pointed to the window at his back. 'I can see out clearly, especially in daylight. But seeing in is well nigh impossible. Whoever entered the window knew that Russell was in his office. And David Russell probably let them in, which means David Russell knew his attacker. It had to be prearranged. '

He turned around again and stared through the window as the doctor's car backed up and drove away. He sat down. He felt that what he had just realised was important, but something still evaded him and he couldn't make any sense out of it. Peter was staring at him, with raised eyebrows expressing the bewilderment that Clement could see on both men's faces. He swallowed.

'It was just a thought,' he said, feeling embarrassed.

Morris nodded and smiled.

But seeing Phillip again reminded him of the villagers in Lewes Hospital. He should have visited them before now, and felt guilty that he hadn't. In a way, they were his patients too.

'Clement, I was wondering if after church on Sunday I could address the congregation before they leave?' Morris asked.

'I think that would be a very good idea.'

'Does everyone attend?'

'Most of the villagers do. But only some of the local farmers.'

Morris nodded.

'If you are finished with me, I'll get back to the filing,' Peter said.

Clement smiled at his friend. He was grateful that Peter could find humour where so many others were despairing.

Morris walked with them both to the front door of the police station.

'You are redecorating, Arthur?' he said, his eye on the newly-painted front door.

'Constable Matthews offered to do it. Someone smashed a bottle on the front step and it damaged the paintwork,' Morris said. 'It seems rather odd to me, in light of the damage to other buildings in the village. But Constable Matthews has found a renewed sense of pride in the place recently and insisted on doing it.'

Clement's mind went to John Knowles. He remembered seeing John stagger past the police station on his way home. 'When did that happen?'

'Monday morning. But it could have been Sunday night.'

He nodded.

'No, Sir,' a voice said behind them.

It was Constable Matthews, holding a piece of board. 'It was not there when I arrived at work first thing Monday. Someone did it during the morning. I heard them and came running to catch the culprit but they had vanished. Kids, probably. No respect.'

Constable Matthews hung the "wet paint" sign on the door and returned to the desk.

He said goodbye to Peter and watched his friend walk away. There was a droop in Peter's shoulders and Clement wasn't surprised. Everything was complicated. Arthur Morris stood beside him.

'You are to come with me tomorrow, Arthur, to London.'

Morris nodded. 'I'll meet you on the platform then, Clement. What time?'

'The nine o'clock will put us into London at about the right time.'

He shook hands with Morris and walked away. He looked down the High Street towards the village green. Most of the shops were in the process of being repaired. All except Peter's lovely Georgian building that was gone forever. Nothing of it remained, except rubble. He saw Peter amongst the jumble of stone and shattered timber. Gazing along the row of familiar buildings, Clement watched as the people he knew went about their business. People stopped and chatted, life was slow and ordered. He smiled. But life was never what it seemed. He had said that before. He thought of John and Margaret Knowles. He had thought he knew them. 'I don't suppose you ever really know anyone that well,' he muttered. He saw two of the villagers standing on the Green chatting. The memory of the day the fighter strafed the village flashed into his mind. So much devastation. Yet he had been proud of the village that day. There was no hysteria. Fear, and later sadness, yes, but not panic. People went about their allotted tasks. They had Mary to thank for that. And Phillip. People were like ants in that respect. When it came to repairing damage the ants were an inspiration. *Go to the ants, you sluggard*, he quoted, and turned to walk home. But the bus shelter caught his eye. It was the dead letter drop where George secreted the reports.

Instead of going home he wandered down the street and sat on the seat in the shelter, his eye on the advertisement poster cupboard. It was a narrow, glass-fronted, locked cupboard that contained posters advertising everything from Defence Bonds to Pears Soap. Shards of broken glass were stuck in the shattered frame. He thought of George, a young man who through inclusion in the unit had found life's purpose. Changing the poster every week had been part of George's duties as postman. George had collected the reports from Clement while delivering post to the vicarage, then visited the bus shelter to change the poster. While doing this he used to wedge the reports between the timber frame of the advertising cupboard and the wall of the shelter.

He stared out, looking in every direction, thinking of the missing report. Directly in front was *The Crown*. He looked at the old Elizabethan building. Upstairs he could see the tiny windows of the guest bedrooms under the overhanging thatch. His eye fell on one in particular. The one he knew to be room six.

Chapter Twenty-One

It was a few minutes before eight o'clock when Clement knocked on the door of Peter's house.

'The men are here,' Peter said.

He heard the sorrow in his friend's voice. But Peter's tone and expression held more than sadness. There was an element of resignation, that the acceptance of death during war was inevitable. But George had not died on the battlefield. He had been murdered. And until it was proved otherwise, his murderer was English.

Three faces looked up at Clement as he entered Peter's small sitting room. It was late and he was tired, but he had to see the men. Reg stood to one side, his right arm resting on the mantelpiece. Clive and Ned were seated. They all stared at him as he sat in one of the chairs.

'I suppose you have heard about George?' he asked.

No one spoke.

Villages. Impossible to keep secrets. But Fearnley Maughton harboured a murderer and it had kept that secret well enough.

'What's going on, Clement?' Reg asked. 'Was George's death connected to our activities?'

It was a direct question and one that he wanted to answer. He glanced at Peter. These men were putting their lives on the line and he needed to be honest with them. They listened as he told them Gubbins' theories about the Germans waiting until they held air supremacy before invasion.

'Well, I wish they would just hurry up and get on with it, if they are going to,' Reg said.

The room was silent. No one really believed Reg. But everyone understood.

'And George?' Clive asked.

It was what they all wanted to know. The Germans were almost a side show.

'Unless Stanley is hiding in the forests, it cannot be Stanley this time,' Ned Cooper said.

'You are right, Ned. If Stanley and the girl are still together, Fearnley Maughton and its environs would be the last place he would be.'

'Unless that is his thinking,' Ned added.

'Stanley doesn't have the brains for that kind of deception,' Reg said.

Clement shot a glance at Reg. Even though harsh, he knew Reg's assessment was correct.

'Unless it was about the girl. George was keen on her too,' Clive added.

He looked at Clive. Whilst there was some logic to Clive's remark, he could not imagine Stanley killing George over Elsie. 'Stanley and George have known each other for too long for that. But I am concerned about the girl,' he added. In his mind he could see Elsie sitting on the bar, her shoe dangling from her toes. 'I do not mean to sound unkind, but why would a girl like Elsie be smitten with a lad like Stanley? What could she possibly hope to gain from the liaison? What's more, we don't really know if the girl and Stanley are still together.'

'Well, if not Stanley then who? Does this Chief Inspector Morris have any ideas?' Reg asked.

'He is a thorough man. And an intelligent one. I'm sure he will find the killer soon.'

'Do you think David Russell and George were killed by the same person?' Reg asked.

It was a question that worried Clement too.

'And what about Constable Newson?' Ned asked.

'Collateral damage,' Reg added.

'I don't know. It is possible someone stumbled on the Operational Base and killed George thinking him an enemy spy,' Clement said.

'So what happens now? Are we to be disbanded?' Reg asked.

Clement looked at Reg. He could see the disappointment. Reg was inherently brave, but Clement wondered if the man was almost too eager to prove his loyalty. With all that had happened, he was beginning to question everything and everyone. Yet Reg had also proven to be one of the best marksmen he had ever seen. The man could score a direct hit from fifty yards without a telescopic sight. But he had to be managed. The solo patrol had proved that. He visualised the hole in George's head, and Constable Newson's blank visage. He thought of the skirting board in Russell's office. But no matter how accurate Reg's shooting was, Clement did not really believe the man to be a murderer. For the sniper, the personal motivation to score a hit was in the accuracy of the shot, not the killing.

'No. In fact, Gubbins wants you to go to Coleshill for a few days to hone your skills. If the Germans are waiting to gain air supremacy before invading, the invasion could be on hold for a while. It gives us some breathing space. Given this and where George's body was found, it is best we stay away from the Operational Base for now. It could all be coincidental, I just don't know. Go to Coleshill, but remain vigilant. And watch each other's backs.'

'You not joining us?' Reg asked.

He shook his head, feeling the division. They had been a team of seven men and they had shared and learned much about each other. That made a team coalesce. But with two members missing, one of them murdered, the cohesion of the team had been shattered. Clement hoped Coleshill would reunite them. But without him it would be a lopsided team, and one where he increasingly felt like the outsider.

'There is something important I must do and about which I can tell you nothing,' he said, hoping it sounded convincing.

The room fell silent again.

'I thought we were a team, Clement?' Peter said.

He nodded. 'It has to do with Stanley. He must be found. And the girl. And Johnny can get Scotland Yard involved,' he said, avoiding any mention of Chief Inspector Morris. He hated lying. But Morris was sure to learn their identities and that was something he had promised would not happen.

He glanced at the faces. Peter, Clive and Ned seemed to accept his excuses.

'Stanley's dead, isn't he?' Reg said, staring at him. 'If not already, then he will be. He knows too much.'

He could feel Reg's eyes on him.

'You doing it, Clement?' Reg asked.

Clive and Ned turned to face Reg.

He could see their incredulity. He believed he mirrored their reaction. 'I don't know where Stanley is, and that is God's honest truth.'

But Reg's face was resolute, as though he had discovered an absolute truth as yet unknown to the rest of mankind.

Clive and Ned were now looking at Clement, but he could say nothing.

He watched Reg purse his lips then pout. 'Right!' Reg said. 'Well, if that's it?'

The reaction annoyed him but there was little else he could say. 'Be at Lewes Station at six o'clock tomorrow morning. That is all for now,' he snapped.

Reg walked towards the front door.

They heard the door slam.

Clive Wade stood, Ned beside him. 'What Reg said, is it true, Clement?' Clive asked.

'Absolutely not!' he said aghast. 'I do not kill innocent men!'

He could feel the stares.

'That is good enough for me, Clement. Sorry, but I had to ask,' Ned said.

He nodded. 'I understand. And thank you, Ned.'

'Do you think Stanley is still alive?'

'I don't know, Clive. I hope so. But he must be found. Soon.'

Peter showed Clive and Ned to the door.

The room was empty now except for Clement and Boadicea, who had not moved from her mat in front of the fireplace. It alarmed Clement that Reg thought him capable of tracking and killing Stanley. Especially as he was endeavouring to find some proof that would exonerate the man. He had, at times, removed his cleric's collar since the *Cromwell* alert but he hadn't abandoned his Christian faith.

Peter returned, and they exchanged glances but neither of them spoke for several minutes. Clement stared at the flames licking the logs in the fireplace. A pine cone cracked in the heat, the popping sound and sudden burst of released embers briefly illuminating the grate.

'At least the Germans haven't landed,' he said.

'Don't worry, Clement. We will do what we must. You just find Stanley and who killed George.'

As Clement left he heard Peter's front door close behind him, and grabbing his bicycle from beside the front fence, he rode into the night. As he rode he stared up at the night sky. It was cold and he could see only stars tonight. But the memory of Reg standing beside Peter's mantelpiece, and what the man had believed him capable of doing, appalled him. Yet that would have been David Russell's fate, and it was what they had been trained to do. Kill. And silently. 'Get used to it,' he muttered. 'It is what you signed up for! Terror by Night,' he reminded himself. As much as he did not like voicing the Auxiliary Unit motto, it was his future for the remainder of the war. At least, the remainder of his war. He cycled back into the village, the moonlight casting long shadows across his way. No one was about. Late-night travel was discouraged, being considered too dangerous and, for those who had vehicles, a waste of valuable petrol.

As he cycled past the common he could smell the burning log fire in *The Crown*. He stared at the building, thinking of Elsie Wainwright. The girl was an enigma. Arthur Morris was staying at *The Crown*, and Clement wanted to ask him if they could leave for Lewes in the morning a little earlier than they had agreed. He wanted to visit the injured in Lewes hospital.

There was the usual group huddled around the bar and seated by the fireplace. Elsie's absence was, no doubt, the reason for the subdued atmosphere in the public bar. He scanned the faces present before opening the door to the dining room.

Morris sat alone in the deserted room, a newspaper spread on the table in front of him, the evening meal long since tidied away.

'It's late to be out, Clement. Everything alright?' Morris asked.

He nodded. 'Arthur, tomorrow, I was wondering if we could leave the village a little earlier than arranged. I should visit those who are still in hospital in Lewes. I feel guilty that I have not visited them before now.'

'Of course. There is always plenty of paperwork to do.' Morris paused. Lifting the newspaper, he slid out a piece of paper with a rough sketch of the village drawn on it. 'Would you mind if I asked you again about the day you found Inspector Russell?'

'Anything to help,' he said, looking at the sketch. Lines and arrows had been drawn all over the paper.

'The vicarage is quite close to the police station,' Morris said.

He stared at the diagram. He could see that Morris had pencilled in his home, the police station and other buildings around the village.

'From your perspective, Clement, what was going on in the village last Sunday and Monday?'

He thought for a moment. 'That was the fifteenth. They are saying it was the worst day of bombing. We saw bombers and fighters all day and well into the night. Our planes and the German ones. Sortie after sortie. I do not know how our brave boys could tell who was friend and who was foe. Do you know the glow of London could be seen ten miles away? I heard that on the wireless. Hard to believe how London has survived. The sight and noise of those planes overhead placed a pall over the village. By Monday morning everyone was worried. But it is amazing how people react. Some went about their business, opening their shops and offices, while others remained indoors listening to the wireless reports. However, the tension was undeniable. Invasion and defeat were in everyone's mind. But I am glad to say not on their lips. The village felt eerily normal.'

'What did you do that day?'

'Church, of course, in the morning,' he replied, and leaned back in the chair remembering. 'In the afternoon, I wanted to go for a walk on the Downs. I saw John Knowles. Not a happy situation. His child had been born that day. There was much gossip about the child's paternity in the bar,' he said, glancing towards the public bar. 'I went home after that.' He paused. He could not tell Morris about his main concern that day, the retrieval of the list from Russell's safe.

Morris nodded. 'And the Monday, where were you, exactly?'

191

He couldn't look at Morris. That was the morning he received the telegram, when life as he knew it changed forever. It was also the morning life changed for Stanley Russell and his father. 'At the vicarage,' he said. 'Then I went to Peter Kempton's office, then to look for Stanley.'

Morris paused. 'Why did you go to see Inspector Russell?'

He nodded. 'I thought David might have known where Stanley was.'

Morris picked up his pencil and drew a dotted line from the vicarage to Peter's office building, out to Stanley's cottage then back to the police station.

'Was Constable Matthews there?'

'Yes. No.'

Morris raised his eyebrows.

'I mean, he was on duty, just not behind the desk when I arrived. I didn't have to wait long, though.'

'Did Constable Matthews say where he had been?'

'He was in the police station. I saw him, through the glass partition, walking back down the corridor. I remember now, he was carrying a dustpan and broom. Of course, the smashed bottle on the doorstep. He must have just cleared it up.'

Morris paused.

'The day of the raid, the seventeenth, you went to check on Stanley. Do you remember anything you thought was out of the ordinary?'

'Other than a German fighter dropping bombs and strafing a quiet, rural English village, you mean?'

Morris pulled his lower lip inwards. 'The plane was quite low, I understand?'

Clement nodded. 'Yes. I did think that was odd. The pilot dropped the two bombs and strafed the village a couple of times and left. Most people were just trying to get out of its way.'

'Did it follow the same path on the second and third runs?'

'Yes, I think so.'

'And most of the damage was around the village green?'

'Yes. One bomb dropped on Peter Kempton's office. It must have been a bigger bomb.'

'Why do you say that?'

'It caused much more damage than the one on Doctor Haswell's garden. And although there was a large hole in the rear wall of Phillip's house, I remember thinking that there was not much damage in the street.'

'Did you see anyone near to or enter the police station?

'There was so much confusion. I saw almost all the villagers at one time or another. I did see John Knowles outside *The Crown*. His wife was one of the victims killed in the strafing. I asked him to help me carry the dead on stretchers to the church. We passed the police station several times. Too many times. But I do not remember seeing anyone enter or leave the police station.'

'When did you last see Elsie Wainwright?'

He thought for a while. 'On the Sunday afternoon. Here, in *The Crown*.'

Morris smiled. 'Thank you, Clement.'

'I am not sure if I have been of any help, Arthur.'

'Timing, Clement. That is how our murderer, or should I say murderers, have done it.'

'You think there is more than one?'

'Without question.'

Chapter Twenty-Two

Saturday 21st September 1940

He was getting used to Lewes station. Even the stationmaster smiled at him as he sat in the waiting room. Mary had packed two sandwiches. Sardines. Italian sardines that Gwen had saved and which he would savour on the journey. He saw the Chief Inspector walk onto the platform.

Morris sat beside him and they exchanged pleasantries.

'You seem quiet this morning, Clement?'

'I have just come from the hospital. The sight of burnt flesh is very sobering, Arthur.'

Morris nodded. 'How is the Doctor coping?'

'The man works long hours. In fact, he was at the hospital even earlier than me this morning.'

'I have yet to meet the Doctor. He is out every time I call to see him,' Morris said.

'Really? I would have liked to have spoken with Phillip myself. I am worried about Mrs Faulkner. She is elderly and has major burns. The Sister says she may be in hospital for months.'

'You didn't see Doctor Haswell?' Morris asked.

He shook his head. 'No. But I know he was there. His car was in the parking area at the front when I arrived. I don't suppose you have heard anything about Stanley and Elsie?'

'No,' Morris paused. 'This afternoon, Clement, after we have met with your people, I might go to Scotland Yard. If you need to get away early, I can make my own way back.'

'Of course.'

Morris opened his newspaper. Clement saw it was the previous week's edition of the *The Evening Argus*.

'I have today's paper if you would prefer it, Arthur?'

'Thank you, Clement. But I'm actually looking at the classifieds section.'

'You are looking for other work?' he asked.

Morris smiled. 'No. I cannot imagine what I would do if I was not a policeman. I am, however, looking at the Hospital and Medical Appointments.'

'May I ask why?'

'I am wondering why a village doctor in Sussex advertises in *The Times*. With all the signage removed, I would have thought a nurse with local knowledge of the area would have been preferable. But, who knows, perhaps Doctor Haswell advertised in *The Argus* as well.'

Johnny met them at Victoria Station, and they sped off towards Whitehall and the ubiquitous beige stone.

Clement smiled at Miss Bradwynn seated behind her desk in Gubbins' outer office.

She smiled back. 'Won't you sit down, gentlemen?' she said. 'Colonel Gubbins won't keep you long.'

The typewriter clacked away, the bell sounding as the carriage was pushed back with every new line of type. Clement wondered if Miss Bradwynn ever went home. Perhaps the Admiralty was her home. War doesn't keep business hours, he told himself.

Colonel Gubbins was seated behind a pile of papers on the desk when they entered his office. He thought Gubbins looked older. Strain does that. And he was about to add to it.

Clement introduced Arthur Morris, and they sat down.

'We couldn't tell you over the telephone, Clement. But we have decided to stand your cell down. It is just temporary,' Gubbins told him.

Gubbins must have seen his concerned reaction.

'Your sector is being taken over by people who are worth a lot more to the Germans than your team.'

It didn't help. He swallowed hard. 'And my men?'

Gubbins looked at him. 'Given that two of your team are no longer with you, your remaining team will be much safer at Coleshill, Clement.'

He felt the weight lift from his shoulders.

'Now, what's been going on in Sussex?' Johnny asked.

Clement explained, and when he finished speaking he glanced at Morris. Morris hadn't interrupted but remained seated, his legs crossed, his hat perched on his knee. Clement saw the smallest reaction on Morris' face when he informed Johnny and Gubbins about George, and the proximity of George's body to the Operational Base. But it was the news of the disappearance of the report that caused furrows in the brows of all present.

Gubbins' office fell silent.

'Chief Inspector, it is vital that you find Stanley Russell and Elsie Wainwright,' Johnny said. 'Kent and Sussex are our top-priority sectors, but if these two people remain at large, they could jeopardise every cell in the country and we simply don't have the personnel to replace them all. Especially now.'

'Have you any leads, Chief Inspector?' Gubbins asked.

'The pieces are coming together. I would like Scotland Yard to run a few checks on the bullets we have recovered from the various crime sites.'

'As long as there is no mention of us here or the Auxiliary Units, Chief Inspector.' Gubbins said.

There wasn't much more to say. Being stood down should have made Clement happy. And as far as it involved his men, it did. But he didn't feel joyful. Failure is what he felt. He and Arthur Morris left the office. There had been no mention of lunches at expensive hotels this time; what's more, he was left in no doubt that Gubbins and Johnny were regretting his involvement. No other group, he felt sure, had caused so much trouble. But at least his men were safe. That alone was cause for celebration. He pushed Johnny and Gubbins from his mind. 'There is a place under St Martin-in-the-Fields where we can get some lunch. It will probably be bread and soup but it's not too bad,' he said.

Arthur Morris shook his head. 'Thank you for including me in your discussions, Clement, but I want to run some checks on those bullets. Even with top priority, it will probably take all day, so I'll make my own way back to Lewes.' Morris paused. 'And rest assured, Clement, I will not mention anything of your clandestine activities.'

He nodded. He watched Arthur Morris walk away, then checked his watch. It was nearly one o'clock. He walked towards Trafalgar Square and St Martin-in-the-Fields.

As he crossed the great square he heard them start.

Sirens.

A most unnatural sound: slow to begin with then heart-racing in their urgency.

The noise bounced off the stone buildings and reverberated around him. A wave of pigeons lifted from the pavements, their wings loud with panic. People began to run. For a second he didn't know what was happening.

He wheeled around.

Above him he heard the repetitive low booming sound, like hundreds of cars spluttering and backfiring.

A second later, the ground began to shake.

'Get in the shelter!' someone bellowed.

He turned again. A warden was yelling at him. He looked around, in the direction of the angry man's pointed finger.

'I'll show you,' a voice said.

He felt the tug on his arm.

He looked down and a young woman was holding his arm, pulling him along.

'Down here,' she said.

They hurried, with scores of others; like a human ribbon they streamed down the steps into the underground. Below, it was dark and it smelled of sweat and urine.

'Quickly now,' the girl was saying. 'If we hurry we can find a place to lie down.'

'Lie down?' he mumbled.

'They're early today. I was hoping to have time to wash my hair before reporting back,' the girl said.

'How long does it last?' he asked.

'You're not from around here, are you?' the girl said.

'No. I'm just in London for the day.'

The girl laughed. 'Well, if it is like yesterday, we could be here all night.'

The girl ran forward and pounced on the wooden-planked station seat. 'Come on!' she called. 'You can share the seat. The other night I had to lie on the steps. Bloody Jerries!'

He removed his coat and sat beside her.

'Oh! Sorry, Vicar. I didn't know.'

'No harm done,' he said. 'I'm indebted to you for ushering me down here. I wouldn't have known where to go.'

The girl stood and removed her coat and threw it over the seat. 'Anne Chambers,' she said, her hand thrust towards him.

'Reverend Wisdom,' he said smiling, shaking the girl's hand. But it wasn't until she sat down that he realised she was wearing a nurse's uniform.

'Do you work hereabouts?' he asked.

Anne nodded. 'Charing Cross Hospital.'

The rumble of bombs rattled above them. He glanced around. No one seemed to be paying much attention. Someone had turned on some lights. But the underground was grimy and dingy. He remembered the crypt at Christ Church, Mayfair. Somehow at Christ Church, sitting among the sarcophagi had seemed more normal than sitting and waiting for the forces of good and evil to transform the world above them as they knew it. He stared at the people. Some sat or lay along the platform. Everyone waited. It was a well-rehearsed routine, but to an onlooker it was the most extraordinary sight. People, probably total strangers, sat side by side along the platform like Gwen's Italian sardines. Women were making tea on small paraffin cookers near a brick column upon which were advertising posters. He stared at the poster. It showed a photo of Weston-Super-Mare, of couples sitting idly in deckchairs, staring at a golden setting sun and enjoying life. Fate sometimes had a cruel streak. He cast his eye around the space. Some women were knitting, the needles clicking hard, the repetitive sound bouncing off the hard surfaces then stopping each time the earth shook. He thought of Mary, and prayed there were no stray aeroplanes over Fearnley Maughton today. A man stoked his pipe and sat down on a chair as though he was in his own home. What Clement saw was visible resilience, but what he smelled was suppressed fear.

'Tell me about yourself, Vicar?' Anne asked, settling on the bench. 'Are you married?'

He looked at the girl. If Anne was afraid, she hid it well. But then he had learned at Coleshill, in interrogation classes, that some people talk a lot when nervous. He knew this from his time in the trenches anyway. Anne had made herself as comfortable as was possible, given their surroundings, her nurse's cape draped over her knees and tucked in under her legs. Thank the Lord for the Annes of this world, he thought.

He smiled at her. He knew her questions were not intended to be either familiar or impertinent. She was being friendly. He glanced around again at the people in the shelter. Groups had formed. He smiled. Even in the underground, the class system prevailed. But neither bombs nor bullets discriminated when it came to maiming and killing. Another lesson learned from the trenches.

He nodded. 'Twenty years. My wife used to work in London. At the Admiralty.' He paused, thinking of Miss Bradwynn. 'What about you?'

'London born and bred,' Anne said. 'I trained at Guys but I have been delivering babies at Charing Cross ever since. I like London, Vicar. Couldn't live anywhere else.'

'Charing Cross Hospital? I don't suppose you ever worked with an Elizabeth Wainwright?' he asked.

'Yes, I knew Elsie.'

The girl's response was so unexpected he felt his jaw drop. 'She worked in my village, in East Sussex.'

'Elsie? In the country? Can't be the same Elsie, Vicar. Elsie hated the country. Particularly East Sussex. Too close to her parents. They didn't get on.'

A child was crying, but Clement almost did not hear the wailing infant.

'She grew up in Eastbourne. Her father was a doctor there,' he said, trying to confirm the few details he knew about the girl.

'That's right. But both her parents died some time ago.' Anne pulled a biscuit from her pocket and broke it in half. She held a piece out to him.

He shook his head.

'I put them there during the shift. I don't steal. But if the patients don't eat them, why waste them? Besides, you never know when you might not eat for a while. She went back there a couple of years ago to see their graves,' Anne continued. 'Elsie, I mean. She met someone. A man. But it didn't work out. And she returned to London. She said she wouldn't leave London ever again. Only get your heart broken, she said. But I know the truth.'

'Do you know where she is now?' he asked.

Anne stared at him, the large green eyes wide. 'But I thought you knew, Vicar? Elsie is dead.'

Chapter Twenty-Three

Clement could feel the ground thumping. The railway tunnels amplified and distorted the noise.

'What?' he mumbled.

The rumbling continued. Sudden gusts of wind came through the train tunnel each time the earth shook.

'She jumped off Westminster Bridge. Well, that is what the police said.'

He stared at Anne Chambers. He felt as though his chest had exploded with the East End.

'When?'

'It's got to be three years ago. Not long after she came back to London.'

'Can you describe her?'

'What is it, Vicar? You look like you've seen a ghost!'

'Please, Anne, indulge me. Can you describe her?'

'About five feet four inches, twenty-three,' Anne paused, 'Elsie would be twenty-six now, blonde with blue eyes. Pretty. The prettiest girl I ever saw. Though she wasn't too pretty when they pulled her out of the Thames.'

'Did she have any distinguishing marks?' Clement asked.

'Elsie? She was about as perfect as God can make a woman, Vicar.'

'Indeed,' he said. But he was thinking of the Elsie Wainwright he knew, who also was a beautiful young woman. 'Was there anything about Elsie that only someone who knew her well would know?'

The girl looked at him. She had the oddest expression on her face.

'Other than being pregnant, you mean?'

'What?'

'What is all this about?' Anne asked.

'I have met a young woman who is calling herself Elsie Wainwright. She is wanted by the police.'

'Then whoever she is, she couldn't be the Elsie Wainwright I knew, Vicar. I saw her. I identified her. And I know that body was Elsie Wainwright.' Anne paused. 'They said that is why she jumped off Westminster Bridge, because she was pregnant.' Anne shook her head. 'I shouldn't be telling you, Vicar, but nurses, well, we work with babies. And some women lose babies, poor sods. Naturally, I mean. But there are always a few from the wealthy classes who don't, if you know what I mean. And the midwives are there to help.'

He swallowed again. What he was hearing astounded him. 'It wasn't quite what I meant,' he muttered, his voice subdued. He felt the numbing sensation of incredulity. His head spun. Not because what Anne had told him very clearly conflicted with his religious beliefs, nor so much for the evident illegality of it, but because Anne Chambers had confided so much vital information he was having trouble taking it all in. Yet the unnecessary death of a beautiful young woman and an innocent baby made it all the more tragic. And sinister. Also unfair. Unfair on people like the real Elsie Wainwright, who had, no doubt, fallen in love with a man who had used the girl and abandoned her. And the unfairness to women like his Mary. There was no justice this side of eternity. Everything he held dear was crumbling down around him.

'You meant was there anything physically different about her,' Anne said, staring at him. 'It was how I knew it was Elsie.' The girl paused. 'She had a mole on the forth toe of her left foot.' Anne let out a short laugh and shrugged her shoulders. 'She used to wear a sticking plaster around it rather than look at it. It was just a tiny mole but Elsie hated it.'

'What did the police say had happened to her?'

'Death by suicide, so they said. But I don't think so. She had gone to meet him. She told me. But she never came back. The police said she killed herself because of the baby. Not Elsie. She was popular. Men fell at her feet. With or without the baby, she'd have found another. Besides, like I said, she didn't have to have it.'

'Did you ever know the man's name?' he asked.

Anne shook her head. 'She wouldn't say. But I know he was in the Navy, based somewhere along the coast. Eastbourne most like. Classified!' The girl shrugged her shoulders. 'They all say things like that.'

Clement stood. He needed to find Arthur Morris before he left London.

'Need the lav, Vicar?' Anne asked. 'I'm afraid it's a bucket down here.'

'No. I need to leave. I must find someone.'

Anne Chambers was shaking her head. 'The warden won't let you leave here until the all-clear sounds.'

He sat back down on the hard bench and ran his tongue over his lips to moisten his dry mouth. He still couldn't believe it. But illegal abortions and unwed young women aside, what he had learned about Elsie sent his head spinning. A void was forming in his chest and he couldn't think. Why had the Elsie he knew attached herself to Stanley? His heart was sinking. For the first time, he began to suspect that Stanley had suffered the same fate as his father. He visualised Reg Naylor leaning on Peter Kempton's mantelpiece, asking if Stanley was already dead. He swallowed. Was Nurse Anne Chambers correct about Elizabeth Wainwright? Or had Elsie Wainwright wanted to disappear and stage her own death? He thought of the mole. Could that be faked? Could a nurse do that as well? Could Anne have lied to aid Elsie's disappearance? He didn't believe so. Anne had volunteered the information and believed Elsie Wainwright was dead. He visualised the girl on the counter in *The Crown*. His heart was pounding. Had the real Elsie Wainwright been murdered because she resembled the Elsie he knew? If the girl he had met was not Elsie, then who was she? And why had she come to Fearnley Maughton?

He pulled his coat around his body and sat with his head leaning back against the wall. He didn't wish to appear unsociable, but he needed to think.

'You alright, Vicar?' Anne asked.

'Yes. It doesn't matter. It must be another Elizabeth Wainwright.' He saw Anne pull a book from a pocket. He wondered what else Anne Chambers carried in the capacious folds of her nurse's cape. But right now his mind was on Elizabeth Wainwright. Elsie Wainwright had come to Fearnley Maughton after answering an advertisement in *The Times*. Why would a girl who did not like the country seek a position in a rural village in East Sussex? It confirmed Anne's innocence in any complicity with any possible staged disappearance of the real Elizabeth Wainwright. The girl Clement knew as Elsie didn't know the real Elsie's dislike for the country. That tiny fact could be her undoing. Morris had said the devil was in the detail. He thought of Arthur Morris and the man's patient, diligent investigation. Morris had checked the *Evening Argus* classifieds section for Hospital and Medical Appointments. 'The pieces are coming together,' he remembered Morris had said in Gubbins' office. Chief Inspector Morris was also suspicious of Elsie Wainwright. He smiled. He needed to speak with Morris, but until he could, he forced himself to focus on Elsie and on all the occasions he had met the girl since her arrival in the village. He had noted at the bus stop in Lewes that the girl had very little luggage. She would, if she did not intend to stay long. Mary had suspected something about the girl. He wished Mary was with him now. The next time he saw Elsie was in the street. But he had not spoken more than a few words to the girl on that occasion. After that he had seen her on the Sunday in church, surrounded by men, then later that same day at *The Crown*. He pictured her again in his mind, sitting on the bar-room counter surrounded by men who were eager for the gossip she was happily supplying. Johnny had described her as a well-educated English rose. Clement himself had compared her to Helen Moore. Elsie was no English rose. Despite Anne's description of the Elsie Wainwright Anne had known, the Elsie Wainwright he knew did not have the manners associated with either a girl described as an English rose or a past pupil of the prestigious school by the sea. He thought back to the day he and Constable Matthews had found Stanley in his cottage, holding the knife. Stanley believed the girl had left to pack her possessions then return to Stanley's cottage. But she did go to *The Crown*. He knew that. But where had she gone after that? And how had she left the village without anyone seeing her? Had it all been staged? Had Elsie killed David Russell and fled? Timing. Morris had talked about timing. Morris had also talked about there being more than one murderer. At the time David Russell lay dead, Elsie would have been at *The Crown*, packing. Or was she? Had she packed previously? Sometime after Stanley was heard arguing with his father, and before the time of death at around half past ten, Elsie had disappeared. The bottle. Why had someone smashed a bottle on the doorstep? Constable Matthews was a little deaf, yet it was loud enough for even him to hear it and investigate. Clement opened his eyes. The safe keys. Whoever killed David Russell had already done the deed. Morris believed that the murderer had entered by the window and had been expected. That had been confirmed in Clement's mind when he stood by the window in the police station attempting to attract the attention of Phillip Haswell. David Russell must have been expecting Elsie. The window was open and Russell would have seen the girl arrive. But once she was inside, and with Russell unconscious, the open window permitted another to enter. He thought of the blow to Russell's head. A woman could have done that. Especially a woman who already knew of David Russell's weakness for a pretty woman and who had prearranged a meeting. Russell would not be expecting trouble. In fact, quite the contrary. It fitted with what Clement had witnessed in *The Crown*. Elsie could have left the police station by the same window and run around the building, smashing the bottle on the steps to bring Constable Matthews to the door. This would give whoever was in David Russell's office time to fetch the keys. Constable Matthews had said that Inspector Russell always kept his office door ajar, but when Constable Matthews was standing in the corridor outside David Russell's office, someone had closed the door. Clement knew now that the murderer had closed it. But how were the safe keys replaced? The keys were there when he went into the police station. Or had they been? Constable Matthews would surely have noticed their absence. They must have been there. He shut his eyes. If Elsie had been watching the building she would have seen both him and Phillip Haswell and Constable Matthews carry the body of Inspector Russell out of the police station and around the building to Doctor Haswell's car. The police station would have been unattended for only a few minutes. Clement thought back to the times he had seen her cycle through the village. She came and went, and almost no one took any notice of the district nurse on a bicycle. He remembered Morris' comment about there always being a witness. The killer could have given the keys to Elsie, who could have dropped them into her nurse's cape, entered the station and placed them back on the hook, all before he and Constable Matthews returned to the station to telephone Lewes Police. It fitted. But how had she acquired the gun? She must have duped Stanley into showing her his pack. He remembered seeing it in Stanley's bedroom. Stanley had made no attempt to conceal it. She must have taken the gun and the knife, but only had time to place the knife in the scullery drawer before Stanley joined her. The gun she must already have taken and hidden somewhere.

He opened his eyes. His mouth was dry and he felt like he had been hit.

'Had a nap, Vicar? That's the way. Forget about it. It's better that way,' Anne was saying. 'Do you want some tea, Vicar? The ladies over there are making,' she said. 'It's really brown-coloured water. Best not to ask what. But you can tell yourself it's tea. Mind my seat and I'll get us some.'

He smiled. Anne Chambers was a well-meaning girl. A real nurse, helpful and caring.

He watched Anne walk away. There was something different about Anne. It was in the walk, the way her feet hit the floor: slap slap. She had the slouch of the weary. It told the onlooker that here was a person used to hard physical labour and who spent most of every day on her feet. Elsie had never displayed such a gait. Whilst he knew the girl to be an impostor, he did believe that Elsie was a nurse. She had delivered the Knowles baby, which proved it. But if Anne was the epitome of the overworked London nurse, then Clement did not believe Elsie had come from London at all. Elsie Wainwright became more enigmatic with every passing minute, and he realised he knew very little about the girl. But then, as he had previously expressed, how well did anyone know their neighbour? But did it follow that Elsie, who was complicit in David Russell's murder, was also involved in George's death? If the answer to that was yes, then it had to mean that whoever this girl was, she was still near Fearnley Maughton. Or still in it! He shuddered.

Anne returned and he sipped the tea. The liquid looked unappealing, but at least it was hot. He remembered the vagrant. Was the vagrant her accomplice? Had he been the man the real Elsie Wainwright had gone to meet on Westminster Bridge? And if Elsie, with or without the vagrant, had the list, what were they planning next? Had Gubbins suspected it and that was why he sent the men to Coleshill? Clement needed to see Morris.

The siren sounded.

'Well, there's a relief, Vicar. The all-clear. We won't be down here all night after all.'

'Do you live far from here, Anne?'

'I live in the Nurses' Home, attached to the hospital. I was on a split shift and hoped to have time to wash my hair and get some much-needed air. Some air! The smells of the London underground! Never mind. I wouldn't have met you, Vicar, had I not come out. Well, good luck to you,' she said.

He lifted his hat. 'Thank you, Anne. You have been such a help. Would you mind if I was to contact you again? About Elsie?'

Anne turned to face him. 'If you can make any sense of it, Vicar, it would put my mind to rest,' Anne lowered her voice, 'because I think she was murdered.'

Clement came up into the light. Trafalgar Square looked much the same. He thanked the Lord for his safe delivery and for Nurse Anne Chambers. Meeting Anne had been a true turning point. Some would say it was luck or coincidence. He felt a smile creep across his lips. He called it divine intervention. But now he needed to find Morris. He wasn't really sure where Scotland Yard was, but he quickened his pace as he walked in the direction he had seen Arthur Morris take. Asking directions, he found the layered white and red brick building and entered the main door. Fifteen minutes later he was sitting in an office with the Chief Inspector.

He told Morris what he had learned from Anne Chambers. 'Can you find out what happened to the real Elsie Wainwright?'

Morris nodded. 'The archived files are downstairs. The raid has delayed the forensic report on the bullets, so we can do it now.'

They left the office. More corridors, more glass partitions, more polished wood and more smiling secretaries later, they stood at a counter and requested the file on Elizabeth Patricia Wainwright.

Records. Regardless of the century or the circumstance, the English are the world's best at record-keeping, Clement thought.

'I never thought I would say this but I have to thank the Germans for their early bombing raid today. I would never have questioned the identity of Elsie Wainwright,' he said.

'It has advanced the investigation. And we may just catch them, Clement.'

He wasn't really sure what Morris had meant by the remark. He would have asked, had the woman not returned to the counter with a file in her hands. They sat at a wooden desk, one of many in the archive room.

'Does it say anything about distinguishing marks?' he whispered.

Morris' eye scanned the document. He saw Morris raise his eyebrows and knew what that meant. But whether the real Elsie Wainwright was pregnant or not was not relevant to their current enquiries.

'There are no birthmarks listed,' Morris said.

'Not a birthmark as such,' said Clement, and he told Morris about the mole on the fourth toe.

His eye ran over the documents as Morris turned the pages. Listed with the deceased's clothing and personal effects was a handwritten comment that upon removal of the deceased's water-sodden shoes and stockings, a plaster covering had been found on the fourth toe of the left foot, but it had revealed a mole not a wound.

He learned back in the chair. 'Was Elsie Wainwright murdered?'

'Cannot answer that, Clement.'

'But you will investigate?'

'Perhaps. But my priority is to find the girl purporting to be Elsie Wainwright, and also Stanley Russell. It must be considered that Stanley might be another victim. Shall we call the impostor Jane, for now?'

He was thinking more Jezebel. 'Why Jane?'

'Plain Jane,' Morris answered. 'The complete antithesis of an English rose.'

He smiled and began to share his thoughts on how Jane had entered the police station, and his theory about the smashed bottle.

'Did you think to ask Anne Chambers where we can find her in future?' Morris asked.

'She lives in the Nurses' Home at Charing Cross Hospital.'

'Good.'

'You seem convinced that Elsie – sorry, Jane – is not acting alone,' he said, but his statement had more to do with confirming the suspicion rather than challenging it.

'I am pleased you have come to the same conclusion, Clement.'

He nodded.

They left the archives office and returned upstairs to the visiting police officer's room. On the desk was a beige envelope marked for the attention of Chief Inspector Morris.

'The report?' Clement asked.

Arthur Morris tore open the envelope, his alert eyes scanning the document. Morris lifted his head and stared at him. 'Nine-millimetre. All three from the same weapon.'

'A Sten?' he asked.

Morris shook his head. The intense brown eyes settled on him. 'Luger.'

Chapter Twenty-Four

By the time the train pulled into Lewes Station, Clement had learned that the Chief Inspector was a widower of his own age, and that Morris and his late wife had not had children. That fact alone created a common bond between them. Morris had told him about his boyhood home in Hampshire, and Clement had shared memories of Rye. But even after so many years, he was ambivalent about his boyhood home. The smell of the sea and long walks on the sands reminded him of his mother. But the town itself did not hold such cherished memories. He thought of his late father, and felt the instant dark and sodden pall he always associated with the man. Reaching up for his gas mask and satchel in the rack above his head, he waited for the train to stop.

Stepping onto the platform, he glanced at the station clock. It was just on seven o'clock. 'Are you returning to Fearnley Maughton, Arthur?'

'If you can wait fifteen minutes while I write up some paperwork, Clement, I would be happy to drive you home.'

'Thank you so much. I can spend the time at the hospital,' he said.

They walked away from the station and separated, Morris going on into the town while Clement turned left up the steep hill towards the hospital. Jane. Elsie. He pondered the chance meeting with Nurse Anne Chambers. What had been revealed was nothing short of cataclysmic. Had the real Elsie Wainwright's death been a convenient cover for the girl they were calling Jane? Or was she murdered so that Jane could replace her? The girl's death, so Anne Chambers had told him, was three years ago. He stared down at his feet as he walked. Was he making more out of it all than had actually happened? Just thinking about Jane and what he knew she had done made him sceptical about everything. But what he now pondered made him angry. If Jane was a German collaborator, then arranging the death of her look-a-like implied a complex and sinister plan that had been implemented at least three years previously. But what could be so important as to lead someone to commit murder, install an impostor and wait three years? Three years ago the war had not begun. Churchill had seen it coming. Could the Germans have planned it so far in advance? He thought of the man in Elsie Wainwright's life with the classified job, and the Naval installation he now knew about at Cuckmere Haven. Clement had not known of its existence and had no idea what went on there. But if it was top secret, could it have been there three years ago? If so, it would be important enough for the Germans to want to know about it. Had Jane taken the money from the safe, he may have thought her just a thief. He walked through the old stone gates of the hospital towards the front entrance. Reaching forward to grasp the handle of the door, he stopped and turned. Off to his right he saw Phillip Haswell's car parked in the front. He shook his head. He hadn't seen much of Phillip but he guessed that since the attack on the village the man had been kept busy. He checked his watch. Morris had told him to be at the police station before half past seven, which gave him only a few minutes to see Mrs Faulkner. He decided that if he saw Phillip he would ask about the old lady's prognosis. He opened the heavy, glass-fronted hospital door, the smell of ether and floor wax greeting him, and walked down the corridor staring at the shiny blue and white striated linoleum.

He stayed with Mrs Faulkner just five minutes. She had expressed her gratitude that he had visited her twice in one day. But something the old lady had said worried him. He made his excuses and left the bedside. Quickening his step, he hurried towards the Matron's office. Fortunately the woman was still at her desk.

'Can you tell me where Doctor Haswell is, Matron?' he asked.

'I haven't seen him all day, Reverend Wisdom.'

He felt his face fall.

'Is something wrong, Reverend?'

'I saw his car parked out the front this morning and it is there now. He must be here. Could you find out if he is in the hospital, Matron?'

He could hear the panic in his own voice. He cleared his throat, trying to suppress his rising fears. Not another death. Not Phillip. He liked Phillip Haswell. His mind flashed to the day the fighter strafed the village. Phillip had been a tower of strength. By the grace of God, Phillip had been in his garden when the second bomb landed on his Anderson Shelter. The Matron picked up the telephone and Clement waited while the woman rang every ward.

Nothing.

In fact, no one had seen Doctor Haswell that day. He left the Matron's office and hurried down the corridor towards the front door. He could hear Matron's feet running behind him.

He walked towards the car. He wasn't sure what he expected to see. Something. Or someone.

Nothing.

He was not a man given to panic, but he could feel his throat tightening. He thought of Arthur Morris. 'We must telephone Chief Inspector Morris.'

'Do you think something has happened to Doctor Haswell?'

'Matron, could you find out if anyone saw the doctor arrive? And don't touch the car!'

He ran back into the hospital and headed straight for the switchboard operator. He felt his heart pounding in his ears. As he waited for Arthur Morris to answer the telephone, his mind raced. Something insidious was happening around him, its tentacles enveloping him and those he knew and cared for. George's dead body flashed into his mind. Everything was connected. He just didn't know how. Morris' steady logical mind would bring reason. He pushed open the door to exit the hospital and waited in the parking area. Within minutes Arthur Morris and a Constable stepped from the police car and stood beside him.

'What is it, Clement?' Morris asked.

He nodded in the direction of Phillip's car. 'Doctor Haswell's car. It was parked here this morning, I saw it. And it is still there. But no one in the hospital has seen him today.'

The hospital door opened and the Matron joined them. 'I asked the Evening Supervisor to check with all the Ward Sisters, Chief Inspector. Doctor Haswell has not been into the hospital since lunchtime yesterday.'

Morris turned and walked towards the car. 'Did you touch the car, Clement?'

He shook his head. 'I looked in but when I saw nothing I telephoned you.'

'Matron, could you ask your staff if anyone saw the doctor leave the hospital on Friday?' Morris asked.

The Matron nodded and left.

Morris placed his hand on the driver's door handle. The door opened and he looked in.

'Anything?' Clement asked as Morris checked the car's interior.

Morris closed the door and shook his head. Walking around the car, Morris reached for the latch to open the car's boot.

The lid lifted.

Morris reeled back.

He stepped forward and stared in. A dark-haired man in a navy overcoat with epaulettes lay curled up in the boot, his hands bound behind his back, a bullet hole between his eyes.

Clement stood beside the Chief Inspector. Neither of them spoke. He knew his mouth was open but he couldn't speak. Neither could he take his eyes from the man's face: the grey-white pallor of death, the out-of-place, repellent purple hole between the eyes, the dishevelled hair. He screwed his eyes shut. In his mind's eye he could see George lying on the forest floor staring heavenward in death, with the exact same gunshot wound: life terminated in an instant. *In the midst of life we are in death*, so the Order for the Burial of the Dead said. He had never before realised just how profound those words were. He blinked and forced himself to look again at the man in the boot of Phillip Haswell's car. He stared at the coat, the rankless epaulettes... the vagrant. But the deceased was not old. Neither was the man a boy. This man was of enlisting age. Clement ran his eye along the contours of the body. From what he could see, the man appeared to be in good physical condition, with little evidence of malnourishment. Neither did the man appear unkempt. Only the navy coat with epaulettes alluded to this man being the vagrant seen by his men in Maughton Forest. His eye looked along the trousers to the shoes. The soles showed no sign of excess wear, and despite the existence of a shadow of a beard about the man's face, Clement was not convinced the man was a vagrant at all. If the man had deserted, it was recent. Leaning forward he looked over the corpse to see the man's hands. Bruising around the wrists indicated that the man had been bound before death. But the nails were short and from what he could see, clean. He looked again at the face. Did the beard suggest the man had fled into the forest? And if so, why?

Morris closed the boot. 'Clement, would you ask the Matron to contact the Coroner? And Constable, please arrange for the car to be moved into the police yard.'

The Constable nodded and left.

In silence Clement watched Arthur Morris' steady gaze. He heard the front door to the hospital open, and the Matron reappeared on the steps.

Clement went to speak with the woman about the Coroner. The Matron left and he rejoined Morris by the car.

Morris looked up as he returned.

'The Matron says that no one saw Doctor Haswell leave the hospital.'

Morris nodded, then turned to face him. 'Do you know the deceased man, Clement?'

'Not one of mine. But he could be the vagrant my men saw. Although other than the beard, this man does not look like a vagrant to me. But the sighting of a homeless man wearing a navy coat with epaulettes was in our report to Gubbins.' He stopped speaking. A hollow knot was twisting in his stomach. 'That report may not have reached Gubbins.' He could feel his chest heave. 'Two deaths because of a report? Is it possible?'

Morris nodded. 'And both killed at the same location and possibly the same time,' Morris said.

'How do you know that?' Clement asked.

Morris sprung the latch on the boot again and reaching in, placed his hand on the dead man's coat. Lifting the fabric, Morris pointed to several leaves in varying stages of decomposition stuck to the man's coat and socks.

He looked up at Morris. 'The second bullet?'

Morris nodded. 'I think it likely.'

'Why didn't the murderer remove the bullets this time?' he asked.

'Good question, Clement. And as I said at the time, I believe our murderer wants us to know something. It is almost like he is leaving clues for us. But he is undoubtedly aware of your subterranean base.' Morris narrowed his eyes. 'But does he want to be identified?'

'He wants to be caught?' Clement asked.

'I didn't say that.' Morris replaced the man's coat and closed the boot again. 'But I do not believe there will be any more murders. Whatever the murderer or murderers came for, they now have.'

'How do you know that?' he repeated.

'Because Jane has disappeared,' Morris said, sucking on his lower lip. 'She was brought into the village for a reason and whatever that reason was, it has either already transpired or is no longer relevant. But first we must identify this man. Then we can work on the motive.'

Clement swallowed hard. Could Phillip Haswell be implicated? Was that what Morris was implying? Phillip had advertised for a nurse. But why had Phillip only advertised in *The Times*? Surely, Morris was right in thinking that a local nurse would have been more appropriate. And Phillip would have known that. Had Phillip Haswell been kidnapped? Or worse?

'So where is she?' he asked.

'I don't know, yet,' Morris said, and stepped away from the rear of the car. Clement watched as Morris stood about ten feet away from the car, the vigilant eye tracing every contour of the vehicle.

Clement said goodnight to Morris and walked up Church Lane. He felt bone-weary. One death was shocking. Two was unfathomable. Three was alarming. But four was one too many. Four murders surely provided too many clues for the killer to remain at large. And if Morris was right, the murderer wanted to be identified, although not caught. But how could the murderer remain uncaptured once identified? Only leaving England would safeguard such a man. Spy or collaborator? Either way, Clement wanted to see the guilty parties brought to justice. But what of Phillip? He could not bring himself to think of a fifth death. Or was it six? Stanley. He thought of Stanley and George. Good and decent young men who had not deserved such a fate. Willing to die for their country. What was happening? George's cold body flashed before his eyes. The stare. The finality of murder. He would never forget it. Cold-blooded murder had nothing to do with defence. And now Phillip was missing. Clement's men had been sent away for their safety. What did Gubbins really suspect? He was now convinced that Stanley would not be found. He let himself into his home. The hallway was dark now. For a horrible moment his heart jumped. 'Mary?' he shouted. He made his way to the kitchen and switched on the light. A note sat propped against the mustard pot on the kitchen table. Mary had gone to Windsor during the day and was not returning until Sunday by the late train. The hours spent underground with Anne Chambers and the ghastly discovery in Phillip's car had combined to delay him. He folded the note and let it fall onto the tablecloth. He felt wretched. He had wanted to see her. It was selfish, he knew, but he wanted to hear those ditties emanating from the kitchen. He needed to see those beans.

He made tea.

Sitting in his study, he sipped the warming drink and thought of the hot brown drink Anne had purchased for him in London's underground. Leaning his head against the antimacassar, he closed his eyes. Jane and someone else had killed David Russell. And Constable Newson. And by assisting Stanley to escape, the lad was, at the very least, an accessory to the murder of his father and the Constable from Lewes. But if Jane and her accomplice had implicated Stanley for the murders, why would they want Stanley with them? Was Stanley a hostage? As far as Clement knew, when people were taken as hostages, a demand of some kind followed. And, again as far as he knew, no such demand had been received. Besides, with Stanley's father dead who would pay the ransom? He took another sip of his tea. Perhaps Stanley had gone willingly? He knew Stanley loved the girl. He reflected on the day he had spoken with Stanley in the cell at the police station. Stanley had been prepared to hang for the girl. Would he commit murder? Did that also include George's murder? Clement shook his head. The big lad had been used, as surely as the real Elsie Wainwright. But where was Stanley? He took another sip of tea and closed his eyes, melancholia settling into his heart. He now accepted the heavy realisation that Stanley had been killed and may never be found. He could hear the clock in the hall, ticking the seconds as they passed. Death had no use for time. He opened his eyes. 'May never be found,' he said aloud. He almost dropped the cup. Clive's words that night at the Operational Base reverberated in his mind. What had Clive said? 'If it had happened during the raid, no one would be any the wiser'. Clive had been referring to the murder of David Russell, but had it been the fate of the son? Clement leaned back in the chair. 'Dear God!'

Chapter Twenty-Five

Sunday 22nd September 1940

The telephone was ringing. Clement threw back the bedcovers and pushed his feet into the slippers by the bed. Reaching for his dressing-gown he pulled the garment on as he descended the stairs. The house was still in darkness and he had no idea of the hour.

'Hello?'

'Clement. I'm sorry to disturb you so early. Can you be dressed and outside in fifteen minutes?'

'Arthur?' he mumbled.

'There is something I would like your assistance with,' Morris told him.

'Actually, Arthur, I wanted to see you today. I've been thinking about Stanley. I am concerned that he might have met the same fate as the others.'

'I'll be around in fifteen minutes, Clement,' Morris said, and rang off.

Clement replaced the receiver and wandered into the kitchen to check the time. Four o'clock. The overpowering weight of anxiety about Stanley, and possibly also Phillip, made him feel old. Almost by instinct he filled the kettle, placed it on the stove and lit the gas. Whatever Morris had to say to him at such an hour could not be good. It had to be about Phillip. He reached for a dish, and filling it with cold water, splashed his face. The icy water seemed to penetrate his flesh. With his realisation about Stanley, he prayed that Morris had not found Phillip dead in some squalid place.

Twelve minutes later he was outside. There was no sound. A light breeze brushed his unshaven face and he shivered. It was still dark but he could hear the familiar sound of the swaying trees which surrounded *All Saints*. Autumn leaves; most of them would be gone by the end of November. He pulled his coat around him. Winter approached. Bad times were always endured better in the summer months. He heard the light footsteps, and turning, saw the familiar silhouette of Arthur Morris walking up Church Lane towards him.

'What has happened?' he asked in a low voice.

'I received a telephone call late last night from your Commander Winthorpe, Clement. Jane has been sighted.'

'Stanley?' he asked, hoping to hear his suspicions were wrong.

Morris shook his head.

'Where is she?' he asked. But he was wondering why Johnny had telephoned Morris with the news.

'She was spotted on a train. And is being followed. But that is only partly why I called you. I need your assistance, Clement. Rather, I need you as a witness.'

He stared at Morris, uncertain what was coming next. 'How can I help, Arthur?'

'I want to break into someone's house.'

'Sorry?'

'I realise it is unusual, but I don't want prying eyes and I don't have time to arrange the official documentation.'

'Whose house?'

'Phillip Haswell's.'

It was the name Clement dreaded hearing. 'You think he is dead, too?'

Morris looked away down Church Lane. 'Something you wanted to ask me about Stanley, Clement?'

'It was something one of my men said, Arthur.' He told Morris what Clive had said.

Morris stood staring into the night sky. 'You could well be right.'

He wasn't sure what Morris had meant by the remark. Was the Chief Inspector dismissing his theory? Perhaps it was too fanciful. If Stanley had died as a result of a bomb, then surely it had been accidental. But if not, then it had been arranged, and that put everything in a different light.

'What do you expect to find in Phillip's house, Arthur?' he whispered, closing the gate to the vicarage.

'I would just like to see inside the house. And as I said, there is no time for official documentation to be sought.'

He felt his stomach cramp. 'You think his body is inside?'

'With me?'

They walked down Church Lane. It was only a short distance. No one was as yet in the street and the blackout curtains in the neighbouring houses were still drawn. Clement looked down the High Street to the village green. Even though the moon was waning, there was sufficient moonlight by which to see. Behind him he heard a door open. He spun around and saw the large, young Constable from Lewes standing in the police station doorway.

Morris motioned to the Constable, and without speaking he walked towards the door to Phillip's house and slammed his shoulder several times into the doctor's front door. A minute later the old panelled door gave way under the Constable's force, the timber door jambs splintering around the lock.

He felt sure someone would be alerted, or at the very least a dog would bark, but nothing stirred. The Constable straightened his jacket and returned to the police station, closing the door behind him, while Clement and Arthur Morris went into the house.

The corridor of Phillip's house was dark and cold. A draught flowed through the house, the open door to the street turning the corridor into a wind tunnel. Clement shivered. A window somewhere was rattling. He remembered the damaged rear wall. Morris flicked on a torch and Clement followed the Chief Inspector into the surgery at the front and off the corridor to the right. The room looked as though it had been cleaned since he had seen it last. A makeshift kitchen had been set up in the corner. Morris moved the torch beam slowly over the floor. Nothing. As they walked towards the door to the corridor, he glanced at the cupboards behind the doctor's desk. It was where Phillip kept his medical bag. Morris was watching him. The bag sat in readiness on the bench, awaiting Phillip's hand. Clement stared at the bag. Its presence reinforced his worst fears. They walked across the hallway. The room opposite had once been a sitting room but it was now used as the waiting room. Chairs lined the walls. Near the fireplace was a desk. The chair was placed under the desk as though the occupant had gone for the day. He saw Morris staring at him, the familiar enquiring tilt of the head. But from what Clement could see, everything looked the same. Morris opened the next door: a store room with patient records. Again, nothing appeared disturbed or unusual, and there was no sign of any dust or debris from the damaged rear wall. Opposite the storeroom was the staircase. Panning the torch from side to side they went upstairs. Off the landing were three bedrooms. Clement had never been upstairs, but he could see there were two rooms at the front on either side of the landing, and another two smaller rooms at the side and rear of the building. All the doors were open. Morris stood in the doorway to the bedroom that overlooked the front of the house. Clement joined him and stared into the room. The beam of light from the torch was directed onto the bed. Empty. He sighed. But not seeing his friend sleeping only increased his anxiety. Morris walked across the room and opened the wardrobe. Phillip's clothes hung on hangers. He felt his heart miss a beat. He knew Phillip was unlikely to travel without his doctor's bag, but no one would travel, even for a short time, without clothing. Clement glanced at Morris. He could feel the anxiety welling up. He strode towards a chest of drawers and opened each. In every drawer were underclothes and vests and other assorted gentleman's undergarments. He turned and saw the shoes lined up under a washstand.

His heart sank.

A pain was developing in his chest. He forced himself to breathe. Leaving Morris in Phillip's bedroom, Clement went into the bedroom on the opposite side that also overlooked the front. Like Peter Kempton's house, the room was filled with old patient records. He stepped back into the hallway and went to the smaller bedroom adjacent to the stairwell. He stared at the bed in the next room. Empty. His eye scanned the room, the walls, the cupboards. He opened the wardrobe. Nothing. He went to the bedroom at the rear. It contained a couch, a few old wooden chairs and a radiator. But he could smell the dust. Fine brick dust has a smell all of its own. He went back to the small bedroom and stared at the room for what seemed like an eternity. What was it about this room? It appeared to be unoccupied. A guest room. But there was something about it that appeared familiar. He walked back to Phillip's bedroom and stood in the doorway staring in.

'Clement?'

'The bed in the next room. Something about the bed. I just wanted to compare it to Phillip's.'

Morris flicked the torch onto Phillip's bed.

Two pillows with white and pink ribboned pillow cases sat side by side on the double bed. For one moment he felt ashamed for trespassing on Phillip's tangible memories of his departed wife. He did not know what he would say to justify such an intrusion if Phillip returned at the very moment. But the bed, although made, was not well made. And he knew from Mary, that if one went away even for a short period of time, beds had to be stripped, blankets and quilts folded and mattresses rolled. Phillip's bed looked exactly as though he expected to return. The blanket was roughly tucked in on all sides and a pink quilt lay folded over the end of the bed.

'What is concerning you, Clement?' Morris asked.

'Come and have a look at this,' he said, and they went into the small bedroom.

Against one wall was a single bed. It was an iron-framed hospital bed, utilitarian and austere.

'Look at the corners,' he pointed, the bed in room number six at *The Crown* flashing into his mind. 'Neat, without a wrinkle anywhere there shouldn't be one.'

Morris turned to face him. 'Hospital corners. Well spotted, Clement. I will make a detective out of you yet.'

'Is that your intention, Arthur?'

Morris' head tilted. 'Nothing in this wardrobe, I suppose.'

'No. I checked,' he said. He looked at Morris' face and knew what the Chief Inspector was thinking. 'But why would she be here?'

'Do you know if Doctor Haswell had anyone to do for him?'

Clement stared at the empty space in the upper hall. 'I don't know,' he muttered. It was possible. But Phillip had never told him of any domestic help. In fact, he recalled that Phillip often complained about housework. That always amused Mary. He stared at the blanket that had been nailed up to cover the damaged rear wall which was awaiting repair. The rear bedroom, which appeared to be more of a store room than a guest room, still had the dust of damaged brickwork on the windowsills and furniture. Only the rooms with public access and the two bedrooms upstairs had been cleaned. 'Why didn't Phillip know?' he muttered.

'Clement?'

'The day the fighter strafed the village, Phillip told me he didn't know Elsie had left. Why wouldn't she be at work on a Tuesday?'

'Good question.'

They went downstairs and walked through the old kitchen. His panic had already given way to something else. Doubt. And suspicion. Even betrayal. Of friendship certainly. And trust. But could this be more? He felt ill. The cold of the morning seeped into his bones. The rear wall of the kitchen and scullery had been boarded up, but again no repairs had been carried out. Why was that? The words resounded in his mind. No need! No need! The insistent realisation clamoured to be heard. And accepted.

'Clement. The day of the strafing raid, you said you came to find Doctor Haswell. Where, exactly, was he?' Morris asked.

'I found him in the garden. His front door was open as usual.' He paused, reliving the day he had run into the doctor's house. He stared at Morris. 'Why was the destruction here so much less than the bomb that demolished Peter's office?'

'Another good question,' Morris said, and stepped outside.

The first tinges of dawn were lighting the heavens. Morris flicked off the torch, and they stood gazing down into the crater that had been Phillip Haswell's Anderson Shelter.

Clement drew his collar up around his neck to ward off the cold air.

'Did you hear this bomb land, Clement?'

'Yes, it was a moment after the other one.'

Both men stood staring at the hole in the ground as daylight increased around them.

'Would you, with your knowledge of explosives, say that it was possible for a fighter to drop two bombs of different tonnage in rapid succession?'

'I am not an aeronautical expert, Arthur, but I do know that a fighter plane can carry bombs. Not really heavy ones and not many, I would have thought. But I do know that light aeroplanes, like fighters, need to be balanced to take off. If it was carrying two bombs I suppose they would be the same weight.'

'I have visited the site of Mr Kempton's office. It was a two-storey building, I understand?'

He nodded.

'Have you been there since the bomb exploded?' Morris asked.

'Yes. I offered to help Peter carry anything that had survived the blast. But there was nothing. The whole building vanished, and everything in it.'

'How deep was the crater?'

'Deep. About twice as deep as this,' he said. 'But the hole is wide. And, of course, filled with rubble.'

He stared at the crater that had once been the Anderson shelter. The hole contained the metal sheeting; a quantity of earth and grass, which had once formed the bomb shelter's roof, now covered the crater's floor. Clement turned and saw the fragmented brick and timber walls of the lavatory lying on the ground where they had fallen.

'It is fortunate that Phillip was not in the shelter at the time,' he said. 'Nor still in the lavatory.'

'Where was he, exactly?' Morris asked.

Clement's eye went to where he had found Phillip standing in the garden. He looked up. In the muted morning light he saw the beans. Beans. And carrots. Phillip had told him he was pulling carrots when the bomb hit. He told Morris.

Leaving Morris staring at the crater, he wandered along the path and walked the rows of beans and potatoes.

He stood in the middle of the patch and stared around himself at all the vegetables growing in the garden, the first streaks of sunlight hitting the tree tops.

'Have you found something?' Morris called.

'It's what I haven't found, Arthur,' he called. 'There are no carrots.'

Chapter Twenty-Six

Sunday 22nd September 1940

Dawn was breaking, and the rising sun had turned black night to pale day. Clement closed his eyes and leaned back in his chair. Even the familiar click of his door could not elicit its usual soothing response. It had been just after first light when Morris jumped into the crater that had once been the Anderson Shelter in Phillip Haswell's garden. He still could not believe it. He visualised the twisted and burnt wires and valves of what had once been a transmitter radio, buried deep in the soil and rubble of the Anderson Shelter.

Clement wrapped his hands around his teacup. He felt numb. He felt betrayed. And foolish. He remembered the verse from Ecclesiastes. But Phillip was not an angry man. At least, the Phillip Haswell he had known. Perhaps, as the Good Book taught, it was only the foolish who expressed anger. The truly wicked never displayed rage. Theirs was the smiling-faced, festering hatred of the psychopathic mind, that contrived and manipulated while maintaining a detached, even charming, cool head. Clement had prided himself on his ability to judge character. But Phillip had made a fool of him. How could he have so misjudged the man? Phillip had been his church warden as well as his doctor, and he had lived among them for three years.

Elsie Wainwright. The real one had met a man in Eastbourne. And had conceived his child. Had that man been Phillip? Had Phillip lured the real Elsie to Westminster Bridge, then pushed the girl to her death? Clement thought of the pink and white pillow cases. The depth of the man's deception astounded him. He now knew how Elsie had left Fearnley Maughton without being seen. If Phillip's car held the body of a man, it would hold a woman. A woman who had returned to London to hide. But where was the girl now? Morris had said she had been spotted on a train. But he had not said in which direction that train had been travelling. Jane, as she was now being called, was being followed. And if Jane was to rendezvous with Phillip, they would catch him. Anne Chambers. He began to smile. Morris had said that finding Anne Chambers was the turning point. He pondered whether Jane had taken the opportunity to flee during the strafing raid, having made arrangements for Phillip to follow at a time and opportunity that would not raise suspicion. He felt his whole body sink. It was more likely that between them they had ordered the raid to disguise the detonation of the shelter. Could it also be possible that they had targeted Peter's House in the High Street because it was so distinctive and easy for a pilot to spot? At the police station Jane had killed Constable Newson and freed Stanley, before taking him to Peter's office via the rear lane knowing a bomb would fall on the house where Stanley and anyone else in the building, including his friend, would be killed, their remains beyond recognition. And the bombing of Peter's office building would be the signal to blow up the Anderson Shelter. Such cruelty and wickedness confounded reason.

The doorbell sounded.

Clement opened his eyes. He felt utterly drained. His eye fell on the clock on the wall. And the papers on his desk. Nine o'clock. Battersby would be arriving soon to take Matins. He walked to the door.

'Arthur?'

'Could I have a word, Clement? Given what we have learned about Doctor Haswell, I wondered if you have also realised that the raid might not have been random?'

He nodded.

'I have arranged a team of men to do some digging on the site of Mr Kempton's former office. Do you know where Mr Kempton is currently?'

'Yes. But he won't be back here until late tomorrow evening,' said Clement. With all that had happened he had not thought about his men. They were safe, and for now that was enough.

'I came to ask if you thought Mr Kempton would have any concerns about us digging on the site?'

He shook his head. 'If Stanley was killed there, Peter would be the first person to assist with the digging.'

Morris tilted his head. 'After you have attended to your correspondence, you may like to come by? If I find anything of an unfortunate nature, I will come and find you.'

'Thank you, Arthur,' he said.

He heard the footsteps before the doorbell rang. He rose from his desk and went to the door. Arthur Morris stood on the doorstep. The man's face was downcast, and Clement feared the worst.

'Come in, Arthur,' he said.

Morris stepped inside and he closed the door.

'It would appear that only Mr Kempton's secretary was in the office on the day of the raid. However, she has told me, now that she has had time to reflect on that day's events, that she remembers hearing noises upstairs. But before she could investigate the source, she heard the aeroplane and left the building to run to the assembly point at *The Crown*. Clement, fragments of bones have been unearthed,' Morris paused. 'And a blood-stained shoe.'

Following Morris into the village, he stood on the edge of the crater. A crowd had formed around the site. Lumps of stone and splintered timber which had once been his friend's historic office building lay in crude stacks along the ground. In a box beside the hole were torn leather strips of book bindings and other pieces of office equipment. It resembled an archaeological dig. But the hole was deeper now than it had been. Morris' team of men had sifted through the debris. Morris went to one side and lifted an object from one of the boxes: a shoe without laces. Clement felt the lump in his throat as he stared at the dark-stained, blood-encrusted shoe. He felt the tragedy. For that was what it was. When so many young men were dying, Stanley's death was so needless. And so wicked. A trusting lad had fallen in love with a girl; the most natural thing in the world. He glanced at Morris and nodded.

He turned and stared at the rubble that was Stanley's resting place. At least the boy would not have suffered.

'What was upstairs in Mr Kempton's office?' Morris asked.

'Storage rooms. Filled with old files. They would once have been bedrooms. But that would have been long ago. Peter has been the solicitor in Fearnley Maughton for at least twenty years, and I think he purchased the building at the same time as he purchased the practice which has operated out of the same location for generations. There must have been thousands of files up there. No wonder there was so much destruction. It was a fire waiting to happen.'

'But there was enough room for someone to hide?'

He shrugged. 'Peter doesn't live on the site. But, yes, there would have been enough room. And of course, there was an external staircase to the upper floor. It had once been the servants' entrance. No doubt Phillip and the girl wanted Peter dead too. Like George. And Stanley. And the rest of my men. I cannot tell you how grateful I am that Peter wasn't here at the time. We have lost too many from the village. Is that what it is all about, Arthur? Eliminating the men of my team? I did not realise the Germans saw us as such a threat. I am so pleased my men are safely away from here at present.'

'Where are they, Clement?'

'I cannot tell you specifically, Arthur, but they are at a training camp in another county.'

Morris nodded.

'How did Jane get out of the building?'

'She would most likely have known when the strafing raid was to happen, and would have made some excuse to leave Stanley here alone.'

Clement hated Jane. He hated Jane more than Phillip who, it now appeared, had orchestrated the whole thing. Jane had crushed Stanley's heart, not just his body.

'When did she leave the village?' he asked.

'Unknown, I'm sorry, Clement. But probably the next day, when Haswell left Fearnley Maughton on one of his routine trips to Lewes to see the strafing victims. Given the bed in the second bedroom, it would appear that Jane hid at Doctor Haswell's until the next day when she could leave the village in the doctor's car.' Morris paused. 'There is something else, Clement. But perhaps we should return to the vicarage.'

Clement picked his way over the rubble and they walked away from the destruction, back to his home. His sanctuary. As he closed the door to his study he heard the click. Its pacifying effect was returning.

He gestured towards the armchair in his study and Morris sat down.

Clement saw the lips being sucked in, first the top, then the other. The room was quiet and cold.

'Where is Mary?' Morris asked.

A cold dread coursed through Clement's body from scalp to toes. He heard himself answer. 'In Windsor, with her sister, Gwen.' But his heart was thumping. And panic was rising. His head spun. 'Why do you ask?'

'I thought that in view of what we discovered earlier you may appreciate your wife being with you. I telephoned the police in Windsor and asked them to send a police vehicle around to her sister's place and drive your wife home.' Morris paused, his face contorted with painful duty. 'She is not there, Clement.' Morris paused. 'The neighbours say she hasn't been there for some time.'

Chapter Twenty-Seven

Morris' voice came to him. 'Drink the water, Clement.'

He stared at the glass in Morris' hand. His mouth was dry and he felt like he had been flattened in the rubble of Peter's house.

'I think it is time we spoke again to Commander Winthorpe,' Morris said. 'I'll call from here, if that is alright with you?'

'Johnny? Why would you call him?''

'Rest here, Clement? I am sorry to have shocked you. But there was no other way. And it could all be completely innocent.'

He looked up at the Chief Inspector. Completely innocent? What did Morris suspect? His mind reeled. Mary had gone to Windsor, to Gwen's. There had to be some mistake. He leaned forward in the seat and grasped the armrests of the chair, his hands shaking. He wanted to telephone Gwen. He remembered the crossed line. But it had been Gwen's number that he had dialled. He was sure of that. Besides, Mary had answered the second time. How was that possible if she had not been at Gwen's house?

'I apologise for worrying you, Clement. I'm sure there is a logical explanation. But in view of all that has happened lately, I think we should involve Commander Winthorpe.'

'You think they have kidnapped Mary?' he said, his voice weak and fearful.

'It should not be ruled out.'

'Dear God!' he whispered. He stood and walked into the hall and dialled Gwen's number. He heard Gwen's voice. 'Hello, Gwen. It's Clement. Is Mary with you?' he asked, trying to sound calm.

'No. I haven't seen her in weeks, Clement. Is everything alright?'

'Yes, Gwen. She went up to London shopping and said that if she had time she would call in on you. Nothing to worry about. But if she does turn up, could you ask her to call me?'

He hung up. It was all he could think of to say on the spur of the moment. His head was spinning. It did not make any sense. Why would she lie?

Morris was beside him.

'I don't know what to think, Arthur,' he said. He felt as though he had been kicked. He faced Morris and saw the kind but detached eyes. But there had to be some explanation. He knew Mary. You cannot be married to someone for twenty years and not know them.

Morris was speaking again. 'There is more to what has been happening than we have been told. At least, that is what I believe. We should speak with Commander Winthorpe. Are you alright, Clement?''

He nodded. But his pulse was still racing. He took a long deep breath, and walking back to his study, sat down. He looked around the familiar room. His room: his desk, his chair, his door, his lock. Arthur Morris sat beside him again.

'I have to ask myself a question,' Morris began. 'Two questions, actually. Why did Commander Winthorpe telephone me, not you, to say that he was having Jane followed?

Clement had wondered the same thing.

'And how did he know it was Jane?'

Clement reached for the glass on the table beside him and pondered what Morris had just said. He thought back to when Johnny had come to Fearnley Maughton. That was before he and Mary had met the girl they had known as

Elsie Wainwright at the bus shelter in Lewes. It was true. Johnny had never met Jane. Clement felt his brow furrow. 'Only someone from the village would recognise Jane as Elsie. Unless,' he paused. 'Johnny knew her beforehand.'

His heart was thumping again.

Morris was nodding. 'My thoughts also, Clement.'

He felt weary. It seemed to come from his inner core and radiate outwards. Had Johnny betrayed him? Had Johnny killed the very people he had helped to unite? And where was Mary? He placed the glass on the table beside him. His limbs felt heavy and he could feel the blood draining from his face. He stared through the drawn curtains to the day beyond. It was like walking into a spider's web. Felt but unseen. Whichever way he looked, he couldn't see the way clear.

'First things first, Clement. We telephone Commander Winthorpe and go from there,' Morris was saying.

He was glad Morris was there with his detached, logical judgement. He reminded himself that he was a vicar, not a policeman.

He stood and walked into the hallway. Reaching for the telephone, he dialled the number. 'Commander Winthorpe, please.'

The telephone line clicked and crackled. He spoke to three male voices before he heard Johnny's voice on the line.

He placed his hand over the mouthpiece and nodded to Morris as Johnny said hello.

'Something else happened, Clement?' Johnny asked.

'Tell me something, Johnny. Who is following Jane?'

There was a short pause.

'We have several people on it. They change every hour or so,' Johnny said.

'Are you going to tell me who?' he asked, his voice becoming insistent.

'Not over the phone.'

He glanced at Morris. He could hear other voices on the line. They seemed to be in the background and he fancied that Johnny was at some meeting and had taken the call in a public place. At least, he hoped that was the case. 'Chief Inspector Morris thinks we don't have much time. Our chief suspect has not been seen since lunchtime yesterday.'

There was a pause.

'Where are you, Clement?' Johnny asked.

'At home, with Chief Inspector Morris.'

'Can you and the Chief Inspector be at Lewes Police Station within the hour?' Johnny asked.

'Yes,' he said.

He heard the line go dead. He stared at Arthur Morris. 'I think Commander Winthorpe is not in London. In fact, he could be quite close by.'

Morris nodded.

'This is more than murder, isn't it, Arthur. We are talking espionage, aren't we?'

'Quite possibly.'

He went to the kitchen and made some tea but everything in the kitchen reminded him of Mary. He couldn't think about it. Yet it was all he wanted to talk about.

'Combe Martin!' he said, holding the teapot in mid-air.

Morris looked up. 'The West Country?'

He nodded. 'That is where she is, Arthur,' he said, shaking the pot. 'I asked her to go there a week or so ago, when I thought the invasion was close at hand. There is no telephone there but I can get a message to her through the postmistress.' His mind flashed to Ilene Greenwood. 'In fact, the postmistress will probably know where she is. They all seem to know everything.'

He saw Morris smile. The brown eyes still held their detachment, but a flicker of possibility lingered.

'May I use the telephone first, Clement?' Morris asked. 'I would like to call the Chief Superintendents in Dover,

Hastings and Eastbourne and ask them to keep a look out for Jane and Doctor Haswell.'

Thirty minutes later they drove out of Fearnley Maughton. The postmistress at Combe Martin hadn't seen Mary. Clement was glad that Morris knew how to drive. He had never felt so desperate or so exhausted in his whole life. Even the trenches of France had not had the same effect upon him. But then the trenches were real; death traps, of course, but honest places of death where one army fought another. Nothing like the world of espionage with its sinister invisibility. His thoughts went to Mary. He loved her. And, he believed, she loved him. What had caused her to lie to him? Yet, if he was fair, he had withheld his involvement in the Auxiliary Units from her. They had been married twenty years. They finished each other's sentences, such was their affinity. That Mary should have a double life was unfathomable. He felt alone. Betrayed. And foolish. It was unfair, but that was what he felt.

Morris pulled the car into the police parking area at the rear of the Lewes Police Station, and pulling on the handbrake, turned off the engine. From his seat in Morris' car Clement could see both Inspector Russell's car and Doctor Haswell's, parked in a compound behind the Lewes Police Station. He got out of the car and stared at the vehicles. Frowning, he realised now how similar they were. He walked towards them and stared at the tyres on both cars.

'I told you I would make a detective out of you, Clement,' Morris said.

'Are they identical?'

'No. Doctor Haswell's car is a Humber Super Snipe, to be precise, and Inspector Russell's is an Austin Twelve. But they both have long wheel bases, four doors and six side windows. They have similar front wheel arches and both have a rounded shape over the boot. And, perhaps more importantly, they are both black. Only the grilles are different but with both cars parked front to curb, as they are in the rear laneway behind the police station in Fearnley Maughton, the grilles are not visible. And with the headlight shades now required to be fitted on all vehicles, and the white painted front bumper bars, cars do look remarkably similar.'

'So it was Inspector Russell's car which drove into Maughton Forest?'

Morris shook his head. 'No. While the body was found in Doctor Haswell's car, I do not believe it was either the doctor's car or Inspector Russell's car which was in the forest.'

He stared at Morris. 'If not either of these cars, then whose?'

'Another good question, Clement.'

'What is going on, Arthur?'

'Do you know something interesting, Clement?' Morris said.

He raised his eyebrows.

'When we brought Inspector Russell's car to Lewes we had to jump-start it. The car keys are missing. They were not on Inspector Russell, and neither were they in or on his desk. Nor were they in the safe. Nor at Inspector Russell's home. Constable Matthews says that the Inspector kept the keys to his car on his person. However, I am also informed that Inspector Russell's car keys have a distinctive key ring with a Celtic cross medallion.'

'You think the car was used?' he asked.

Morris nodded. 'I do. Find the car keys and we find the murderer.'

'But if the murderer returned the safe keys why wouldn't he replace the car keys?'

'Because the car was used after Inspector Russell's body was removed from the police station.'

'How was the car used?'

'I'm not sure yet,' Morris replied.

They heard the sound of the approaching vehicle.

'But I think we are about to find out some of the mystery,' Morris said, his head tilted towards the unknown black car which pulled up in the parking space nearest the door. 'That must be the fastest trip from London on record,' Morris said. 'If that is where Commander Winthorpe came from.'

Johnny got out of the black car and stood waiting for them to join him.

'Commander Winthorpe, would you like to come into my office?' Morris asked.

Without ceremony they walked into the police station and along a linoleum corridor towards Morris' large office.

'You came from London, Commander?' Morris asked, placing his hat on the stand in his office.

Johnny shook his head. 'Not even I can drive that fast, Chief Inspector. In fact, I have been at a meeting at Petworth on an unrelated matter. I couldn't say over the phone, Clement, but Jane is heading south east. Possibly Eastbourne. But it could be somewhere further east. Tell me what's been happening.'

He told Johnny what they had found in the Anderson Shelter.

Johnny listened without interruption.

'All the murder victims are from the village except one, the man my men believed to be a vagrant,' Clement said. 'A description of him was in our report, which was stolen and for which at least two people have died.'

'Is the body of the vagrant still in the mortuary?' Johnny asked.

'I have arranged for you to be taken to Lewes Hospital's mortuary to see the body of the seaman, as we are calling him, on your arrival,' Morris told Johnny. 'Perhaps we should do this first. Once you confirm the identity of your man, if it is your man, perhaps you would like to inform us what is really behind the murders in Fearnley Maughton?'

Clement saw Johnny lean back in the chair. Johnny was staring at Morris, a slow smile spreading over his lips.

Twenty minutes later they were back in Morris' office. They hung their coats and hats on the stand and sat down.

'How were you so sure he was my man, Chief Inspector?' Johnny asked.

Morris stared at Johnny, the familiar tilt of the head preceding his response. 'If he had been a deserter, I would have been given a name and a description. And I would have had a visit from the Military Police. Likewise, if he had been a German spy I would have been deluged with telephone calls from London and Special Branch. That no one was asking about this man led me to only one conclusion.'

Johnny smiled. 'Quite so. And a lesson for us all, Chief Inspector. The seaman, or the man you believed to be a vagrant, Clement, was Naval Lieutenant Roger Ellis. Ellis is, or rather was, one of my men. Sorry, Clement, but church duties for me have really taken a back seat. And the Archdeacon thing is only temporary. For the duration of the war. It allows me to travel around Britain in clerical garb and I always have a place to stay away from hotels and other more public places. Ellis was stationed at a top secret location in Cuckmere Haven, known as *His Majesty's Ship Forward*. It is there that all Royal Navy battle plans are formalised. So you see just how vital it is that the facility at *Forward* remains secret. However, it had become apparent from intercepted German chatter that the enemy had become aware of some activity at Cuckmere Haven. That being the case, we saw little point in trying to conceal it from them. And, in fact, rather than attempting to hide it and thereby making the Germans even more curious, we saw it as a golden opportunity. It has taken over a year for Ellis to establish his cover and, more importantly, for his information to be believed. His death is a major blow.'

'He was feeding misinformation?' Clement asked.

Johnny nodded. 'Yes. We know he had a contact in Fearnley Maughton, although we never knew who. The man went by the code name *Phoebe*. Ellis would deliver the information to *Phoebe* in Maughton Forest. That contact would then send the information onto the Abwehr by wireless. But Ellis had become suspicious about *Phoebe* and had reported it to me. The interesting thing about our work is not only listening to what is said but also what isn't. *Phoebe* had changed and even failed to make the rendezvous on several occasions. Never a good sign. Insignificant, perhaps, but changes in habit have to be investigated. Perhaps Ellis asked too many questions and *Phoebe* became suspicious. Unfortunately, we will never know the answer to that. And, Ellis, of course, was the only person who could identify *Phoebe*.

'Doctor Haswell,' Clement said, thinking of the times he had seen Phillip Haswell drive away from Fearnley Maughton. He had always believed the doctor was visiting the sick in Lewes Hospital or doing rounds, not keeping appointments with Naval Lieutenants.

'He must have seen the Royal Engineers on one of his rendezvous in the forest, and found the Operational Base,' he continued, thinking of George.

Johnny nodded. 'Knowing *Phoebe's* real name now is of little use. We suspect the bird has flown, although we do not know where, precisely. We hope he will rendezvous with Jane.'

'Who recognised Jane?' Clement asked.

'Just one of my people. But we cannot get too close. We don't want her disappearing before she makes contact with Doctor Haswell, if he really is *Phoebe*.'

'Is there any doubt?' Morris asked.

'Until the individual is caught, there is always the possibility of error.' Johnny added. 'I understand you grew up on the coast, Clement? Considering Jane is heading east, it could be useful if you were to come along.'

'Of course,' he said. But he couldn't stop thinking about Phillip Haswell. 'Doctor Haswell lived among us in Fearnley Maughton for three years. Why now? What changed?'

'It could have been the establishment of the Auxiliary Units,' Johnny said. 'But I don't think so. Especially as Doctor Haswell could not have known about the team's existence. Or perhaps someone was just getting too close.'

'Or he had what he came for?' Morris added.

Johnny raised his eyebrows. 'Perhaps. But I think he would have remained in situ for the duration of the war. It is my opinion that he would only break cover if he had a vital piece of information that could not be sent by wireless, or if he was in danger of discovery. I feel certain that the strafing run was arranged for no other reason than to blow up the radio transmitter.'

Clement glanced at Morris. But his thoughts were on Stanley.

'And the murders of David Russell and Stanley Russell?' he asked.

'Jane was called in to assist Haswell's escape and to aid in any other sabotage. Perhaps the murders of your team, Clement, were for no other reason than that Stanley Russell had told her about the group and shown the girl the weapons. While the Auxiliary Units could well have been the catalyst for Haswell's flight, the information from Cuckmere Haven would appear to be the real reason for Doctor Haswell to break cover.' Johnny paused. 'But I don't think so. I think that is what they want us to think. While *Phoebe* was receiving what he believed to be accurate information, why would he leave? But, if *Phoebe* learned of the existence of Coleshill and its location, that would be a real coup for the Abwehr and an excellent reason for breaking cover. Every cell in the country would be wiped out and the training camp targeted. The elimination of Coleshill and every Auxiliary Unit cell would render us vulnerable to invasion. If they can win the war in the air before we can properly regroup and rearm after Dunkirk, there would not be much stopping them on the ground. It would be a complete walkover. And even if we did somehow stop the Germans from landing, the elimination of Coleshill and its work would set our war effort back at least twelve months. This knowledge is a major coup for the Germans. Certainly worth breaking cover for. They will probably award *Phoebe* the Iron Cross.

Morris spoke. 'Stanley must have told her. She certainly knew about his pack. And finding the list in Inspector Russell's safe gave her the names of the other members of the team. It is the only answer.'

'But Stanley didn't know about the existence of the list,' Clement told them. 'Moreover, the list contained nothing else but the names. No mission, no regimental identification...' he stopped.

'Clement?' Johnny asked.

'It was in an official envelope. Ministry of Home Security. That would have been reason enough for them to open the letter.'

'But how did they know it was there?' Johnny asked.

The room was silent. It was the definitive question.

'Inspector Russell must have told someone. He was the only other person who knew it existed. Other than me and Johnny. And Gubbins.'

'Perhaps they opened the safe as a matter of course,' Morris said.

'Well, no point speculating on it now,' Johnny said. 'We have a nurse and a doctor to find.

The large Constable appeared in the doorway. 'Sorry to interrupt, Sir, but there is an urgent telephone call for Commander Winthorpe.'

'May I?' Johnny asked, gesturing towards Morris' telephone on the desk.

Morris nodded.

Three minutes later Johnny replaced the receiver.

'Do you have enough petrol for a trip to the coast right now, Chief Inspector?' Johnny asked.

'Where exactly?' Morris asked.

'That was Gubbins,' Johnny said pointing to the telephone of Morris' desk. 'He has just heard from Y-section. Y-section listens in on our enemy's conversations. They have just correlated some chatter they heard a day or so ago with a deciphered Jerry message to a U-Boat in the North Sea. There is to be a pick-up. Scheduled for the high tide at zero four hundred hours tomorrow morning.'

'Where?' Morris asked.

'Winchelsea Beach.'

Morris looked up at the clock on the wall in his office. Half past three. 'Are you with us, Clement?'

He nodded. He felt exhausted. They had been awake since four o'clock in the morning. But he was not going to miss out on confronting Phillip Haswell. He pictured all the dead and injured from the strafing raid. George Evans' pale face was locked forever in his memory. Lieutenant Ellis, Constable Newson. Even David Russell. But the one he particularly wanted to avenge was Stanley. Gullible Stanley, whose only crime was to fall in love.

'And,' Johnny continued. 'Elsie, or Jane as you are calling her, is on the train for Rye.'

Chapter Twenty-Eight

As they walked towards the car Clement checked his watch. Four o'clock. Twelve hours since he had slept. Eleven hours since he had eaten. And another twelve hours until the pick-up time for Jane and Phillip Haswell. Morris had arranged a car with a police driver so Clement could get some sleep as they drove. He had wanted to speak with Mary. But the telephone in his front hall had rung and rung without answer. He visualised the hallway at the vicarage, the ringing phone and the darkened corridor in his empty house. He knew it was unlikely she would be home yet. But he had had to try. And now they could wait no longer.

He looked across to Arthur Morris as they drove east. He and Morris had taken the rear seat while Johnny sat in front with the driver. Morris had his eyes closed but Clement was sure he was not asleep.

'How was Inspector Russell's car used?' he asked.

Morris opened his eyes. 'Not one hundred percent sure, but I think it was where Lieutenant Ellis was stored overnight before being transferred into the doctor's car. Remember I told you; there is always a witness. But unless it is blatant, that witness may not even be aware of what they are seeing. And as the police station is at one end of the village, a car could come and go in that back lane without raising suspicion. In fact, as long as the cars are similar and are parked in the same place, it is assumed by any casual observer that it is the car belonging to either Doctor Haswell or Inspector Russell. But what if the cars were switched in their parking places or even substituted for a few hours... would anyone take any notice?'

He stared through the window at nothing much, reflecting on what Morris had just said. 'I saw Phillip drive away on Friday. It was when Peter and I were in your office at the police station. The day we found George. I even waved to him. Though I couldn't say if it was his car or not. But it was his car in Lewes Hospital. And the body of Lieutenant Ellis must have already been in the boot of his car when Phillip left Fearnley Maughton,' he said.

'Not necessarily. And it is possible that Doctor Haswell might not have even known the body was there.'

'You think Haswell is innocent?' Clement asked.

'I don't know yet,' Morris replied.

'But either way, Lieutenant Ellis was put into Doctor Haswell's car on the previous night,' he added.

Morris nodded then closed his eyes. 'That would be a safe assumption.'

'Brought out of the forest in David Russell's car, then transferred to Doctor Haswell's car during the night,' Clement said.

Morris opened his eyes. 'Not necessarily. As I said earlier, Clement, I do not believe it was Inspector Russell's car that went into the forest. There was no sign of leaf matter in the tyre treads of either car. Of course, they might have been washed, but someone would have witnessed that. But I do, however, believe that Inspector Russell's car was used for storage and retrieval.'

Clement stared through the window again. He remembered seeing Phillip drive into the rear lane one evening. He had waved then, too, but he knew his gesture would have been too late for Phillip to have seen it. Timing. Morris had said it was all about timing. He wasn't even sure now that it had been Phillip's car. He had seen the headlights and made the assumption. 'When was that?' he muttered. He realised that it had been the night he had cycled out to Peter's to enquire about the report. George was already dead, lying in the leaves of Maughton Forest.

And Lieutenant Ellis? He lay dead in the boot of Haswell's car. Clement closed his eyes. He needed sleep.

They drove into Rye just on dusk. He had slept in the car during the drive east and he was glad for it. Stepping from the car outside Rye Police Station, he breathed in the salty air. He knew every corner, every twisting byway in the town, perched as it is on the hilltop. His eyes darted to his left. Against the skyline he could see the spire of St Mary's, his father's old church, in the dwindling light. But even if he could he had no wish to go there; the place held too many memories. Closing the door to the police vehicle, he walked with Morris and Johnny towards the front door of the police station.

Morris introduced himself to the Sergeant.

The Sergeant was a man Clement recognised from his school days. He remembered the shock of dark hair and large, hooked nose. His father had said that the boy had French blood. In those days, that was an insult. He suppressed a smirk at his father's prejudices. But the sergeant had changed little in forty years.

'Since you telephoned earlier, Sir,' his old acquaintance informed them, 'we have had the railway station under constant surveillance.'

'Thank you, Sergeant,' Morris said.

'Now, how can we be of assistance, Sir?' the Sergeant asked.

'Is there a telephone I can use?' Johnny asked.

Clement watched Morris' hands as the man poured some tea that had been left for them. Hands say a lot about the person. Or so Mary believed. Morris' were not the hands of any physical labourer. But they were not delicate either; they were showing the signs of arthritis, and the brown spots of old age were visible on his skin. Clement thought of Mary and the way her hands peeled and sliced beans and carrots. His heart was heavy. He longed to speak to her. But even the thought of Mary peeling carrots reminded him of Phillip. He felt the wave of betrayal and shook his head in disbelief. Such deception astounded him. He glanced at the clock on the wall. It was just after seven o'clock. She would be at home. He determined to call her. 'Has Jane been sighted?' he asked as the Sergeant re-entered the room.

The Sergeant nodded. 'But not intercepted.'

'Where?'

'Not far away, as it happens. *The Standard Inn* in The Mint.'

'I know it,' Clement said. 'She will probably take the Needles Passage to Wish Street, then head across the Strand Quay for Winchelsea. It is only about three miles.'

Morris glanced at the local police Sergeant. 'You have someone watching her, Sergeant?'

'One of my people, actually, Chief Inspector,' Johnny said, re-entering the room. 'On the inside. They followed Jane to the inn and took rooms. They will telephone us here when Jane makes her move,' Johnny said, taking a cup of tea from the table.

'What about Phillip Haswell?' Clement asked.

'Hasn't been sighted yet,' the Sergeant said. 'We have checked all the inns. But, of course, he could be using an alias.' The Sergeant looked at Morris. 'The description of the suspect could fit any number of men in the town.'

It was true.

'Only Reverend Wisdom would recognise Doctor Haswell in the dark,' Morris said.

He frowned, remembering what Morris had told him about Phillip always being unavailable. Morris had arrived in the village the afternoon of David Russell's death, and Phillip Haswell had not left the village until the following Friday. Four days. Yet in those few, event-filled days, Phillip Haswell had contrived to evade the Chief Inspector. Clement knew why, now.

'At least we know where Jane is,' Johnny said. 'If Haswell and the girl are to rendezvous, it will either be here or on Winchelsea Beach. My guess is that they will meet up here. Travelling separately and meeting up on the beach is too risky. And they will not make their move for a few hours yet. It's a waiting game for now. But one thing is certain: they will be on the beach at zero four hundred hours tomorrow morning, because that sub will not wait any longer than its prescribed time.'

But it didn't make the waiting any less tedious. 'Could I use the telephone, Sergeant?' he asked.

The sergeant took him to the other room.

Clement closed the door and went into the vacant interview room. It was exactly like the one in Fearnley Maughton Police Station. He picked up the receiver and dialled his home number and waited.

He closed his eyes.

He prayed for Mary and his team. And he prayed for himself. Whatever happened this night, it would end badly for someone. He glanced up at the half-frosted window in the room. From the diminishing light outside he could tell it was now dark.

He rejoined the group. Johnny was sitting in the only armchair in the room, his legs crossed and a plate of toasted scones under his chin. He couldn't resist smiling. Johnny's composure never ceased to amaze and amuse. On the table beside the pot of tea was a plate of dry toasted scones with a smear of butter. Dry though they looked, he was grateful. It had been some time since he had eaten anything.

The Sergeant unrolled a map of Rye and spread it out over the table. They gathered around. A pencil mark had already been drawn on one street, indicating *The Standard Inn* on The Mint. Clement's eye followed the route he believed Jane would take to leave the town.

'How many people do you have available?' Morris asked Johnny.

'Just the two. But both are seasoned operatives. Jane will not detect them. Sergeant? Do you have a police motorcycle?'

'Yes, but no petrol, Commander,' the sergeant said.

'Have your Constable drain some from our car. It would be best to have it available as a diversion, if required.'

'Would you prefer, Commander Winthorpe, that this was handled as a security matter or a police matter?' Morris asked.

He glanced at Johnny.

'Police matter, Chief Inspector,' Johnny answered.

He saw Morris suck on his upper, then lower lip. Clement knew Johnny. And he knew that Johnny didn't take orders from just anyone. It was a mark of respect for Arthur Morris. Or perhaps Johnny didn't want the responsibility if it all went wrong. He chastised himself again. He had become cynical. Not something he had ever been before the war. Or was it before the formation of the Auxiliary Units? He shot a glance at Morris, who he thought was thinking along similar lines.

Arthur Morris stood, poring over the map on the table. 'To summarise then; the woman we are calling Jane is at *The Standard Inn* on a street named The Mint. Commander Winthorpe has a person on the inside who will telephone here the moment Jane makes her move. We also know, from the deciphered message, that the rendezvous is at the high tide at zero four hundred hours tomorrow morning off Winchelsea Beach. If we are to have any hope of apprehending the suspects, some of us must be in place at the beach well before four o'clock.'

'You are proposing we divide, Chief Inspector?' Johnny asked.

'Yes. Jane will recognise Reverend Wisdom. We cannot allow her to abort now or we will not catch Haswell whose current location remains unknown. I am proposing that Reverend Wisdom and myself go to Winchelsea Beach. We can conceal ourselves somewhere along The Ridge.' Morris pointed to the strip of roadway that hugged the beachfront. 'It is a bit exposed, but that should not be too great a problem at that hour. We will also see the landing craft sent to collect them. Clement, the beach at Winchelsea: is it sand or shingle?'

'Shingle.'

'Pity.'

'What about ordnance?' Clement asked, looking at the Sergeant.

The Sergeant reached for a folded map and spread it on the table. They stared at the line of green circles on the map.

'The large circles are anti-tank mines,' the Sergeant said.

'And the smaller ones with spikes?' Clement asked.

'Anti-personnel,' the Sergeant added.

He stared at the clusters of green circles evenly spaced along the beach. Each cluster had been placed at twenty-foot intervals along the land-side edge of the beach, about ten feet in from the roadway. He could feel his eyes widening. Whilst the anti-tank mines presented no problem for a man on foot, it was a different story for the anti-personnel explosives and ordnance maps were notoriously inaccurate.

'How far apart are the anti-tank mines from the anti-personnel mines?' Morris asked.

'About a yard either side,' he said glancing at the legend on the side of the map.

Clement flicked a glance at Morris and Johnny. Fleeting though it was, their eyes held the same reaction. If he had not believed the mission to be suicidal before, he did now.

'Perhaps I should go separately, Chief Inspector. I can take the motorcycle and leave well before you,' Johnny said. 'That way, I can remain concealed at the Rye end of that straight section of The Ridge adjacent to the beach.' He pointed to the section of roadway on the map. 'Once Clement has identified Haswell, you can both run overland. Then as soon as Haswell and Jane are on the beach we move in around them. Once I see them pass me I will start the motorcycle. When you hear the motor, you can run onto the beach. What is the wind forecast for tonight, Sergeant?' Johnny asked.

'Around two knots, Sir, South South-West,' the Sergeant said. 'So quite calm.'

There was silence for some minutes. Clement glanced at the faces of the men alongside whom he was soon likely to die. He recognised that look. He had seen it before in the trenches moments before the whistle sounded. The interesting thing about impossible missions is the silent acceptance of them. Fear disappears when death is inevitable. At least, that had been his experience of the men with whom he had served. There was a job to be done. That was all they needed to know about now.

'When they hear the motorcycle they will start to run, surely,' he said.

'It doesn't give us much time,' Johnny agreed. 'But by then everyone is exposed. It should be expected that they will be armed. And the boatman may well have a machine gun mounted in the craft.'

Clement had signed up for a two-week life expectancy. Now it was a matter of hours. He wriggled his ankle. But a knife, even a commando knife was a risky venture on the beach with a younger man who was also the enemy. And not worth a farthing against a mounted machine gun. A Sten was what he needed.

'We will need some binoculars or at least a telescope. And a pistol or Sten if they have one here,' he said, thinking of his pack in the filing cabinet in the church office.

255

'Already thought of, Clement. And both my operatives have hand pistols, as do I. And binoculars.'

'We have some also,' the Sergeant added.

'And Clement has his knife, I'm sure,' Morris said.

Somehow, thought Clement, he was not surprised that Morris guessed he carried a knife.

'Clement and I will position ourselves midway along the roadway, adjacent to the beach and opposite the most northern groyne. The topographical map shows a ditch on the opposite side of the road, from which there would be a clear view of the beach and both sides of the groyne. According to the ordnance map there is a gap between the buried mines directly opposite the line of sight from the ditch to the groyne pylons. Commander Winthorpe, as you will be at the beach before us can you cut the wire there in advance? That way you will know exactly where Clement and I will station ourselves. Once we see Jane and Haswell we can cross the road and run onto the beach in a straight line to the pylons. We should have a reasonable chance of cutting them off.'

'Sir, all the horizontal boards on the groynes have been removed. Only the uprights remain,' the Sergeant said.

'Even better,' he said.

'How tall are these pylons, Sergeant?' Morris asked.

'Well over a man's height, Sir, and spaced about ten feet apart.'

'But enough to offer some protection?' he asked.

'Limited,' the Sergeant added.

'Morris is right,' Johnny said. 'The landing craft may not beach. It could stand offshore but the pylons offer the only protection while the targets swim out and board the dinghy.'

'Would the Germans know the locations of the mines?' he asked.

'It is wise to assume they do,' Johnny said.

Johnny must have seen Clement's sceptical expression.

'Intelligence of that sort is much prized and highly paid for, Clement. We cannot assume that everyone is a patriot.' Johnny paused. 'Paid for,' Johnny muttered.

He looked up. 'Using five-pound notes, perhaps?'

'It is possible, Clement,' Johnny responded. 'Although, those notes would be very useful for any other future German spies arriving in England.'

Clement wondered about the notes. Not that he believed the whole business had ever been about the money. But if five-pound notes lined the pockets of Jane and Phillip, their presence would provide the tangible link to the murder of David Russell.

The room was quiet. He knew they were all pondering what lay ahead on Winchelsea Beach. He did not believe Phillip and Jane would ever allow themselves to be caught. Much less stand trial for either espionage or murder. The best he could hope for was to kill them before they, or the machine gun in the dinghy, killed him. His thoughts shocked him. Several times since he had become involved in the Auxiliary Units he had said to himself that he felt less and less like a vicar. Once, he could never have imagined even thinking such thoughts. Killing. He remembered Gubbins' words. But this had become personal. Phillip Haswell was a man he knew. At least, thought he knew. He pushed his feelings aside and tried to remain detached, hoping his motives were not revenge but duty. He understood now why Johnny had referred to them as 'targets'. It depersonalised what they were about to do. For regardless of what he thought, the man was the enemy, and the location of Coleshill had to remain secret. That was what Clement had signed up to do: to defend his country and, if necessary, to die to protect it from Nazi aggression.

'Sergeant, would you inform the local Home Guard of our activities tonight? It is better that they know and stay away,' Morris said.

The Sergeant made an entry in his notebook.

'Where do you think Haswell is hiding?' he asked.

'You are our Rye expert, Clement. Where would you go?' Morris asked.

'I do not believe he would be close to *The Standard* in case Jane was picked up. But I do believe he could be somewhere where he could see her departure.' Clement stared at the map of the streets he knew so well. 'Will they walk to Winchelsea Beach?'

'I think it likely,' Morris said. 'If not, they would have to steal a car or motorcycle, which would be too noisy and with too great a risk of there being no petrol in it.'

'And they cannot afford to miss the rendezvous,' Clement said, almost to himself. 'It is my opinion that they will leave Rye separately and join up once away from the town,' he said. He stared at the map. In his mind he walked the streets, the waterfront and the Winchelsea road. He ran his eye around the edges of the town on the seaward side. The view from Ypres Tower spanned more than two hundred and seventy degrees across the surrounding environs and more than one hundred and eighty degrees across the harbour. But at night the shifting sands were too dangerous for anyone not familiar with them. Besides, the local Home Guard had a post in Ypres Tower and at the foot of Watchbell Steps on the eastern end of the Strand Quay. Watchbell Steps. They led from Watchbell Street down the steep escarpment to the waterfront. But Clement also knew of the tunnels that connected the houses of Watchbell Street with the infamous smugglers' haunt, *The Mermaid Inn,* in Mermaid Street at the end of which was the laneway known as The Mint. 'There,' he said, pointing to the steps. With his left index finger on the steps at the end of Watchbell Street, his right finger traced the route of Jane's anticipated departure. 'Jane leaves *The Standard* and walks from the inn towards the Needles Passage, then into Wish Street and across the Tillingham River to Winchelsea Road. Phillip is watching from the steps in Watchbell

Street. Even in the darkness, with a pair of binoculars and with the moonlight reflecting off the water, there is sufficient light to see her cross the bridge. Especially since Jane's departure will most likely be at a specific time. But Haswell will not take the steps to the waterfront because of the Home Guard sentry. Once he sees her, he returns to the house at the end of Watchbell Street and takes the underground tunnels to *The Mermaid*. Once he leaves the inn, he walks down to the Strand Quay to cross the Tillingham, the Home Guard sentry now behind him and obscured from sight.'

'You're sure about the tunnels?'

He nodded, but he was thinking of his mother and all the stories she had told him about Rye's smuggling past.

'Sergeant, telephone the Captain of the Home Guard and tell him to remove the sentry on duty tonight at the foot of the Watchbell Steps between the hours of midnight and four o'clock tomorrow morning. I do not want another unnecessary death,' Morris said.

'Where exactly does this tunnel surface, Clement?' Johnny asked.

'Behind a bookcase in one of the bedrooms at *The Mermaid*. I have seen it. Phillip takes the tunnels from Watchbell Street to *The Mermaid*, then runs the short distance towards the bridge over the Tillingham. Once across, he joins Jane on the Winchelsea Road.'

'How do you want to play this, Chief Inspector?' Johnny asked.

Morris stared at the map. 'It would be wise to check the steps near Watchbell Street.'

'The local boys should do it,' Clement said, interrupting Morris' train of thought. 'If Phillip sees any of us, especially me, he could vanish. If the local police could station themselves in a house in Watchbell Street with a view of the steps, once they see Haswell or any man watching the seafront return to the house with the tunnel, they could telephone you here at the police station. However, the sergeant and I should position ourselves in another house opposite *The Mermaid* as soon as we know Jane has left *The Standard*. We will need as much time as possible to get into position. Sergeant, can you arrange it with a patriotic resident?'

The Sergeant nodded. 'Leave that to us'.

Clement continued. 'Phillip's departure from Watchbell Street will be but minutes after sighting Jane crossing the bridge. I estimate that the Sergeant and I have about three to five minutes before Phillip emerges in Mermaid Street. Once I identify Phillip and see him leave *The Mermaid*, the Sergeant and I will return to the police station and you and I, Arthur, will run overland for Winchelsea Beach. Johnny should go at midnight. That will give him more than enough time to locate the best and safest course across the beach and cut a section of barbed wire for us and the motorcycle. When Arthur and I arrive at the beach, we will locate the ditch adjacent to the cut wire opposite our surveillance post. Then we wait for Jane and Phillip to arrive.'

They stared at the map of the ancient town.

Phillip Haswell flashed into his mind again. But if Clement had learned anything about human nature it was that he didn't really know anyone. He wondered if that also included Mary. Coleshill had made him question everyone and everything. Even himself. Especially himself. It was what the training stressed. Know your own abilities and limitations. Waiting until one is faced with the muzzle end of a gun in the enemy's hand is not the time to philosophise about killing. Especially if that enemy was somebody one knew. Besides, Phillip Haswell had not been won over to Nazism recently by the prospect of a negotiated peace to mitigate grievous times. Phillip and Jane had killed the real Elsie Wainwright in order to contrive and maintain a history for him; a legend, he believed, was the word they used for such deceptions. Phillip had been sent in to watch and wait and to provide information that was so valuable that the Nazis would wait years to acquire it. Coleshill House. The discovery of what really happened at *HMS Forward*, thanks to Lieutenant Ellis' misinformation, was still intact, even if the location was known. But the existence of Coleshill and what went on there was dynamite, especially now with the invasion imminent. That is what it had really been about. That was why Phillip had broken cover. Clement was pleased that the Germans were receiving misinformation about *HMS Forward* but that was not his concern. Ensuring that the Germans would never know about Coleshill was what was important now. *Phoebe* had struck gold. And it was his job to stop *Phoebe*.

Chapter Twenty-Nine

Monday 23rd September 1940

Midnight.

'I'll go now,' Johnny said. He reached for his coat. 'Once I see the targets, I will start the motorcycle. If there is anything unexpected, I will flick on the headlight.'

Clement shook hands with Johnny. They held each other's eye for a moment. There was no need for words.

Johnny turned to go. 'See you on the beach, Clement, Chief Inspector. Just be prepared for the unexpected. Always best.'

He could hear Johnny's footsteps disappear along the corridor. He didn't really need Johnny's warning. The unexpected was what such missions were all about. He thought of his men. He would have liked to have had them with them. Especially Reg for his ability with the rifle. Yet, he believed he was as prepared as anyone, given the circumstances. But he took Johnny's comment as he believed it was meant: for reassurance.

The Sergeant had found two Home Guard uniforms for him and Morris. He was grateful for the Sergeant's foresight. The cloth was rough but incredibly warm, and Clement thought it fitted better than his own.

By the time they returned to the interview room wearing the Home Guard uniforms, the Sergeant had refilled the pot of tea. But what Clement really needed was sleep. He couldn't. Not yet. When it was over he would sleep like a baby. He wondered whether it would be in this life or the next. Sleeping for a thousand years had appeal. Just as well, he thought, because that is what lies ahead for you, Clement Thomas Wisdom. He turned his mind to the weapons Johnny had brought, and reaching into the pack, lined them up along the table. The Sten was closest to his hand. He checked the magazine of ammunition. But his preparation was routine. He didn't expect trouble. Not this time. The initial sortie was for reconnaissance only. Yet despite this, he would not go unprepared. In his mind he heard Major Bannon's voice telling them that preparation and adaptability are the keys to a successful mission. Keys. His mind drifted to Inspector Russell's car keys and what Morris had said about them. Finding the five-pound notes on Jane or Phillip implicated them, but the car keys with the Celtic cross would see them hang, if they were not already dead by morning.

He wriggled his foot and felt the Fairbairn Sykes knife, strapped to his inner left leg, digging into his calf. He never went anywhere without it now. He ran his eye over the remaining weapons. He intended to take three grenades and four more magazines of ammunition when they went to Winchelsea Beach. His eye rested on the trip wires and explosives. But there was no time for laying explosives; besides, there were enough already on the beach. He glanced at the knuckle duster, stiletto and garrotte. The knuckle duster could be useful, but the other items he decided to leave behind. Stealth might have been possible if the beach was sand, but it was impossible to disguise running footsteps on shingle. The small, rounded stones had a way of falling and sliding beneath one's feet. As a child he had loved both the feel and the sound of the crunching, slipping stones. But now their sound meant death. Frontal attack was the only way. And that required bravado as much as it did bullets.

He checked his watch. Thirty minutes had passed since Johnny had left the police station. And, he guessed, it would be another hour and a half before they received word that Jane had left *The Standard.*

263

Morris went to lie down in one of the cells. Despite his body yearning for the panacea of sleep, Clement couldn't. He had never been one for cat-napping. Yet, despite the lack of sleep and his age, he felt alive. Adrenaline did that. He hoped it would last for a few hours yet. He swung his feet onto a chair as he leaned back, closed his eyes, and pulled his Home Guard uniform jacket around him as the temperature dropped.

The telephone rang.

Clement could hear the Sergeant's voice. Then the even, determined footsteps.

'Jane has left *The Standard*,' the Sergeant said as Morris joined him.

Clement glanced at the clock on the wall. Two o'clock. Reaching for the Sten gun, he checked it one more time then fitted the silencer. Morris reached for his police-issue service revolver. Clement watched Morris check the weapon and place extra ammunition in his pocket. He knew the weapon would be next to useless but he couldn't say so.

He smiled at Morris, a man he had come to respect and admire. 'Be ready to leave the moment we return, Arthur,' he said.

Morris nodded. 'I'll be ready. And Clement, good luck.'

Clement smiled, and he and the Sergeant ran along the corridor.

The Sergeant opened the door to the street. Cinque Port Street was deserted. A cool wind slapped their faces as they ran into Market Road. Crossing High Street, they ran up West Street, their distorted shadows leaping over the cobblestones in the moonlight like the departed spirits of the smuggler gangs. He knew their footsteps were echoing off the buildings, but there was little he could do about it. As they approached Mermaid Street, he began to tiptoe along the cobbles. Slowing at the corner, he ran his fingers along the Sten and slipped off the catch. Peering around the edge of the corner building, he saw that Mermaid Street was deserted. Rounding the corner, he leaned against the walls and peered down the descending, narrow street, his eye scanning and checking every window and doorway in the darkness. He edged forward and glanced upwards. The roofline of the houses was visible against the moonlit sky. But the light did not penetrate into the narrow streets. In the darkness, human forms blended into night air. He listened. Beckoning behind him to the Sergeant, he hunched low and they ran along the cobbles to the doorstep of a house diagonally opposite *The Mermaid Inn*. Clement kept his Sten close to his chest, his finger poised on the trigger. Glancing around, the Sergeant tapped on the door. A man of advanced years opened the door, and Clement and the Sergeant slipped inside.

'Thank you for helping us tonight,' he said. He didn't know the couple's names but he could see their wide-eyed enthusiasm. The old man pointed to the stairs and they ran up to the bedroom at the front of the house that overlooked the street. A minute later the telephone rang and Clement heard the old man answer. As he squatted by the window, the resident came into the bedroom to give them the message that a man had left Watchbell Steps. The house owner left the room and Clement heard the elderly man's footsteps return downstairs. Squatting on the window seat, he opened the window and leaned his head out, his eye on the front door to *The Mermaid*. The street below was deserted and still. He checked his watch. It had taken them three minutes to reach the house. In the dim light, the street below exuded its sinister past. Silent, macabre even in the black-blue light. He gripped his Sten. He recalled the terrifying tales his mother had told him when he was a boy of the infamous Hawkhurst gang of the early eighteenth century, who tortured and murdered anyone who dared oppose their smuggling activities. *The Mermaid*, even then, had been the chosen haunt of criminals. He saw the door open.

Two men stepped out into the street, their boots tapping on the cobblestones, a wisp of condensed air escaping from their warm mouths.

Clement stared at the dark shapes.

'Is that him?' the Sergeant whispered.

He leaned further forward, his head out of the window. Staring at the backs of the two men wrapped in coats with hats pulled down over their heads, he fixed his gaze on their silhouettes. He had not expected two men. He squinted, his eyes straining for any sign he recognised. Were they innocent people walking the streets? Who walked the streets during wartime at two o'clock in the morning? He stared again at the darkened shapes as they walked away from the inn and down the street towards the waterfront, their shadows elongating as they went, the moonlight picking up their presence. He continued to stare. Time was passing. He needed to make his decision. The figures were almost at the junction of Mermaid Street and The Mint. He visualised the day of the strafing run, when he had watched Phillip Haswell run towards the village green. Were these the same narrow shoulders? He shifted his eyes to the other man. From the gait, he sensed that the second man was larger and also older. But even though he was weighed down under the heavy coat, there was a spring in the man's step. He stared at the forms as they walked close together. Too close. Something about the way the men walked was wrong. He couldn't see the thinner man's arms. He felt the frown crease his forehead. 'That's him!' he said, but he felt something was not right. He stood, and without waiting for the Sergeant, ran from the room and descended the stairs. Opening the front door of the obliging resident, he stood in the doorway and checked the street. The two men had disappeared from Mermaid Street and were now somewhere close to the waterfront and out of his sight. Turning right, he ran to the top of the street and sprinted towards Cinque Ports Street. Three minutes later he ran into the police station. Morris looked up as he entered the room.

'Something is not right. There are two men,' he said.

'Two!'

He nodded. Lifting his foot onto a chair, he unstrapped his commando knife from his calf and strapped it to his left wrist. 'Are you ready?' he asked Morris again, while grabbing the weapons lined up along the table.

Morris nodded.

Almost without thinking, Clement slipped the knuckle duster, three grenades and four magazines of ammunition into the webbing around his waist, and strapped a pouch containing the binoculars to his right thigh. Glancing at Morris, Clement held the Sten in front of him, and they hurried from the police station into the night.

They ran as far as Wish Street, pausing just before the last building. Leaning against the cold wall, he peered around the corner. His eye panned the open space between the last building in Wish Street and the Tillingham Bridge. He scanned the opposite side of the river. If he had been Phillip Haswell, he would wait in some obscure hiding place on the other side of the river just to make sure no one was following, before running along the Winchelsea Road. His eye searched the low bushes on the other shore for movement.

'What's happening?' Morris whispered.

Clement reached for the binoculars and scanned the opposite shoreline. He saw the huddled forms. Three shapes coalesced into one dark mass, then parted again into three. Standing, the three separated and began to run. Jane was on the far left, the slight shape immediately recognisable. The centre figure, from the running gait, Clement recognised as Haswell. But the other man was hunched and appeared to be carrying something. As he stared, the light caught the object. A glint of light, just a second in duration but it was enough. The older man held a machine gun. Within seconds the group had disappeared from sight.

He replaced the binoculars and signalled Morris. They ran across the bridge, and climbing through low scrubland, headed south-east for Winchelsea Beach. His eyes oscillated between his feet and the night air in front of him. He could hear Morris' breathing as they ran. Flaring his nostrils, Clement breathed in the salty air. He had not run along this stretch of land since boyhood but nothing was different. The short cuts and tracks to the beach had not changed in forty years.

From the top of the beach head, he and Morris lay belly down in the grass. He fancied that he could hear the gulls. But he knew it was his imagination. Reaching for the binoculars again he panned the barbed wire, looking for the break Johnny had cut through it two hours previously.

'There,' he whispered. His eye scanned the area again, but he could not see Johnny. He replaced the binoculars in their pouch and stood. He could see the old wooden pylons about fifty yards along the beach, black like tall burned tree trunks against the shingle. Hunching low, they ran through the low grass towards the ridge opposite the line of pylons. He stopped and again, using the binoculars, scanned the beach before he and Morris descended from the low scrubland, across the track and onto the ridge overlooking the beach. Opposite the now deconstructed groyne was a narrow ditch. It had once been used as a drain in the event of an unusually high tide. He and Morris lay there, their bodies spread on the sloped wall. He flattened himself into the ground, and lying on his belly pulled the binoculars to his face and checked the length of the barbed wire barricade. He smiled when he saw the break in the wire. Johnny had cut a gap for them, and had even placed some driftwood over the fallen, razor-sharp wire.

Morris dropped beside him, the man's back pressed against the ditch. Clement could hear Morris' heavy breathing.

'Anything?' Morris whispered.

He shook his head. He hadn't expected there to be anything yet, he just wanted to be familiar with the beach and the structures on it. With the binoculars to his eyes, he panned the length of the deserted beach. In the half-light he could see the low waves crashing onto the shingle. Halfway along the beach were the remains of a fishing shed and another series of pylons. He focused again on the tall pylons opposite their position. There were the remains of twelve pylons. He knew, from his boyhood, that each pylon was taller than a man but the horizontal planks that formed the groyne had been removed, just as the Sergeant had said. Five of the pylons stood on the beach out of the water, seven extending into the waves. A boat could tie up to the outer one but there would be little in the way of protection from onshore attack. An individual, however, would be afforded some protection. Clement looked out to sea. The night sky and the sea had merged into one dark mass. If it had not been for the moon's half light he believed they would see nothing. Silver flecks of light played over the water. He lowered the binoculars.

'Do you know the time, Arthur?' he asked, his voice low.

Morris slipped his hand under his coat and flicked on a torch. 'Two forty-five.'

He nodded.

Much too early.

The wind blew in his face. He should have been feeling nervous but he was surprised by his sense of calm. He felt alert and alive, almost like a young man again. But above all, he felt in control. It was as though every minute of his life so far had been a preparation for this day. This hour. This mission. And his stomach had not troubled him since arriving in Rye. Was it just that he was on familiar ground? Perhaps he felt the familiarity of past actions? He had lain in trenches before, his eyes scanning horizons for German tanks. Now in the dead of night he searched for German submarine periscopes. Somewhere out there, just beneath the surface, was a German U-boat waiting for the allotted time.

He placed the Sten on the grass beside him and checked his watch. Zero two fifty-eight hours. Taking the binoculars, he panned the sea again.

Morris' breathing had returned to normal and the man lay on the ground beside him, the police service pistol in his right hand.

'Have you done this sort of thing before, Arthur?' he whispered.

'I was once involved in an altercation involving guns. But not one with a German submarine.'

'Are you an accurate shot?'

'Yes. But I am not sure how I will fare against automatic weapons.'

The ensuing silence told him they both knew how it was likely to go.

Clement gazed upwards and silently recited the Lord's Prayer. It is amazing how many stars are visible when there is no ambient light. He wondered why he had spent so little time doing things like stargazing. The view at night would be spectacular from the Downs. He closed his eyes. He would never see it now.

'What do you think of our chances, Clement?' Morris asked.

'Not good.'

Silence.

Some minutes passed. The only sound was the lapping water, the rhythm of the endless waves crashing on the shingle shoreline. Clement closed his eyes, rolled over and listened to the hypnotic sound. Soothing, gentle. He burrowed his shoulders into the shallow depression, seeking any measure of comfort and warmth the cold earth afforded. The temperature dropped. So did the conversation; there was nothing to say. Besides, voices at night carry for miles, especially with the light wind. He pushed his hand under the pack and flicked on the torch to check his watch. Zero three forty-five hours. Soon. Fifteen minutes. He rolled onto his belly, and holding the binoculars, once more scanned the foreshore. Morris lay on the grass beside him, his hat over his face. Clement nudged Morris and the man rolled over, his eyes staring out to sea.

'Do you see anything?' Morris whispered.

He shook his head. But it wouldn't be long. He shivered. It seemed colder to him, but perhaps it was just that he knew the time was approaching. They say that the night is coldest at four o'clock. He trained the binoculars on the shoreline, panning right to left, then out to sea, scanning and sweeping over the waves. Moonlight, silver and bright, cut into the part of coast he was watching, like a dagger plunging from the horizon and pointing straight at them. The light played and sparkled over the ever-moving surface.

It appeared: the thin, black periscope slicing through the water. Then the hull followed, rising from the depths. Even though he was expecting it, actually seeing it sent shudders through Clement's body. The periscope pierced the thin line of silver light for no more than two seconds, then vanished again into the darkness. He lowered the binoculars and stared into the night.

'What is it?' Morris whispered.

'They have arrived,' he said.

He passed the binoculars to Morris.

'The sub, not the targets,' he said, reminding himself that Phillip Haswell was his enemy.

He checked his watch again. Zero three fifty-eight. The trio would be on the beach within minutes. He held the binoculars again to his face and relocated the periscope. What he saw made his heart skip a beat. In the moonlight the dark form took on a shape and a presence of satanic evil. He had never felt or witnessed anything like it. The black mass, sinister and silent rose before him. It had appeared without any sound and was lying in wait for its prize. Clement's open mouth was dry and he knew his eyes were wide. He could feel his eyelids had opened so wide it was almost uncomfortable. But the sight was mesmerising. He screwed his eyes tight and blinked several times.

'How far off the shoreline is it?' Morris asked.

'About half a mile.'

He watched as the coning tower hatch opened. A minute later he saw a silhouette climb out and descend onto the submarine platform. A small dinghy was lowered into the sea and the man climbed over the side of the submarine and into the dinghy. Clement watched the coning tower. No one else left the deadly hulk.

A crunching sound cut into the cold air. In an instant the mesmeric hold of the submarine on his concentration vanished. Several sets of feet were running over the shingle. He held the binoculars steady and focused on the sound of running feet.

'Now!' he said, grabbing his Sten. He and Morris stood, and ran forward. As they crossed the road they cleared the ridge top and descended onto the beach. The motorcycle engine roared somewhere off to his left. A shaft of light from the motorcycle's headlights coursed over the beach. He stopped and he saw the beam of light cut into the night. In its glare he saw legs, torsos, then arms, running, two men, one woman. Within seconds, gunfire exploded in rapid staccato cracks. He saw one of the men turn and drop to the beach, the flash from the muzzle of the gun strobing yellow in the blackness as the bullets sprayed the beach. He heard the motorcycle engine still going but the motorcycle was stuck in the shingle, lying stationary in the loose surface. Bullets shattered the machine, and the headlight was extinguished. Within a second the fuel tank exploded, the noise and searing light piercing the night around them. For one second he could see three figures on the shingle at the water's edge. Another round of bullets sprayed the burning motorcycle. Clement wondered about Johnny. In the confusion, he and Morris ran for the break in the barbed wire, his feet falling on anything, his eye searching for the driftwood plank over the barbed wire. Rushing forward, he crossed the break, his feet pushing on, the shingle sliding and slipping beneath his tread. 'Arthur, stay behind me and off to my right,' he shouted, turning his head back to see the Chief Inspector only a few paces behind him. The machine-gun fire stopped.

Silence.

He fell to the beach, his Sten in his grasp. He heard Morris fall onto the shingle behind him. He couldn't see the group now. But in the confusion he and Morris had advanced across the beach about fifty yards. Lying on the shingle, listening to his own breathing, he was convinced that his enemy did not know of his and Morris' presence.

But everything was silent. He waited. He could hear, in the light wind, the sound of oars in the water followed by a bump. Repeated. The light wind was bringing the sounds to them. He knew it was the dinghy. The small craft was hitting the last pylon, the waves buffeting the boat against the wooden pole.

The silence continued.

Then he heard running feet.

As the feet ran across the shore the rapid firing started again, the yellow strobing flashing, coursing across the beach, fanning the shoreline. He thought the firing was random, and he guessed his position was still unknown to the gunman. He could hear the bullets hissing and pinging off the shingle. He lay on the beach, his head down, and waited for the barrage to stop. Turning his head to one side, he saw the gunman strafe the beach again. The yellow flicker of the bullets leaving the muzzle exploded in the night and he caught a glimpse of the gunman, backlit from the firing weapon. An outline of the face only, but it was enough.

'Stop firing!' a panic-stricken voice screamed into the night air.

Clement recognised Phillip's voice in the hysterical shriek. It shocked him for one moment. Standing and holding the Sten to his shoulder, he fired at the face he had known for three years. He saw Phillip fall. He dropped and rolled several times to his left over the round, hard stones. But the hail of bullets was not directed at him. He rolled once more. The firing started again. The gun was in another's hands now. Another round of shots strafed across the beach, followed by the sound of feet running again. But the pattern was different. The running was laboured. Someone was injured. The running stopped again. He looked up from where he lay on the shingle. The yellow flashes were coming from behind one of the pylons. The pattern continued. Running. Firing. With each round a spray of short, staccato shots flew across the stretch of beach, but the gunman was moving to the next pylon with each burst. Clement could tell that the firing was wild and not aimed with any accuracy. He watched the glow from the muzzle move further towards the sea. He could hear Morris behind him, then another set of feet. He hoped they were Johnny's. Standing, he ran forward and lined the Sten up with the pylon at the end of the old groyne.

He heard the sound of an engine. A low sound. He dropped again to the beach. He thought it was a diesel motor; the low chugging sound of a small launch. From where he lay on the shingle, he looked up. Out of the blackness a searchlight lit up the shoreline. He lowered his head, his Sten on his chest, and rolled sideways away from the shaft of light, their position no longer unknown.

274

Lowering his head, he waited for the rapid fire. Bullets skittered across the shingle, pinging off the stones. The light was on the pylons now. Each one was illuminated in turn until he saw the targets, bright in the intense beam, break cover and run into the low waves. He could not tell if the launch was friend or foe, but it no longer mattered. He would use it. He stood again and ran forward. The old rotting pylons of the groyne stood out, brighter than day in the blinding light. He heard splashing. Then he saw two people, a woman and a man holding hands as they ran into the water. He saw the man toss the weapon into the sea and swim towards the dinghy. They had separated, the woman still behind the last pylon. Machine-gun fire coursed from the motor launch. He could hear the bullets splashing and skipping across the water; the high-pitched spitting continued, several rounds hitting the water-sodden timbers of the pylons. Clement stayed low. He rolled sideways, then two seconds later he rolled away once more as the bullets fired again. Although he could not be sure, the bullets from the launch did not appear to be directed at the beach. Keeping low, he tucked his head under his arm and looked back. The light strobed across the beach again, then swept over the water. In that instant he had seen Morris and Johnny lying flat on the beach behind him, lit up in the glare. He stood, and running forward, fired the Sten, sending a sweeping spray of bullets into the sea. The light swung off the beach and onto the water. Morris had been off to his right, lying flat on the shingle and about twenty feet behind him. To his left Johnny was closer, a Sten in his hand. He did not know if either or both were hit. He stared into the night. The launch worried him. Yet he believed the vessel was not German. The light went away from the shore again and onto the water surface. He looked up. In the distance he could see the outline of the submarine, its sinister dark presence impassive to the mayhem around it. The man in the dinghy was standing now, his blond hair caught in the fierce glare of the launch's light. The man was firing in a wide arc, defiantly spraying bullets across the water towards the motor launch. Clement rolled again, over and over away from where he had lain on the stony beach. Laying his head along the barrel of the Sten, he closed one eye and stared down the sight at the dinghy. Pulling the trigger, he heard the bullets skimming the water. He rolled again, left then right. The man in the dinghy once again directed his fire onto the beach, the bullets striking the beach where Morris and Johnny had been pinned down. The strafing continued, the yellow light from the machine gun indicating the arc of the gunman's aim. Spitting bullets were still hitting the water. He guessed that the man who had swum towards the dinghy was now either dead or in the craft, but the girl, if not already dead, was still behind the pylon. He wondered why they would sacrifice themselves waiting for her. He stood and ran forward firing at the last pylon, running across the shingle for the pylon nearest the water's edge. The bullet hit hard. His upper left arm was stinging as though he had been bitten by a large dog. It felt warm. He dropped again. He couldn't see the girl any more behind the pylon. Holding the Sten to his right shoulder, he laid his head along the barrel, his eye on the sight. His arm was painful, but he fired again into the night in the direction of dinghy and unleashed the remaining contents of the magazine.

The searchlight flashed again. Clement saw on his left that the man in the dinghy was down. With the boatman down, the two escapees would have to swim to the boat, board it and row away themselves. But for some reason the man, if he was alive and in the dinghy, was waiting for the girl. In that instant Clement knew he had them. He looked again at the dead boatman, whose body was half in and half out of the small boat. Another man, the older one, was hunched over in the dinghy, his body still as the boat floundered in the waves. Clement fired the Sten and saw the hunched body move only slightly with the impact of the bullets. The girl, Jane, was in the water, her arms raised in the waves.

It was over.

The motor launch's engine roared, and although he could no longer see the craft, he heard it disappear into the night. Lying on the beach, he grabbed his binoculars and panned the sea, about half a mile offshore. The black coning tower was sliding down into the waves. He watched it, spellbound, until it disappeared.

'Everyone alright?'

It was Johnny's voice.

'Yes,' Morris responded.

'Fine,' he heard himself reply, but he wanted Jane. And he wanted the dead traitor, the unknown third person. Standing, he reached for another magazine in his belt and reloaded the Sten as he ran forward across the shingle. He heard his boots splash into the water and felt the rush of cold water around his ankles. He held the Sten chest-high and let off another round of bullets into the air. 'They are all dead, and you have nowhere to run! Come out with your hands over your head!' he shouted. He kept the barrel of the gun on the girl as she swam towards the shoreline.

Johnny stood and ran forward towards the girl.

Clement tossed the Sten back towards the beach and plunged into the sea. He swam out through the waves towards the dinghy, and grabbing the rope on the bow of the small craft, he pulled the boat towards the shore.

A line of people now stood on the beach. From their naval uniforms he guessed they were Johnny's people. He glanced at Arthur Morris. Chief Inspector Morris had been allowed to do his bit but it had been Johnny's call all along. Strangely, he found it insulting. More for Morris than himself. The unknown silent men moved forward into the water and dragged the dinghy high up the beach. Two men now had Jane at gunpoint. Clement glanced at the girl, but he needed to know. Standing, he clutched his arm and walked towards the craft. Morris was standing beside him. The Chief Inspector reached forward, and grasping the coat of the dead man, rolled the body over and switched on a torch.

Chapter Thirty

Clement felt himself starting to shake. The pain in his arm was intense now and he wasn't sure if he was falling. He could hear the waves. He could hear the sound of feet on the shingle. Were they his feet? The waves; always the waves: incessant, shushing, caressing the shore and the ears. But he could no longer see; everything was dark now. Yet he could hear voices. Falling. He had no concept of the physical world around him. Time had stopped. The gentle hush of the waves penetrated his consciousness. He felt himself falling. He heard the soft thud. He was floating, downwards. And it was hot. His skin prickled with the heat. Something hard was under his head and he could hear raised voices above him. He closed his eyes.

'Clement?'
He heard her calling. Was he dreaming?
'Clement?'
The voice in his ear was coming from another dimension. In his mind he sensed a comforting glow. But the pain in his arm stabbed him awake. He winced, then despite the pain, smiled. Mary. Mary was with him. He allowed the sound of her voice to linger in his subconscious. Where was he?

In his mind he saw the running legs. Crunching. Running feet over shingle. Strobing yellow flashes. Machine-gun fire. Rapid. Fall! Roll left. Roll right. Shafts of piercing light. He screwed his eyes shut as the yellow light flashed in his memory. They were exposed, the blinding light lit them up like actors on a stage. Shoot at the beam. 'Get it out or we will all be dead!' he screamed. The blond man in the dinghy was firing. Now the man lay slumped over the gunwale of the dinghy. U-boats. Phillip. Was he dead? The searing light from Johnny's exploding motorcycle. Johnny. Roll right! Roll left! Fire! Jane. He had to get Jane. He remembered the beach. Pain, hot and stabbing. 'Stop!' he shouted. He felt a restraining hand on his chest.

'Clement? Can you hear me?'

He breathed hard and deep. He knew the voice but it was outside, coming from another place. He opened his eyes. 'Mary?'

Her face was before him. She was smiling at him. He stared at her.

'You are alright, Clement. And you are safe now,' Mary told him.

Someone was beside him. He felt the needle enter his other arm. The pain was subsiding. He closed his eyes.

He woke. Mary. He watched her knitting the socks, the needles clicking, the thread unravelling.

'What time is it?' he whispered.

The needles stopped and she leaned forward. 'About eleven o'clock,' Mary said.

'What day is it,' he asked.

'Thursday,' she said.

'Where were you?' he asked, reaching for her hand.

She smiled. 'In London, Clement. I still do some work for the Admiralty. Johnny Winthorpe recruited me last year along with many other former secretaries. I'm sorry, Clement, but I was not permitted to tell you. And Gwen knows nothing about it. I haven't had to do anything until recently. And certainly nothing as exciting as you. I follow people and courier things. It was I who spotted Jane. I saw her at Victoria Station as I was returning home; that unmistakable travel bag was in her hand. So I followed her onto the train. But not before I got a message to Johnny via the stationmaster.'

He understood all her absences now. 'I suppose it was you who put my name forward to Gubbins?'

She smiled. 'You have always been my hero, Clement.'

He smiled and struggled to sit up. 'Where are we?'

'Rye Hospital. You were shot, Clement. We will be home tomorrow if the doctor says you are well enough to be moved.'

Doctor. Phillip Haswell. 'Is Phillip dead?'

'Yes,' she said. But he could hear the sad note in her voice. He wondered why. He looked around the hospital room. They were alone. 'Am I the only sick man in Rye?' he asked.

'Johnny arranged the private room.'

He looked at her and she smiled.

The door opened and Arthur Morris entered. 'How are you, Clement?'

'I'll live, Arthur. What's happening?'

Morris nodded. 'Commander Winthorpe is still in Rye. He and I have been interrogating the girl. Her real name is Katarina Klausmann and she has confessed to luring Stanley Russell to his death. Bundles of five-pound notes were in her pockets. Stanley died at Mr Kempton's house in the raid as we thought. But it appears that there is another sad note to all this, which we decided not to tell you until you were better.'

'Which is?'

Mary reached for his hand and held it.

'It appears that Phillip Haswell was innocent.'

Clement stared at Morris, a shiver coursing through his body.

But before he could speak Morris continued. 'When we picked up his body on the beach, we found that his hands were bound. And just like Stanley was implicated for the death of his father, so Phillip was made to appear like the

German infiltrator. It may be, Clement, that it was not you who killed Phillip. There are several bullets wounds in Doctor Haswell's body, and his companions might have shot him and let you think it was you. The Coroner's report will confirm whether the shot that killed the doctor was fired from close range.'

Clement stared at Morris. Could betrayal get any worse? The depth of it was confounding. It was as though someone had taken a cricket bat to his head. He felt insensible.

The door swung open and Johnny entered the room

'Is it possible *he* was another victim?' he asked, his gaze on Johnny.

Johnny shook his head, but it was Morris who spoke. 'We found the keys to Inspector Russell's car in his pocket.'

He heard the words but he could no longer comprehend. Whether or not he had fired the fatal shot which had killed Phillip Haswell, it did not change what he had done. He had shot Phillip Haswell. Deliberately. It had been his intention to kill the man he believed was a murderer and a traitor. And he had based his conviction on circumstantial evidence. He would have to live with that. But he had been betrayed by another. He felt the pain in his chest. 'It tells me who, Arthur. But it doesn't tell me why.'

'I have telephoned my men in Lewes and they have found the car in a side street near the hospital. I am fairly sure we will find forest leaf matter in the tyre treads.'

'But his wife was Jewish?'

'A lie, Clement,' Johnny said. 'Katarina is quite a handful, but she eventually told us what we wanted to know. I suppose she is hopeful of a mitigated sentence. Unlikely. It appears that Peter Kempton's wife Muriel is alive and well and working for the Abwehr. Of course, his name isn't Kempton. It is Klausmann, Pieter Klausmann.

The girl we were calling Jane is his daughter by his first wife.'

'That is why he waited,' Clement muttered, remembering the dinghy. 'But Peter is English? Everything about him is English. Even his dog.'

Johnny shook his head. 'Peter didn't come to England until after he married Muriel. His daughter, Katarina, remained with her mother, Peter's first wife, in Germany, but Peter did stay in contact with his daughter. Katarina Klausmann came to England on holidays before the war, but Peter was careful never to bring his daughter to Fearnley Maughton. The Germans then sent Katarina to England the year before war broke out.'

'The year Muriel was supposed to have died in Switzerland,' Clement said. 'But what about Elsie Wainwright and the man from Eastbourne?'

Morris spoke. 'I placed a telephone call to Nurse Anne Chambers to ask her if she knew where Elsie Wainwright was buried. She told me that in view of Elizabeth Wainwright having no spouse or other living descendants, Elizabeth Wainwright was interred alongside her parents in Eastbourne Cemetery. We exhumed her remains yesterday. The real Elizabeth Wainwright is dead, just as Anne Chambers said. All the Klausmanns had to do was locate a single, dead girl of the same age. They may have even found a photograph of the late Doctor and Mrs Wainwright and their daughter in the local newspaper records. And if Katarina resembled the parents even slightly, the illusion would be sufficient, as long as she stayed away from Eastbourne and anyone who actually knew the Wainwrights.'

'And the man in Elsie's life wasn't Phillip Haswell?' he asked.

Morris shook his head. 'It appears not. The murders of Inspector David Russell, George Evans, Stanley Russell, Constable Newson and Lieutenant Ellis, and the kidnapping and possible murder of Phillip Haswell, were all by the hand of Pieter Klausmann.'

Clement stared at the foot of the bed, his mind reeling. It was as though they were talking about a stranger; a dead but unknown enemy agent. Not a man who had been his friend for twenty years. His head spun. It felt like he had been shot again. He couldn't comprehend it now but he knew he wouldn't stop thinking about it. He would trawl, in his mind, twenty years of chats, of times spent walking the Downs, of philosophical debates, life ambitions, politics, the war, anything and everything that would help him to understand. But right now, today, all he felt was utter betrayal. Tomorrow it would be anger. He hoped that next week it would not be hatred.

'Ecclesiastes,' he muttered. He shook his head and looked up at Morris. 'How did...' he paused, he couldn't speak the name, '*he* find out about the list? I told no one.'

'It was a routine visit to Brighton Police Station to see a client arrested for theft,' Morris answered. 'According to Katarina, her father saw, while having tea with the Chief Superintendent in Brighton Police Station, an envelope on the Chief Super's desk with the Ministry of Home Security crest in the top left corner. When the Chief Superintendent left the room for a few minutes, Mr Kempton opened the letter and saw that it contained a list of names. On his return to Fearnley Maughton he decided to check David Russell's office. But Mr Kempton realised that he would need an accomplice, so he arranged for his daughter to get a job in the village by talking Haswell into believing the doctor needed a nurse. Kempton then arranged for Katarina to visit David Russell in his office, which she did, entering through the window. After Katarina rendered Inspector Russell unconscious, Mr Kempton entered the police station, also through the window, opened the safe and found the list. Once he saw his own name, he knew what the lists were about and, in view of the list in Brighton

Police Station, it was a fairly safe assumption that there would be similar lists with other senior police officers around the country.'

'The odd thing is,' Johnny interrupted, 'that in every sector other than yours and Brighton, the local Police Chief personally vets the selected men. But the patrol leader in Brighton had reservations about their Police Chief, just as you did about yours, Clement. This is why Gubbins so readily agreed to the sealed list idea. We had done it before. Of course, Peter had also attended the course at Coleshill and not only knew what was taught there, but also, and more importantly, the location of Coleshill. Perhaps he never intended to kill David Russell, just render the man unconscious, but whatever happened, Klausmann killed Russell, then had to devise a plan to implicate someone else and extricate himself from the scene. You might recall, Clement,' Johnny added, 'that it was Peter you asked to assist the Royal Engineers to choose a suitable place for the Operational Base. Peter had been meeting with Lieutenant Ellis for some time in Maughton Forest, so he did not want the Auxiliary Unit group stumbling upon his rendezvous with the naval lieutenant. So Peter made the Operational Base location convenient for his purposes. However, when George stumbled on Peter receiving information from Lieutenant Ellis, both George and Lieutenant Ellis were doomed.'

Clement looked at Johnny. 'But Peter was in the Operational Base the day David Russell was killed, on patrol with other members of the team.' He paused, and corrected himself. 'No, he wasn't. Reg had done the solo patrol to Cuckmere Haven; I remember now Reg said they had become separated. Peter must have doubled back to the village. He would have had plenty of time. Peter was good at charming people and getting them to do things. And he had a skill at blending into the background. He also compiled the watches and who patrolled with whom. I even left him in charge on more than one occasion.' He stared at the window in the otherwise white-painted room. 'But why now?'

Johnny sat on the edge of the bed. 'In a word, Clement, *Scallywags*. Peter believed the invasion was happening. We had sent out the code word for you to assemble in your Operational Base. Peter knew what the Nazis would encounter on arrival and wanted to warn them. But he could not risk his radio message being intercepted, so he thought it was time to leave. It would have been a major coup for the Jerries, if he had succeeded. And a disaster if they had ever discovered the real purpose of *HMS Forward*. But we will miss the opportunity to mislead. Never mind. There will be others. And perhaps he thought you would find out about him if he stayed any longer. Once he had made the decision to leave, he radioed for the fighter to destroy his own office, and the gullible Stanley Russell, then hid the radio transmitter in Doctor Haswell's Anderson shelter. The fighter did the rest. And when you and Chief Inspector Morris discovered the wires in the rubble, you suspected Haswell. It is possible that Klausmann was hiding in the garden when the fighter strafed there, and saw Phillip holding the carrots. Perhaps it had been Klausmann's intention to kill Haswell, but when he found the doctor in the garden during the raid, he decided to make full use of the unsuspecting doctor. He would also have overheard your conversation. Once you and Haswell left the garden to attend to the strafing victims, Klausmann was free to remove all the carrots from the garden, which, if Haswell was questioned, would implicate the man further. Peter then returned to the Operational Base. And placing the dead Ellis into Doctor Haswell's car was all the evidence needed to implicate Haswell as the enemy agent.'

Clement's heart was heavy. He wasn't sure whose bullet had actually killed Peter Kempton, or whatever name the man chose to use. But he believed he had killed Phillip Haswell. In a way, Kempton had killed him too. He looked up at Johnny and Arthur Morris. 'I knew Peter Kempton for twenty years. Played chess with the man every week. How is it possible I did not know about his Nazi leanings or that he was not an Englishman?'

'Don't beat yourself up too much over it, Clement. Klausmann fooled more than just you,' Johnny said. 'As a result we are re-evaluating the psychological assessments and other procedures at Coleshill.'

'Everything about him was English,' Clement said. 'How could I have missed it?'

'While Klausmann was born in Germany, he preferred living in England. But when the war came, Muriel, who of course spoke English, offered her services to the Abwehr and a plausible story was devised to explain her absence. Peter evidently decided that his Nazi fervour could best be demonstrated by remaining in England. He visited Germany on the anniversary of Muriel's supposed death, to see his wife and his daughter and to update his handlers. Klausmann was about as convincing an enemy agent as could be devised. His death will, no doubt, be a major loss to the Reich. We hope not to have too many more like him.'

'And the team?' Clement said, looking at Johnny.

'The invasion has not happened as yet, so there is plenty of time to make decisions about the fates of the remaining members of your group. Just get well, and we can talk again as soon as you are stronger.'

He shook hands with Johnny. He watched the brisk gait as his old friend from seminary school left his hospital room. For Johnny and men like him, the war had become the *raison d'être*. He glanced at Arthur Morris, who smiled and stretched out his hand. 'Thank you for all your assistance, Clement. I could not have done it without you.'

Clement smiled. 'I'm not sure that is correct, Arthur. But perhaps, if you have some spare time, we could play some chess.'

Morris reached for his hat, smiled, and nodding to Mary, left the room.

Clement lay in bed in the old Rye hospice, staring at the river and several small fishing boats lined up on the expansive sands. He could hear the gulls now. But their distinctive and formerly comforting cry did not help. He turned his head and smiled at Mary. He watched her deft fingers slide and twist the wool over the knitting needles, the familiar shape of a sock now evident. She and thousands of women like her was what it was all about. Home. And security. A land free from fear and treachery. He closed his eyes. Yet all he could see in his mind's eye was the dark form of the menacing U-boat. The effect of the craft was like something he had never previously experienced. Its presence was more than foreboding. He believed it was actually satanic. And it wasn't just a memory for him. He could feel the cold dread of its presence even now, days after the sinister craft had slunk back into the water; its invisible malevolence lingered. It represented the antithesis of everything decent men valued and cherished. What kind of world lay ahead if the Nazis won the war? And what sort of people devised such a pernicious regime that contrived for men to deceive and entrap? It was an alien and sinister force, which had to be stopped. He lay back in the bed, feeling the soft pillows under his head. How long could Britain hold out against such wickedness? Days? He hoped years. He hoped forever. But one thing was certain: life as he knew it would never be the same. The war that had seemed so remote for him had been brought to his doorstep. No longer was it the enemy in the sky or a faceless man who dropped bombs on the innocent. Peter Kempton had seen to that. The impersonal had become profoundly personal. Clement looked out to sea as the evening light fell. But the war was not yet over. In fact, for many it had only just begun. Winston Churchill had said it was the end of the beginning. Clement felt it. The Prime Minister had been referring to Britain but could just as easily have been talking about him. And he now believed it would not be over for many months, if not years to come. It was time for him to open his eyes. He loved Fearnley Maughton, and its people, but now he knew where his future lay. And it was not in the church pulpit.

Author's Note

The Auxiliary Units were created in 1940 in response to the impending threat of a German invasion of Great Britain. They were not disbanded until 1944. With hindsight, we know that these units never had to face the enemy on home soil but this in no way diminishes the courage and bravery these men demonstrated. They were prepared to die for their country and kept their involvement in these units secret for a great many years.

While much of what I have written about the Auxiliary Units in *In Grievous Times* is factual, other parts are entirely fictitious. Likewise, some is also open to speculation. The idea of killing the local senior policeman came from an online search and while the article is keen to dispel this as myth, any hint of murder is a flame to the Crime Writer moth.